Roaring Fork
WRANGLER

USA TODAY BESTSELLING AUTHOR
HEATHER SLADE

ROARING FORK WRANGLER

© 2024 Heather Slade

This book is a work of fiction. The names, characters, places and incidents are products of the writer's imagination or have been used fictitiously and are not to be construed as real. Any resemblance to persons, living or dead, actual events, locale or organizations is entirely coincidental.

979-8-88649-397-9

A complete list of Heather Slade's series and titles is available at the end of this book or visit her website: heatherslade.com

Table of Contents

Prologue

Cord

January

"Motherfucker," I groaned, opening my eyes and trying to get my bearings. I was on the ground—I knew that much—and my head was pounding like someone had hit me with the sharp end of an anvil. When I reached up to where the pain radiated from, and brought my hand back down, my glove was soaked with blood.

I tried to prop myself up on my elbow, but didn't have the strength. Blinking away the spots before my eyes, I patted my jacket, looking for my phone. When I found it, I swiped the screen, but the damned thing was dead. How the hell long had I been out here?

I was conscious, and it was still daylight. Both good signs. I raised my head, looking for some kind of land-mark that would tell me where I was. A few feet away was a lean-to. If I could get that far, at least I'd have shelter. As cold as it was, I wouldn't last much longer if I didn't at least try.

I had to drag myself since my every attempt to even get on my knees failed. I made it what I figured was halfway, but the black spots were back, and this time, I couldn't blink them away.

"Fuck!" I cried out with the little strength I had left. What a goddamn way to go. Freezing to death after riding out to find cattle that were probably dead too.

1

Cord

Previous June

Three hundred and sixty-six days after my father's attorney—a guy we'd nicknamed Six-pack in high school—originally read my father's will and the conditions set forth in the Roaring Fork Trust, my three brothers, one sister, and I returned to his office.

"I heard you got married," Six-pack said to my oldest sibling as we took our seats at the conference table.

I could tell by the look on his face that Buck had no desire to make small talk. Neither did I. None of us did.

Last year, shortly after our father died, Six-pack had called us into his office for the reading of our father's will. What happened next was the last thing my siblings or I would ever have anticipated.

There was a codicil within the Roaring Fork Trust stating the date and amount of the distribution of my inheritance, along with that of my siblings, after Buck successfully carried out two stipulations. If he failed to do one or both, none of us would inherit a penny. The ranch that had been in our family for over one hundred years would be sold, and the proceeds, along with any other assets, would be given to charity.

The first demand was for Buck to maintain full-time residency at the ranch, agreeing not to be away from the property for more than forty-eight consecutive hours. Given he worked in private security and intelligence, this meant Buck had to put his job on hold in order to ensure the rest of us would receive our inheritance.

Second, at the end of the year, the ranch had to be profitable. Roaring Fork had been operating in the red for the last five years. Turning that around in twelve months was next to impossible, but we'd done it.

"Can we get on with it?" I pressed.

"Of course." Six-pack cleared his throat. "I've received the ranch's financial reports from the accounting firm chosen by the trustee, and it appears you were profitable."

"It doesn't appear that way; we were profitable," Porter muttered.

"Let's just wrap this thing up," said Buck, as impatient as I was.

Nothing would make me happier than to put all this behind us and move on with our lives. Truth be told, I never wanted to think about my father or his controlling ways ever again.

"Certainly." Six-pack sighed, opened the manila envelope in front of him, pulled out a document, turned on the microphone, and looked directly at me.

"The second codicil reads as follows. 'The Roaring Fork Trust further stipulates that Porter Hayes Wheaton must…'" Six-pack's eyes scrunched, and his brow furrowed. "Sorry. I misspoke." He looked at the document more closely. "'The Roaring Fork Trust further stipulates that Cordero Rooker Wheaton must comply with two stipulations to be named at a later date.'"

A later date? What the fuck did that mean?

While I remained too stunned to react, my two older brothers were angrier than I'd ever seen them. Buck knocked his chair back, stood, and slammed his fist on the table.

"Enough of this goddamn bullshit," he roared. "I did what the motherfucker required. End this, Richard."

The attorney didn't flinch. "I don't have that power, Buck, and you know it."

"Who does? It's a trust. Someone has to be the executor. Who is it?"

"The Roaring Fork Trust LLC."

I raised my head. "An LLC is the trustee?"

Six-pack turned to me. "That's right."

"Is that legal?" I asked.

"It is, and it's common, Cord. The trustee can be an individual, a corporate trustee, or a combination of both."

I was about to ask why my father would do this, but I knew the answer. The bastard had controlled us one way or another all our lives. Why did we think it would end with his death?

"Who are the members of the LLC?" Buck asked.

Six-pack looked him in the eye. "That is confidential."

"It's public information. Either you tell me, or I'll find it on my own." Buck leaned forward and rested his hands on the table. "If I find out it's you, I'll get you disbarred."

When my brother turned to me, his expression softened. "I'm sorry, Cord."

I shook my head. "This isn't your doing. It's the old man's. And, Buck? I mean no offense by what I'm about to say."

He nodded.

"This isn't your battle to fight. You did your part. Now, it's up to me to do mine."

Buck picked up the chair that had toppled to the floor and took a seat.

I hated that the tactic I used with him was the same I'd employed with our father. I was the only sibling, other than my sister, who was able to diffuse his anger. Most of the time, I'd take the blame for whatever had sent him into a blind rage. I couldn't explain why, but instead of meting out a punishment, he'd stare me down, then walk away.

Buck's outburst and reaction to what I'd said, reminded me so much of the old man. No doubt, everyone in the room felt the same—him included.

"I have some questions," I said to Six-pack.

"I doubt I'll have answers."

"Can you excuse us?" I asked, glancing at my brothers and sister, hoping they'd respect my request and leave. Buck and Porter, in particular. As the two oldest, they'd always felt responsible for Flynn, Holt, and me. However, I was a grown-ass man, perfectly capable of handling my own shit.

"You sure?" Porter asked.

"Positive."

"We'll be outside," he said, motioning for the rest to join him.

"As I said, I don't know anything beyond what's stated in the codicil."

I lowered my voice and looked directly at him. "If I don't fulfill whatever it is, we'll lose everything, right?"

He nodded once, and his shoulders dropped. "Look, Cord, I wish there was a loophole, but I sure as hell haven't been able to find one. That highfalutin attorney Buck hired couldn't either."

"So, I wait."

"That's right."

"In the meantime, none of us know our fate or the ranch's."

"I'm not the trustee."

I looked into the attorney's eyes. "I know you're not."

"And I don't know who is other than an LLC."

"Gotcha." I pushed my chair back and stood. "I guess you'll keep in touch."

Six-pack looked down at the paper he'd read from. "I wish I could say when."

On the return trip to Roaring Fork Ranch, I tried hard not to stress about what our dad had in store for me. Given what he'd required Buck to do was something my brother swore he never would, I thought about what I might've told the bastard I hated. The only thing I could come up with was leaving the ranch.

Out of the five of us, only Porter and I felt that way, mainly because we shared the same dream for it. Originally, Flynn and I had thought about turning the place into a dude ranch. That plan came apart when she fell in love, got married, and had twins.

By that time, Porter had already approached me about starting a roughstock business. His side of it was to contract with rodeos to provide horses for both bareback and saddle bronc riding along with bucking bulls. I was in charge of all the livestock we raised, which included cattle, along with overseeing the maintenance of the property.

Neither of us was interested in providing steers or calves for tie-down roping, team roping, or bulldogging, but another ranch in Gunnison Valley, the Flying R, which the Rice family owned, did. Their participation made it easier for our team to either caravan with them to the bigger events or combine hauling to the smaller ones.

The work Port and I did had played a significant role in the ranch turning a profit in the last year, and we were damned proud of it. If I was required to leave for any reason—or if Porter was—I didn't know how in the hell we'd be able to stay in the black.

2

Cord
December

"Cord, can you come to the office this afternoon?" Six-pack asked when I answered his call.

"Weather's bad over here in Crested Butte. How urgent is it?"

"I've received word regarding the trust's codicil."

We'd already gotten two feet of snow, and there were another two on the way. The last thing I wanted to do was get stuck in Gunnison overnight. While there were only thirty miles between there and home, driving to and from in a blizzard also meant running the risk of getting stranded out in the middle of nowhere.

"Let's get together one day next week," I suggested.

"No time, Cord. You need to be there on Monday."

"Be where?"

"A place called East Aurora, New York. It's near Buffalo."

"This isn't even a little bit funny. There's no way in hell I'm traveling to New York, especially at this time of year."

"You've got no choice, Cord. The truth is, if I could get you there tomorrow, I would."

None of us had looked forward to Christmas much when our dad was alive, but now that Buck had a little guy of his own and Flynn and her husband had the twins, our whole family was looking forward to it being different this year, like it was before our mom passed away. "Come on, Six-pack. I can't leave before Christmas."

"As I said, you don't have a choice. You know what's at stake here. If you don't get there on the stipulated date, you and the rest of your family will lose everything."

I shook my head and scrubbed my face. "I'm expected to get from Colorado to New York in the dead of winter in less than a week?"

"You could fly."

"How long do I have to stay there?" I asked.

"You already know the answer."

"Tell me anyway."

"Three hundred and sixty-five days."

"Fuck," I muttered under my breath, knowing if there was any way possible to get out of this, Buck would've figured it out.

"I'll send the details via email. You do have email, don't you, Cord?"

"You're an asshole," I said, ending the call. It was a tossup as to whether he'd heard me or not. Either way, I didn't care. Six-pack might only be the messenger, but something told me he took a perverse pleasure in sticking it to us Wheatons.

I sent a group text to my brothers, asking them to meet me in the main barn as soon as they could. Each one of them must've sensed what was up since no one asked why.

"I heard from Six-pack," I said when Buck, the last to arrive, walked in. "I have to be in New York by Sunday night."

All four of us sat on hay bales, but no one spoke for several minutes.

"Where in New York?" Buck asked.

"Near Buffalo."

He rubbed his chin. "As you know, I've spent time in New York City, not that I know much about it. I know even less about that part of the state. Did Six-pack say why?"

I shook my head. "He's emailing the details."

Porter stood and walked over to one of the horse stalls. "Good thing National Finals Rodeo is over, or we'd be fucked." It was the biggest event of the year for roughstockers and where we made the majority of our money. Unfortunately, the second biggest was right around the corner.

"National Western Stock Show starts mid-January," I reminded him.

"We'll get the Rice boys to send some of their animals," he said, chewing on a piece of straw.

"I'll go," Buck offered. "I'm sure we've got enough hands on this ranch who would jump at the chance to go to Denver for a few nights."

Porter nodded at Buck, then looked at me.

"What?" I asked.

"It's your decision, Cord. I'm sure as hell not going to answer for you. This operation is just as much your creation as it is mine."

"Whatever you do about NWSS is fine with me. My hands are tied, Port."

I stared down at the dirt, then at my phone and the email I received from the attorney, and read as far as the line saying I'd be required to remain somewhere called the Lilacs for a period of one year from the day I arrived.

"I'll head out at zero dark thirty tomorrow." I kicked the same dirt I'd been staring at. "Guess I'll see you guys next Christmas."

I made better time than I thought I would and pulled into East Aurora—a Podunk of a town, but not any more so than Crested Butte—at eight, Saturday night.

"Welcome to the inn," a guy younger than me said as he opened one of the two big, wooden entrance doors. "Are you in town for the holidays?" he asked.

"No."

"Can I help you with your bags, sir?"

"No," I said a second time. "Thanks," I added as an afterthought.

"Right. Okay. Well, check-in is right over there," He pointed to a desk. As I got closer, I saw two women.

One was seated behind it, the other in front. I stood a few feet away, waiting for them to finish.

"Hey, Juni. We've got a check-in," said the doorman.

"Sorry," she said, getting up.

"Take your time. I'm not goin' anywhere."

"I am, though."

I'd removed my hat when I came inside, but with my square-toe boots, barn jacket, and flannel shirt, I had to look like someone straight out of a Western movie to whoever she was. "Cord Wheaton," I said, taking a step forward and holding out my hand. Her grip was strong when she shook it, and her eyes met mine straight on. I liked her already. Not to mention she was about the prettiest girl I'd seen in as long as I could remember. She stared up at me with her big gray-green eyes and smiled, then glanced over at the guy who stood not too far from us. Boyfriend, I'd guess. Pity.

"I'm Juni—Juniper—Chance. That's my brother, Grayson."

I turned to the other woman. "I'm guessin' you must be their sister."

She blushed. "I'd tell you complimenting me wouldn't get you a room upgrade, but it looks like it already did." She stood and approached me too. "I'm Patricia Chance, Juni and Gray's mother."

When I shook her hand, I knew where her daughter had learned how to greet people. Her eyes met mine, and her grip was firm.

"Patricia's my mama's name."

She studied me. "Is she from around here?"

"No. Colorado."

She cocked her head. "Do you have other family you're visiting for the holidays?"

"He said he's not here for that."

Patricia shot her son a look. "Pardon my Grayson's interruption. He's about to take a dinner break and is teetering on the edge of *hangry*."

I looked over at Grayson. "I'm teeterin' there myself. Anywhere you can recommend I get a bite to eat?"

"This way." He motioned for me to follow him.

"Gray, Mr. Wheaton hasn't checked in yet," said his mother.

"Please call me Cord, ma'am." I turned back to her son. "They serve burgers wherever you were takin' me?" I asked.

"The best," Juniper answered for him. "How do you like it?"

"Medium rare with bacon and cheddar if they've got it."

"Fries?"

"Why not? Thanks. Hey, hold up," I said when she followed her brother. "Let me give you some money."

"It's okay. We'll just put it on your room."

I could feel her mama's eyes on me as I watched her daughter walk away. Tight jeans, boots—although more for the snow than riding—a flannel shirt like mine, and long brown hair that swayed just above her perfect little ass.

Dreading looking at her mother, I reached into my pocket and pulled out my wallet. "Figure you need ID and a credit card," I said, handing both to her.

"Have a seat, cowboy." She winked and I smiled. "So, are you just passing through?"

"Nah, I'll be here a while."

She cocked her head.

"I, uh, got a job at a place called the Lilacs."

Her eyes opened wide. "You must be taking over for JD. Such a shame."

"JD?"

"He worked for the Coverts his whole life. And his father did before him."

"Did you say Covert?"

"I did. Do you know the name?" she asked.

I shook my head. There was something familiar about it, but I couldn't place it.

"You're all set," she said after typing a few things into the computer. "Looks like you're with us until Monday."

"That's right."

She handed me an old-fashioned skeleton key. "The room is on the second floor, at the end of the hall. Kids are in the bar."

"Thanks so much, ma'am. I'll just drop my bag and freshen up."

"Welcome to East Aurora, son. I hope you enjoy your time in our little village."

"I hope so too."

I was about to take the stairs up to the second floor when Juniper stuck her head around the corner. "Don't be long, or your food will get cold."

"Yes, ma'am," I said, winking at her like her mama had at me.

"What do you want to drink?"

"Whatever beer is on tap would be great."

"That'll be a Blue."

"Sounds good." Before I took the first step, I caught Juniper's mother out of the corner of my eye. Her arms were folded, but she was smiling. That was a good sign.

The burger was one of the best I'd ever had, or I'd been hungrier than I thought. I even considered ordering a second one. I settled on another beer instead.

"How long are you here for?" Grayson asked as he cleared our dishes.

"As I told your mom, I've got a job at the Lilacs, starting Monday."

Juniper's eyes opened wide. "What will you be doing?"

I shook my head. "I wish I knew. I was told to report there, so here I am. I hope that whatever comes next involves some kind of wrangling since it's about the only thing I'm good at."

"There are horses on the estate," she said.

Grayson started to say something, but his sister shook his head, and he closed his mouth.

"So, uh, horses are a good sign. You know much about the place?"

"Some. I mean everyone around here does," said Juni.

"Why's that?"

"The family's wealthier than that god, Midas," said Grayson.

Juniper shook her head at her brother. "He was a king, not a god, and he was known for greed and foolishness. You're thinking of Plutus."

Grayson rolled his eyes. "Who I was thinking of is beside the point, nerd-girl." He turned to me. "The Covert family is rolling in money. They're kind of like the Rockefellers."

Juniper opened her mouth like she was about to contradict her brother a second time, but shut it.

"The Coverts own the Lilacs?"

Both of them nodded.

"Who are you supposed to be working for?" Grayson asked.

I pulled my phone out of my pocket. "I'm supposed to get in touch with someone named Hoss."

The two made eye contact, but neither commented.

"Somethin' you wanna tell me?" I asked.

Juniper shook her head. "We don't really know him."

But they knew *of* him. It made sense they kept whatever they had to say to themselves since I'd be working for the guy. Honestly, it wouldn't matter what they told me. I'd be here for a year, no matter how much of an asshole he was.

When Grayson walked through a swinging door with the dishes, I took the opportunity to study Juniper, who was staring at her glass of wine. The longer I looked, the prettier she got.

"Where are you from?" she asked.

"Colorado. What about you?"

"Here. I've never lived anywhere else except for at college. Even then, I didn't leave New York State."

"Where'd you go?" I doubted her answer would mean anything to me, but I wanted to hear her talk anyway. Her pronunciation of certain words gave away an accent, albeit one very different from the one person I knew from New York City—Buck's wife.

"Syracuse."

I made a mental note to look it up later. "Major?"

"Dual enrollment. Business management and information studies." She raised a brow, maybe challenging me to ask more questions.

"You're on to me," I said instead. "I basically have no idea where the town you named is or what information studies means."

She laughed. "Computer programming and analytics."

"You're talking about college now?" asked Grayson, coming out of the kitchen and shaking his head.

I chuckled. They reminded me of how my brothers and I were with each other. We didn't tease Flynn, our younger sister, as much as Grayson did Juniper, but that was because our father had been so cruel to her when she was a kid.

"Is everything okay?" Juniper asked.

I realized I probably had the same sneer on my face as I always did when I thought about how much of an asshole he was to all of us. Flynn, in particular. "Yeah, everything's fine."

"Juni, are you ready to go?" Grayson asked.

"I'll stay until Mom can leave," she responded.

I got the impression her brother wasn't crazy about her hanging out with me but kept his mouth shut, given it wouldn't be a great idea to let a stranger—me—know their mom would be here on her own.

"I can stay," he offered.

"You did last night."

He nodded, then turned to me. "Nice to meet you, Cord. Enjoy your stay."

I stood and shook his hand. "Nice to meet you, Grayson. Cool name, by the way." I looked over my shoulder at his sister. "Yours too."

"Thanks."

When her cheeks turned pink and she lowered her gaze, my cock immediately hardened. Juniper was the perfect mix of self-assured and shy, and damn if I didn't want to whisk her upstairs and get her naked in that big ol' bed. Good thing her mama was here—a thought that halted any move I'd make on Juni.

"So. Juniper. Where'd your mother come up with the name?"

"It was actually my dad, and he can't really take credit. It was his great-grandmother's name. She was the twelfth child out of fifteen, so I suppose they ran out of ideas. My dad said they must've looked out a window and settled on Juniper instead of Tree."

I laughed out loud. "Regardless of how it came about, I think it's a beautiful name"—unable to stop myself, I reached out and touched a strand of her hair—"for an equally beautiful girl."

Her cheeks flushed, but she didn't look away this time. Instead, her gaze met mine. "You aren't so bad yourself, Cord."

"There you are, Juni," her mother said, walking into the bar just as I dropped my hand. "The night manager is here, so we can head home."

She jumped down from her stool. "Nice meeting you," she said.

I stood too. "Maybe I'll see you around if you work again this weekend."

"Oh, I don't work here. Actually, only Grayson does."

My eyes scrunched, and I looked over at her mother.

"We're helping out so the family who owns the inn can take a few days off for the holidays," she explained.

"Nice of you."

She shrugged. "I'm sure they'd do it for us if the situations were reversed."

"So, uh, do they serve breakfast?"

Juniper leaned closer. "They do, but Charlie's Diner is much better, and it's just down the block."

"Sounds good, then. Thanks for the recommendation. What time do they open?"

"Around seven, I think," she responded.

"Perfect."

"Are you an early riser, Cord?" her mother asked.

"I'm a rancher, ma'am. Seven will be sleepin' in for me."

"I'm sorry to inform you that you won't find anything open earlier than that in the village."

"I'm good. Might as well take advantage of a couple more days off if I can."

Patricia handed her daughter her jacket, but before I could offer to help her with it, she had it on.

"Can I walk you out?" I asked instead.

Juniper nodded. "We're this way. Thanks."

I opened the passenger door for her mom once we stepped up to the only car in the back lot. When I glanced over and saw Juni's door still closed, I went around to open it for her.

"I can get it. I was just wondering if maybe you'd like to meet at Charlie's tomorrow. I can show you around or tell you more about the village."

"Seven too early for you?"

She grinned, and her cheeks flushed.

"Damn, you're pretty," I said under my breath.

"You're very kind."

I shook my head. "Actually, I'm not. I am honest, though. Would eight be better?"

"You wouldn't mind waiting?"

"For you? Never."

I went inside, took the stairs up to my room, and sat on the bed in the suite Mrs. Chance had upgraded me to, not that I needed it. I would've been just as happy in a smaller one, given how nice this place was compared to where I'd slept on the road.

I opened and read the attachment on Six-pack's email for what had to be the tenth time.

The Roaring Fork Trust stipulates that the disbursement of the assets listed herein will be reevaluated after a period of one year from the date designated by the attorney of record.

The terms of the trust require that Cordero Rooker Wheaton maintain residency at the Lilacs, an estate in East Aurora, New York, full-time, meaning he cannot leave for more than forty-eight consecutive hours. Also, at the end of the year, the ranch must continue to show a profit. If either of those things don't happen, then the proceeds of the estate will be distributed at the discretion of the trustee, in their entirety, to include proceeds from the sale of the aforementioned assets, to local charities including, but not limited to, the Miracles of Hope Childrens' Charity of Crested Butte, Colorado.

On this read, the words "maintain residency" jumped out at me. I sure as hell hoped there was a place for me to live on the estate.

3

Juniper

Since Cord wouldn't walk away until I was inside the car with my door closed and the engine started, I waited until then to release the deep breath I'd been holding in.

I glanced over at my mom. She was looking at me but didn't say anything. Never a good sign.

"What?" I finally asked after backing out of the parking place and turning onto Main Street.

"I didn't say a word."

"I know. That's the problem."

"He seems like a very nice young man. Maybe a tad old for you."

"Mom, I'm twenty-three."

"And according to his ID, he's twenty-eight. Not to mention, I don't get the impression he'll be here longer than he has to."

"I don't think five years constitutes 'too old.'"

"It would if you were twelve."

"Ew. Well, I'm not. Jeez, Mom." I glanced over at her. Her hand was over her mouth, and she was trying not to laugh.

"He is hot. I'll give you that."

My eyes opened wide. "Mom!"

"What? I'm not Miss Cena's age. Although, if she met Cord, she'd probably think the same thing."

I shook my head, thankful our drive home was a short one. "I'm having breakfast with him tomorrow."

"At seven?" My mom gasped.

"We compromised. We're meeting at eight."

Since we were both exhausted from the long day at the inn and Grayson and Dad were already in bed, I kissed my mom good night and made my way upstairs as soon as we got home.

I took a quick shower to rinse the smell of the grill off me, then hurried and crawled into bed. Eight would come too soon and, at the same time, not soon enough. While I couldn't wait to see Cord tomorrow, I hoped I'd dream about him tonight.

I was up at seven, showered and ready to go, wishing I hadn't suggested meeting at eight since, now, I had time to kill.

"You're up early," said my dad, shuffling into the kitchen in his bathrobe and slippers.

"She's got a breakfast date," said my mom, walking in behind him and straight over to the coffeemaker. "And I love her so much right now," she added, pouring two cups and handing one to him. "Thanks for getting a pot brewing, sweetheart."

She leaned in and kissed my cheek.

My dad took a sip, then looked up at me. "A breakfast date?"

"Did you just pick up on that?" my mom asked, nudging him.

"My brain won't process anything until I've had caffeine. So, what about it?"

"A guest checked into the inn last night—" I began.

"He's starting work at the Lilacs tomorrow," my mom told him.

"Anyway, I offered to tell him more about the village. Maybe show him around."

"That'll be a long breakfast date, considering it's Sunday and nothing opens before noon, if that."

I shrugged. "I could take him ice skating. Or we could go for a walk." I filled my cup halfway. "Also, this close to Christmas, I think some of the shops have earlier hours.”

My dad leaned in and kissed my cheek like my mom had. “You’re a nice girl, June-bug. Some might say too nice, considering you offered to get up this early.”

“You haven’t seen this guy,” said my mom, taking eggs and milk out of the refrigerator. “Not that he’d have the same impact on you that he did us.”

When he raised a brow, she set the things in her hand on the counter and hugged him. “He’s a cowboy from Colorado.”

My dad kissed her temple. “He must be taking over for JD.”

We both nodded. “Makes sense, except he said he’s supposed to call Hoss tomorrow.”

My dad made a face. “Hoss Schultz is a criminal.”

“He hasn’t actually been charged with anything, Jay,” my mom reminded him.

“Doesn’t make him any less of one.” My dad turned to me. “The last thing I want to do is rain on your parade, sweetheart, but if this guy is mixed up with Schultz, I’m going to suggest you keep your distance.”

"Understood." My parents let Grayson and me make our own decisions, particularly after we became adults. So when one of them made a "suggestion," as he'd put it, I listened. So did my brother.

"He seems like a nice young man," my mom added, cracking the eggs in the bowl she'd taken out of the cupboard. On instinct, I grabbed the flour and sugar and put a stick of butter in a cup in the microwave.

Every Sunday, my mom made cinnamon cake as a treat for Dad since it was the only day he took off. The Goat, our family's bar and restaurant, was still open, but the staff had ganged up on him, saying they wouldn't let him come in unless it was a dire emergency. Grayson and I were pretty sure our mom had bribed them to do it.

"Have you heard how Miss Cena is?" he asked.

"I haven't."

I looked at my mom, who shook her head. "I haven't, either."

Miss Cena, as we all called her even though she'd been married, was ninety-nine years old. I heard a rumor that she'd turn one hundred sometime around Christmas. Not that she'd ever admit it.

I thought back to when I last saw her. It was at least a year ago. Then, she'd asked me to bring my diploma over to show her when I returned home in May.

"I've never met someone who got two master's degrees at one time," she'd told me the last time I visited.

According to her housekeeper, Mrs. Miller, who answered the phone when I called, Miss Cena wasn't receiving visitors, but she'd let me know if her condition improved. Nine months had passed, and I still hadn't heard from her. Maybe I'd try calling again when I returned home later today.

"You best be off if you don't want to be late," said my mom, motioning to the clock.

I was stunned to see it was a quarter to eight. "Yeah, I gotta go." After kissing the cheeks of both my parents, who told me to have a good time, I walked out the door.

As I sat in the car, waiting for it to warm up, I gazed at the house I grew up in. It was an old Victorian that my father had purchased and painstakingly renovated shortly after my parents were married.

When I came home from college after graduation, I figured living at home would only be temporary until I got a job related to one or both of my degrees. I'd had a few offers but turned them down because they were mostly on the West Coast. Someday, I might want to leave East Aurora, but right now, my parents needed my help at the Goat, especially on the weekend.

Or at least that's the excuse I told myself. The truth was my life hadn't turned out the way I thought it would. All the dreams I'd once had ended the summer between my junior and senior years of high school.

I shook my head, refusing to go down the rabbit hole of that memory. It was over and done, and I wasn't that person any longer. The hardest part was I still hadn't found anything else that excited me enough to build my life around.

That Grayson hadn't gotten a place of his own when he graduated, either, made me feel less like a loser about it. I thought about asking if he wanted to share an apartment, but if I did that, I might as well stay at home since I'd have the same level of privacy.

I pulled the car out of the driveway, then onto Main Street. There weren't many people out this early on a Sunday, so parking places were plentiful. When I saw a truck with Colorado plates, I parked right behind it on the street, then ran across to the diner.

"Hey, Juni," said Mary Beth, a girl I'd gone to high school with.

"I'm, um, meeting someone."

She motioned to the left, and I saw Cord walking toward me.

"Good morning," he said. "I got us a table by the fireplace. I hope that's okay."

"It's perfect." I removed my hat and gloves, shoved them in my pocket, and was about to shrug out of my coat when Cord stepped behind me, helped me take it off, then hung it next to the barn jacket he was wearing last night.

He motioned for me to go ahead. The place was half empty, but the eyes of all those seated landed on Cord and me as we made our way to the table. Most murmured hello, but didn't say anything.

Cord got my chair and, as I went to take my seat, leaned forward and whispered in my ear. "Everyone in here knows you, don't they?"

"How could you tell?"

He sat down before responding. "There's a place in my hometown just like this one. It's called McGill's, and if you and I walked in together, news would spread before we were finished eating that I was with someone they didn't recognize, and everyone would be scrambling to find out who you were."

I laughed. "Must be as small as East Aurora."

"Smaller." Cord picked up the menu. "What's good here?" he asked.

"Everything, but my favorite is the Italian French toast."

He raised a brow.

"French toast made with Italian bread," I explained.

"How's their bacon?"

I laughed. "At least as good as the inn's. Maybe better."

He set his menu down. "I don't know if that's possible. That burger, last night, was so good I thought about ordering a second."

"You should've asked. I would've made you another one."

He rested his elbows on the table. "Did you make the first one?"

"I did."

"That explains why it was so good."

I felt my cheeks flush, and I lowered my eyes to the menu I knew by heart.

"Juniper?"

I raised my gaze and met his. "Yeah?"

"It makes me crazy when you do that."

My eyes opened wide. "Sorry."

"Don't be."

I studied him. "What is it I do that makes you, err, crazy?"

"The way your cheeks turn pink and you lower your gaze. It makes me wanna…"

"What?"

"Ready to order?" asked Mary Beth, standing over us.

"May I?" Cord asked.

"Um, sure," I responded, even though I had no idea what he meant.

"Two orders of Italian French toast and two orders of bacon, make mine crisp. Juniper?"

"Crisp for me too, thanks."

"What to drink?" Mary Beth asked as she jotted the rest of the order on the notepad.

"Coffee for me, please."

"Same," said Cord. "I'll tell you later," he added once she walked away.

"Tell me what?"

"What it makes me wanna do."

My cheeks flushed, and I looked away. Not on purpose. I hadn't realized, until now, how often I did it. When I raised my eyes, Cord was brushing his lower lip with his index finger, and based on his expression, it appeared he wanted me for breakfast.

4

Cord

Alarm bells were going off in my head. I'd met this girl less than twelve hours ago, and for the second time, I was thinking about how soon I could get her into bed. Seducing a woman who'd lived in this small town her whole life was a terrible idea.

Crested Butte was just as small, but that it was a ski town meant, during the winter, the place was overrun with tourists, including lots of pretty girls looking for a hookup with a cowboy—a fact my brothers and I had taken full advantage of in our youth.

We'd all settled down as we got older, not that any of us, besides Buck and our sister, Flynn, were married. Holt, who was the youngest other than her, still sowed his wild oats plenty, but he was also in an über-famous rock band.

As far as long-term relationships were concerned, all of us had someone from our past we'd stayed with longer than we should've because it was easier than the drama of breaking up. For me, it was Sandy Volk, whose ancestors were among the founding families of our town—like mine were. We'd known each other since we were kids, started dating as teenagers, hooked up when she was home from college, and broke up more times than I could count. She was certain we'd get married someday. I was equally sure we never would.

While on the road between there and here, I got a couple of text messages saying she was home for Christmas and wanted to see me. I probably should've responded, but I had no idea what I'd say. If I told her I was on my way to New York, where I'd be living for the next year, she would've been full of questions I didn't have answers to.

"So tell me about the history of East Aurora," I said, resting against the chair.

"Let's see. First, there's the Roycroft."

"The inn, right?"

"Yes, but so much more. A man named Elbert Hubbard started the American Arts and Crafts Movement here in 1897. For twenty years, it flourished, with craftsmen of all kinds traveling to the village to live on the campus he constructed." She rolled her eyes. "I sound like a tour guide."

I chuckled. "Why only twenty years?"

"He and his wife died on the *RMS Lusitania*."

"Right. Was that the one torpedoed by the Germans?"

"It was."

When she smiled, I was damn glad I'd paid attention in history class.

"Anyway, the campus still exists, but it will never thrive the way it did when he was alive. You still see his influence throughout the village, though."

"What else?"

"It's the home of a successful toy-making company, but manufacturing was moved out of East Aurora decades ago."

"Anything else?"

"Millard Fillmore had a home here." She looked out a window. "There are a lot of villages like this one in New York, but few are still flourishing in the same way."

"What about the Lilacs?"

She sat up straighter, and her eyes sparkled. "The history of the estate is *fascinating*. Miss Cena's life in particular, but I might be biased." She shook her head. "As my brother said, I can be pretty nerdy, so be careful when you ask questions because I might go overboard with my answers."

It was on the tip of my tongue to say I loved hearing her talk, that the sound of her voice intrigued and captivated me, but I stopped myself.

"Is that June-bug?" said a guy wearing a cop's uniform as he approached our table from behind her.

"Hey, Pete," she responded, glancing over her shoulder.

"Who's this?" he asked, bending down to kiss her cheek.

"Cord Wheaton, meet Pete Chance, my uncle."

I stood to shake the man's hand. "It's a pleasure, sir."

"Likewise. What brings you to town?"

I chuckled. Like I'd told Juniper earlier, this place was just like Crested Butte. Everyone knew who belonged, as well as those who didn't. "A job."

"At the Lilacs," Juniper added.

"Oh yeah? Workin' with Schultz?"

"That isn't who hired me, but if you're talking about Hoss, I'm supposed to check in with him tomorrow morning."

He raised a brow.

"What do you know about the guy?" I asked, quickly learning the man wasn't well-liked and deciding to take the bull by the horns, as they say.

He glanced around the room. "Where are you staying?"

"At the inn tonight. Not sure about tomorrow."

He nodded, then looked at his niece. "Juni, give Cord my number, and we'll chat later," he suggested.

"Appreciated," I said, taking a seat when he left.

"Pete's a good guy. Whatever he tells you is worth listening to."

I sensed it just from the brief conversation. "Gotcha."

The waitress brought our coffee and food at the same time, which Juniper appeared to notice but didn't comment on. It was yet another thing I liked about her.

Like the burger the night before, breakfast was so good I thought about ordering seconds.

"It's yummy, right?" Juniper asked, pointing at the plate I'd nearly cleaned while she hadn't eaten half of hers.

"If all the food in town is this good, I'm going to need to up my physical activity." I nearly groaned. Despite my resolve to rein in my desire for Juniper, the first thing I thought of—again—was getting her under the sheets with me.

"It's a mile walk from one end of town to the other. You could start there," she said, smirking.

"Yeah? What else?"

"There are a couple of parks that maintain trails for Nordic skiing. Plus other areas where you can snowshoe. The town has an ice rink too, if you're into that sort of thing."

"All of the above. What about you?"

Her smile was broad. "I'm game if you are."

While Juniper fussed, I insisted on paying for breakfast since she was showing me around the place.

We started out Nordic skiing on trails that were well groomed and pretty, like the woman I was with. Though, she was even more so. I continued to tamp down my attraction every minute we spent together when each new thing I learned made me like her more.

"Tell me your faults," I said after we'd turned our skis in and were walking from the trails into town.

Her eyes scrunched. "You want to know my faults?"

"So far, I haven't found any, so, yeah."

She shook her head. "As my brother said last night and I confirmed this morning, I'm a nerd." She shrugged. "Hand in hand with that is I spend too much time reading."

"Yet you're still athletic."

"I'm competitive," she confessed.

"Which is why you're athletic?"

"Let's just say I wasn't about to let Grayson best me at *anything*."

"What else?"

The smile left her face. "I'm twenty-three years old and still live at home."

"I've got five years on you, girl, and I do too." I waited, but she didn't say anything else. "So far, I don't see any of what you said as a fault."

She nodded. "Sometimes, I think it's easier for others to see our faults than it is to see our own. That's true for our strengths too."

"Insightful."

She looked to her left, stopped walking, and motioned to a shop door. "You should see this."

"What is it?"

"An original five-and-dime. There aren't too many left in the world, and certainly not one like this."

"That's cool," I said when I saw a mechanical pony that had to be from the fifties, maybe before.

"Everyone who's ever lived in the village has taken a twenty-five-cent ride on Sandy. And we all have embarrassing photos to prove it."

"Damn," I muttered, pointing to a sign that said no one over the age of eight was allowed. "That hardly seems fair. I wanted a picture."

Juniper glanced around the store. "Get on and give me your phone."

I swiped the screen, and she took it. Since I was tall enough to straddle the thing without actually needing to sit on it, that's what I did. Juniper giggled as she snapped shots of me, including one with me holding my hat in the air like I was on the back of a bronc.

All of a sudden, her expression changed, and she thrust the phone at me. "Ironic," I heard her mutter as she walked over to the bins of candy.

I swiped the screen and cringed. Not only was there a text from *Crested Butte* Sandy, but she'd sent a *revealing* photo with it. One I quickly deleted. "Hey, sorry." I picked up a candy bar and held it out to her.

"What's that for?"

"I don't know. I feel like a jerk and thought chocolate might make up for it."

"Don't worry about it."

"She's…" I took a deep breath.

Juniper thrummed her fingers on folded arms, and her eyes bored into mine.

"Someone from my past."

"At least you know her."

I laughed out loud and shook my head. "I guess you're right. But, seriously, I'm sorry you had to see that."

"Not sorrier than I am, considering I can't *unsee* it."

I pulled my phone out of my pocket and did what I should've done months ago. "There. She's blocked."

"I hope you didn't do that for me."

"More for me."

She shrugged, and I followed her from the candy to the toy section.

"I can't believe they still make some of these," I said, picking up toy after toy I remembered from when I was a kid.

"It's like the entire store is a time capsule." She pointed to her boots. "Including the creaky wooden floorboards."

"I could spend hours in here," I mumbled, finding a lunch box I was pretty sure I had in third grade.

"This isn't even a quarter of it. It goes three storefronts to the left and then there's downstairs."

"Damn."

Juniper grabbed a T-shirt, held it up, and laughed out loud.

"Oh my God," I said under my breath and scrubbed my face with my hand.

"What?" she asked with wide eyes and an infectious giggle.

"*I rode Sandy.* Seriously?"

"Well, you did, right?"

I grabbed the T-shirt from her hand, snaked my arm around her waist, and breathed in the scent of her. "You make me wanna…"

Juniper leaned into me instead of away. "You make me wanna, too."

5

Seeing the image of someone from Cord's past pop up on his cell phone was like being doused with ice-cold water. It was an almost cruel reminder that he was a hot AF cowboy from Colorado who was in town to take a job at the Lilacs for what he'd told my mom was a period of one year.

He'd also said he wasn't sure what the job entailed, but he hoped it involved wrangling since it was the only thing he was good at.

The amateur detective in me went rampant with every new piece of information I stuck in the mental file I'd created for Cord Wheaton.

First of all, who took a job without knowing what it was? That in itself was fishy. Obviously, he did know; he just didn't want to say. And, I supposed, people did take contract jobs for certain periods of time, but still, already knowing he'd only be here for a year seemed odd too.

Another point of information worthy of me sitting up and taking notice was that the only contact he'd mentioned in regard to the job was Hoss Schultz. Rumors were that Miss Cena's great-nephew, Jimmy Rooker, was the one who'd signed the contract with Schultz Winery Management to take over the grape-growing and wine-production operation at the Lilacs. Not that anyone could confirm it, but I doubted Miss Cena would've ever given someone like Jimmy the power to negotiate business agreements on behalf of the estate.

The man had a lengthy arrest record and, according to Mrs. Miller, the head housekeeper, had been banned from setting foot on the property. Not that Miss Cena had any means to enforce that once JD, who was Jimmy's father, passed away.

Finally, the photo Cord had been sent via text message could only be described as pornographic. While he seemed flustered by it, he hadn't been mortified, which, to me, meant receiving something like that wasn't uncommon.

Given all that, I should've thanked him for breakfast, wished him luck in his new job, and left him on his own in the five-and-dime. But I couldn't. In fact, I found myself watching him as he discovered all the gems the store offered. He seemed truly delighted as he added yet another item to his already overflowing basket. That alone made me swoon.

"Wanna trade?" I asked, offering to swap it for an empty one so he could keep shopping.

"Juni?" Someone said my name before Cord had the chance to answer.

"Mr. Reynolds? It's so nice to see you."

"I thought I'd stop in today and check on how my grandson was managing the holiday rush. Running into you is certainly an added bonus."

When Cord glanced over, I motioned for him to join us. "Mr. Reynolds, this is Cord Wheaton. He's in town from Colorado."

"Pleasure to meet you, son."

As the two shook hands, I explained that the Reynolds family had owned the store since it opened in 1929.

"That job offer is still open, Juni," Mr. Reynolds said.

"Job offer?" Cord asked.

"I'm a Syracuse grad myself, and we could sure use someone with this young lady's education and background to step in as GM of the place." He patted my shoulder. "I know your mom and dad need your help as much as we do, but that doesn't mean I'll ever stop pestering you about working for us instead."

"I appreciate it so much, Mr. Reynolds."

He looked between Cord and me. "And yet, she still won't accept. Doesn't matter how much I up the salary." He winked.

"You know it isn't about the money," I said.

"You're right. I do." Mr. Reynolds glanced at Cord's basket. "Let me take that for you."

"I'll get it, Pops," I heard his grandson say before reaching out to set it on the counter near one of the registers.

"Hey, Juni," he said to me.

"Hi, Ross."

He stepped closer. "How've you been?"

Ross and I had dated for a few months once we both returned home after college graduation. I was the one who broke it off, and it was the reason I couldn't accept a job at the five-and-dime.

"I'm good. You?"

"I miss you," he said, leaning into me so our arms brushed.

My eyes met Cord's unintentionally, and he raised a brow. While it would be polite for me to introduce the two, I didn't want to.

Maybe picking up on my general discomfort, Mr. Reynolds struck up a conversation with him, and the two walked to another part of the store.

"Who's that?" Ross asked.

"A guest at the inn. He's here for work, and I offered to show him around today."

"Juni, I was wondering—"

"It was good to see you, Ross. Take care." I rushed off in the direction his grandfather had led Cord.

Mr. Reynolds' eyes scrunched when I approached, but I didn't offer an explanation. Whatever had happened between his grandson and me was no one's business but ours. It wasn't even all that dramatic. I just wasn't as interested in him as he appeared to be in me, which meant I felt better about ending it sooner rather than later.

"It was great to see you," I said, leaning up to kiss Mr. Reynolds' cheek. "I've got to get going but hope you and your family have a wonderful Christmas."

The man shook his head slowly, but smiled. "You too, and please give my regards to your parents and Grayson."

"I will," I said as he walked away.

Cord leaned closer. "Is everything okay?"

"I'll explain later."

He nodded once. "I guess I should check out. If you have somewhere you need to be, don't let me keep you."

"I don't," I said with a sigh.

"I hear you. Things seemed a little awkward."

"Sorry."

Cord shook his head. "Don't be. If anyone gets it, it's me."

We left the five-and-dime a few minutes later, ducked into the bakery next door, ordered a cupcake each, then sat at the table by the window to eat them.

"Mr. Reynolds told me the theater across the street is showing a movie filmed here, in East Aurora. He also said it was a venue I shouldn't miss seeing if I had the chance."

I glanced over at the marquee to see which one it was because several had been made here, especially those with Christmas themes.

"He said there's a matinee today," he added.

"Yeah?"

"Wanna see it with me?"

His tentative expression endeared him to me even more. "Sure. That sounds nice."

Since the movie was starting soon, we finished our sugary treats and rushed across the street to get tickets.

"Sick of me yet?" he asked on our way into the theater.

"Not yet," I responded, winking.

He gasped when we walked inside. "Wow!"

The box office and concession stands were both constructed with carved wooden panels and etched glass. Beyond them were two murals that had been painted for the theater's grand opening in 1925 and restored and remounted a few years ago.

Like at the five-and-dime, I looked around the theater, where I'd seen so many movies, through different eyes—imagining what my reaction would be if I were seeing it for the first time. It was stunning, with plush velvet-covered seats, art deco sconces, and heavy draperies that hung from ceiling to floor.

"I feel like I've stepped back in time," Cord said after we'd chosen seats in the center of an aisle. "This place—and by that, I mean East Aurora—is really special."

"I've always thought so."

"I wonder why I'm here," he murmured absentmindedly.

"Isn't it for a job?"

He rested his head against the high-back seat. "Yes, but it's complicated."

When he didn't elaborate, I didn't ask.

A few minutes later, the lights dimmed and previews started.

"Hey, Juniper?" he leaned over and whispered.

I turned to face him. "Yeah?"

"How many times do you figure you made out in here?"

I laughed out loud, then covered my mouth with my hand, although it wasn't necessary. Cord and I were the only people in the place.

I counted on my fingers, then turned to him again. "Not once," I said with a straight face.

"Not even with your five-and-dime boyfriend?"

"Nope," I said, not bothering to challenge the fact he'd referred to Ross as my boyfriend. I supposed it was obvious enough.

Cord stretched both arms across the back of my seat and the empty one on his opposite side. "You've got to be pulling my leg, but on the off chance you aren't, I'd be happy to be your first."

"You're right. I'm joking. The number of times I have is far too high to count." I winked.

"Damn. I thought I'd come up with a pretty good reason to kiss you."

My breath caught. "Do you need a reason?"

His eyes darted between mine. "Juni…"

I shook my head and was about to pull away when his hand came up from behind me. He weaved it under my hair and gently squeezed the back of my neck.

"You make me wanna kiss you, Juniper."

I kept my eyes riveted to his, basking in this moment for as long as I could and allowing anticipation to wash over me as I watched his lips move closer to mine.

Except he let go of my neck, removed his arm from behind me, and scrubbed his face with his hand. "Incoming," I heard him mutter.

I nearly jumped out of my seat when, a second later, I heard my father's voice. "June-bug? What are you doing here?"

I shifted to look at him, my mom, my grandmother, and Grayson. Since when did my family all go to a Sunday matinee, especially considering the movie that was just starting ran several times each holiday season on local TV stations?

"What are *you* doing here?" I whispered back at him, even though the six of us were still the only people in the theater.

"We wanted to get into the holiday spirit, dear," said my grandmother, loudly enough to probably be heard out in the lobby. "Who's your friend? I don't recognize him."

Thankfully, my mom intervened, shushed her, and said she'd introduce him after the movie was over.

She nodded, and just as I was about to turn around to face the screen, I saw her tug on Grayson's arm. "Be a darling and bring Nana some popcorn, would you, Gray?"

"Of course."

"Want some popcorn?" Cord leaned over and asked.

"If you do."

When he got up and followed Grayson out, Nana put her hand on the seat in front of her and leaned forward. "He's very handsome, dear."

"Shush," my mother repeated.

"Settle yourself, Patricia."

I faced forward, shook my head, and laughed under my breath. Apart from when we were skiing, Cord and I hadn't gone to a single place today where we didn't run into someone I knew. My family being here, at the movies, was by far the most awkward. I just hoped Cord was really getting popcorn rather than racing to his truck and hightailing it out of town.

I closed my eyes, remembering how close we'd come to kissing. Or at least I thought that was what he was going to do. But why would he? And why would I want him to? We'd only met last night. Going to the movies wasn't a date; it was just me showing him something else of note in our town.

So why was I so disappointed?

6

Cord

When I met Juniper, her brother, and their mother last night—which felt like days ago—Grayson had been friendly. Today, he was standoffish. I got it. If a stranger came to town and, in less than twenty-four hours, looked like he was about to kiss my sister, I'd be tempted to knock some sense into the guy.

I hadn't known it was her family who sat in the seats behind us until I glanced over my shoulder and saw Patricia, who, like the night before, winked at me. Had she seen us? Did she know how close I'd come to kissing her daughter?

That they'd showed up when they did and chose the seats they had when there were two hundred or so others empty definitely meant I wouldn't be tempted to try it again. And that was a good thing. I reminded myself I had no business starting something when my life was in such upheaval, particularly in a place I couldn't wait to get out of and head back home.

I also had to figure out a way to talk with Juniper's uncle, preferably before I met Hoss Schultz.

As far as the job, I had no idea what to expect. A ranch manager was on call twenty-four hours a day, seven days a week, unless they had a number-two guy they could rely on without question. I doubted there was such a hand at the Lilacs. If there had been, he or she would likely have taken over for JD rather than me.

I shook my head and scrubbed my face. Everyone who heard I'd be working there assumed I'd be taking over the man's job. That didn't mean they were right. For all I knew, I'd be the bottom-rung ranch hand, spending my days mucking stalls and cleaning up horse shit.

Then there was the other, more important question about what I was doing here in the first place? In hindsight, it was easy to guess the reason our father had forced Buck to spend a year on the Roaring Fork was so he'd realize how much the place—and our family— meant to him. Before he came home for the old man's funeral, I often wondered if we'd ever see him again.

Now, he, his wife, and their son, who they'd nick-named Buckaroo, were living in the original homestead house, which they'd renovated in the months before their baby was born. I could honestly say I didn't remember seeing Buck happy, let alone to the degree he was now. That our father had had a hand in that was almost unfathomable, considering he made our lives as miserable as he possibly could until the day he died.

So why was I here, in a place I'd never heard of? Meeting Juniper was definitely a bright spot in what I suspected were going to be some dark days, but I sure as hell couldn't rely on her to keep me entertained for the next several months.

I stood next to Grayson, waiting for our popcorn.

"If you're playing a game with my sister, I'll make you regret ever coming to East Aurora, and I won't be alone in that." His tone was low, and there was an edge to his words.

"I'm not," I answered, lame as it was. "I'd say we're friends, but how can we be even that? I mean, I can't explain it, but have you ever met someone you feel as though you've known for years after only a few hours?" And what the fuck was with me running my mouth like I was? And to Juniper's brother of all people.

Grayson turned to me and rolled his eyes. "Seriously? You couldn't have said something to make me hate you? You had to deliver a line as sappy as the ones in the movie we're missing?"

I laughed out loud and, at the same time, breathed a sigh of relief. Everyone I'd met in the Chance family seemed happy and good-natured. Truth was, everyone I'd met in East Aurora appeared that way.

"It's my dad and his family you really have to worry about. His brother's a cop."

"I met him. He wants to talk to me about Hoss Schultz."

Grayson's lip curled. "He's bad news. So is Miss Cena's nephew, Jimmy. Everyone thinks they're in cahoots to somehow take the Lilacs away from her. It's just no one knows what to do to stop them. By the time there's proof, it might be too late."

"Do you really think that's possible?"

He shrugged. "I have no idea, but it's what most of the town fears."

"It seems like the community is tight-knit."

"We are. We're also protective of our own."

The girl behind the counter handed each of us a tub of popcorn.

"Six waters, please," Grayson said to her before turning back to me. "You'll want to grab a few napkins too. My sister's been known to use my shirt as the ideal place to wipe the butter off her hands."

I stuffed several into my pocket, then took three of the waters Grayson had ordered. I was headed into the theater when my cell phone rang.

"I'll be a sec," I said when I saw it was Porter calling.

Grayson grabbed the second popcorn and walked away.

"Hey, Port. What's up?"

"Just checkin' in. How are things in New York?"

"It's a cute little town. Like CB, but without a ski area."

"Have you seen the place where you're supposed to work yet?"

"Nah. Tomorrow. How are things there?"

"About the usual."

"You sure, Port? You sound off."

"See ya, Cord."

I held the phone so I could see the screen. "What the fuck was that about?" I said under my breath.

"Did you get another photo message?"

I turned around and saw Juniper standing behind me.

"Thank goodness I didn't since it was my brother calling." We both laughed.

"Is everything okay?"

"I get the feeling it isn't, but when I asked, he ended the call."

"So, do you want to go back in, or…"

"I do."

"But?" she asked when I didn't make a move in that direction.

"I'd like to talk to your uncle."

Her eyes opened wide. "I forgot. I'll send you his number now."

I read mine out, then called him once I got the text she sent me. He picked up on the first ring.

"This is Cord Wheaton."

"I was wondering if you were going to get in touch."

I leaned against the wall and covered my mouth when I yawned. "Sorry, it's been a full day."

Juniper wriggled her fingers like a wave and returned to the auditorium.

"You got time to meet?" Pete asked.

"Sure. When?"

"My shift ends in a few minutes. Where are you?"

"Outside the movie theater." I rolled my eyes like Grayson had. *Technically*, I was.

"There's a tavern right next door. I don't know about you, but I could go for a beer."

"Sounds good. See ya there."

I stuck my head in the theater and saw Juniper had moved to the row where her family sat. Rather than disrupt them all again, I sent her a text, saying I was meeting Pete next door but would be back as soon as I could.

When I saw him walk by, I hurried out to meet him.

"Seein' a matinee?" he asked, looking up at the marquee.

"Juniper and her family are in there."

He shook his head. "Paying to watch a movie they've seen a hundred times."

I followed Pete inside the bar. "What are you drinking?" he asked.

"Whatever's on tap is fine."

"That'll be a Blue," he said just like Juni had last night, then motioned to a table in the back.

I nodded and took a seat with my back to the door. It made me uncomfortable, but I figured Pete would be more so.

A couple of minutes later, he set a beer in front of me, then slid into the booth.

"Let's start at the beginning, Cord. What's a cowboy from Colorado doing in East Aurora right before Christmas?"

"You wouldn't believe it if I told you."

"Try me." Based on the look on his face, I doubted he'd relent until I did.

I got it, though. If Hoss Schultz was trouble, it didn't look good that I'd just rolled into town, saying he was my only contact.

"My father died about a year and a half ago," I began. I told him about the trust, its stipulations, and how my siblings and I would lose everything if I didn't adhere to what was required of me. "Four days ago, I got a call from the attorney, saying I needed to be here by Monday morning."

"And you have to stay a full year?" he asked.

"That's right."

He signaled, and the bartender came to the table.

"Two more Blues and a couple shots of the good stuff. I figure you could use it," he added after the guy walked away.

"You got that right."

"Did the same guy tell you to make contact with Schultz?"

"He did," I confirmed.

"Tell me about him."

"If you mean the lawyer, I can assure you he's not mixed up in whatever Schultz is. I've known him since we were kids. To be honest, I have no idea how he graduated from high school, let alone got a law degree."

"He's got brains enough to hold this over you and your siblings."

"I don't think he knows much more than we do. It seems more like he's the messenger."

"Somebody's controlling this from behind the scenes."

I nodded. "The trustee is an LLC."

When the bartender delivered the shots and beers, Pete raised his glass. "To three hundred and sixty-five days in East Aurora. May you make the best of them."

"Cheers," I responded before downing what was in mine.

"Now, let me tell you what I know about the Schultz brothers. They're some rough customers. You might want to watch your back."

"Understood."

"What I've heard is they've been contracting with wineries, distilleries, and brewers around the state. They look for outfits that aren't doing well, typically mom-and-pop places. They promise them big returns with no upfront costs, saying they can turn their business around inside of a few months. Then they negotiate a monthly management fee and bleed the business dry."

"You'd think it would catch up with them."

Pete took a drink of his beer. "That's where the rough stuff comes in. They threaten the family, saying they'll bury them if they pursue legal action. I'm not talking about criminal. This would be civil stuff. Of course the family has little left as it is, so the idea of hiring a lawyer and facing a court battle is enough for them to drop it. There have been a few who tried to take matters into their own hands."

"What happened to them?"

Pete leaned forward. "Obviously, there's not enough evidence to get a conviction, but at least one guy is in a coma after the Schultz boys *allegedly* beat the shit out of him."

"No witnesses?"

"Only seeing the victim leave a bar. Nothing after that. But some of his family members gave statements saying Schultz did, in fact, threaten him."

"So they somehow got the owner of the Lilacs to hire them? I heard she's pretty old."

"Miss Cena will turn one hundred in a few days—on Christmas. Unfortunately, her health is so bad we've been unable to question her. However, according to a lawyer here in town, there's a bona fide agreement in place."

I studied the beer in my glass, then looked up at him. "You're not telling me all this just so I'll watch my back."

"You catch on quick."

"What do you want from me?"

"I doubt very much Schulz is behind you reporting to the Lilacs for a job. Whatever's driving that is something else entirely."

"You haven't answered my question."

"There are a couple of things I want," he admitted.

"Let me hear them."

"First, keep an eye on what's going on at the estate. If it looks like someone's sabotaging the operation, let me know."

"Next?"

"Your eyes and ears. Anything you see or hear that might lead us to make an arrest, I want to know about immediately."

I took a sip of beer, wishing we'd ordered a second round of shots. "I mean no disrespect by what I'm about to say."

Pete nodded. "Go on."

"What's in it for me besides an ass-kicking if they catch on?"

"I'd think that would be obvious." He was grinning, so I did too.

"If this has anything to do with Juniper, I'm out."

Pete raised his head, then lowered it. "Shit."

"What?"

"I think she may have heard you."

I got up but didn't see her in the bar.

"She hightailed it outta here."

I sat back down. "I'll call her when we're done. I'm not seeing what's obvious, Pete."

"I'm gonna help you figure out what you're doin' here." He rested his forearms on the table. "A minute ago, you said that if Juni is involved, you're out."

"I don't want her or her family getting mixed up in this."

Pete nodded. "I'm glad you said that, because neither do I."

"Look, it isn't like I even know her. She offered to show me around town, and we had a fun day. That's the extent of it."

"Again, glad to hear it. If anything were to happen to her because of your involvement, it's you I'd be coming after, not Schultz."

"Understood."

"You've got my number. Stay in touch." He stood and threw some bills on the table, more than enough to cover a couple of beers and two shots. "As far as what my niece overheard, I'll handle it. For now, I think it's best if the two of you aren't in contact."

While I nodded, I didn't like it. As I'd said, we had a fun day, but there was more to it. I liked Juniper. I wasn't crazy about her thinking I meant anything against her by what she'd overheard.

On the other hand, maybe it would be better if she did. I already knew that resisting reaching out or wanting to spend time with her was going to take every ounce of self-control I possessed.

I made my way back to my truck, but rather than move it after I'd just had a few, I walked the rest of the way to the inn. The feeling that letting Pete talk to Juniper on my behalf wasn't going to turn out well kept nagging at me.

Maybe she, her mom, and Grayson would show up at the inn again tonight and I'd have a chance to apologize.

That idea was quashed when I walked in and saw the same guy behind the desk I had last night after they'd left.

7

Juniper

Could I have been more of an idiot? God, I was behaving like a sixteen-year-old. One would think I'd never had a man pay attention to me or flirt with me. Cord must've been mortified when I'd challenged him to kiss me. I flopped on my bed, wishing I could wipe what I'd said from my memory.

"Do you need a reason?" I'd responded when he jokingly said he thought he'd come up with a good excuse to kiss me.

I was one of those people who remembered every single, stupid thing I said or did, even from when I was a child. I knew those words would play over in my head from now until I was Miss Cena's age.

When I heard a knock at the door, I put my pillow over my head. I was tempted to tell whoever it was to go away, but I didn't.

"Juni, is everything okay?" my mom asked, walking in and sitting beside me on the bed.

"Everything's fine. I made a colossal fool of myself, but what else is new?"

"What happened when you went over to the tavern?"

I peeked out from under the pillow. "I'd rather not talk about it."

"Okay. Well, it looked like we might've interrupted something when we walked into the theater."

"I definitely don't want to talk about that."

"Juni, I've been thinking about something."

I moved the pillow to the side and rolled to face her. "What?"

"Christmas is one week from today. It seems like maybe Cord will be alone for the holiday."

I shook my head. "No."

"It isn't like you to be callous, Juniper."

"Giving the guy a break from the Chance family isn't callous, Mom."

"How do you know that's what he wants? Maybe he appreciates knowing someone here."

I cringed. "You know that thing I don't want to talk about?"

"Which one?"

"What happened when I walked into the tavern."

"Yeah?"

My eyes filled with tears that I blinked away. "Let's just say I know for a fact he wants nothing to do with us. Or at least with me."

My mom moved my hair from my face. "I find that hard to believe."

"I don't, but can we please drop it now?"

"Of course." She got up. "Dinner will be ready in a few minutes."

"I feel like all I've done is eat today. I'm really not hungry."

She nodded. "There will be leftovers in the fridge if you change your mind."

I thanked her, and she shut the door behind her when she walked out. I grabbed the pillow again and put it over my face, then reached over to my phone on the nightstand. After swiping the screen, I hit delete on the text exchange between Cord and me, which meant I also deleted his number.

I lay there, feeling sorry for myself for longer than I should've, when something dawned on me. Maybe it was time I flew the nest, as they say, before my parents chucked me out of it. Not that they would. I was sure it wouldn't bother them if Grayson and I lived here a few more years. And how pathetic would that be?

I opened my laptop and scoured job postings. Those I found had been up for a while. A couple of them were from places that had offered me a position after graduation. While they might not have that exact post open any longer, perhaps they'd be willing to let me interview for another.

It seemed unlikely many people would be in the office this close to Christmas, but I filled out the online applications anyway. Maybe after the first of the year, I'd at least have interviews scheduled.

Nothing I did distracted me enough to stop thinking about Cord. The man set my pulse racing. But more, he made me laugh. I'd never been with a guy like him. Someone who wasn't from here. Even the guys I dated when I was at Syracuse were all from New York, not somewhere as intriguing as Colorado.

The last words I heard him say resonated more than all those we'd said to each other between last night and this afternoon. If I was involved, he wanted no part of whatever Pete had proposed.

Why not? I mean, I'd admitted to being a nerd who was also über competitive. Then he'd had the pleasure of meeting Ross, a guy as "small town" as I was. As soon as Mr. Reynolds mentioned he'd been trying to get me to come work for the five-and-dime, I was sure Cord figured it was what I'd do, eventually. He probably thought I'd end up taking Mr. Reynolds' offer, then I'd marry Ross, stay in East Aurora for the rest of my life, and breed the next generation who would ultimately take over for us when we retired.

The whole scenario turned my stomach. It wasn't like I thought I was above spending the rest of my life in my hometown. I just couldn't see myself with Ross or working for his family's business. If I did stay, I'd much rather work for mine.

When my phone buzzed with a text from a number I knew all too well—Ross'—I deleted it, then removed him as a contact. I didn't go as far as Cord had when he blocked Sandy, though. If he actually had. After hearing he wanted nothing to do with me, I doubted he was even telling the truth.

8

Cord

When I contacted Hoss the next morning, he told me to report to the Lilacs on Wednesday. I was in a near panic, remembering the document the lawyer had sent via email stated I had to "maintain residence" there for a period of one year.

The next call I made was to Six-pack. When I reiterated what Hoss had said, he assured me he could adjust the date of my arrival. I asked him why the hell I'd had to get here so fast and miss Christmas if that were the case, and he repeated that he had no control over the stipulations in the codicil. While he clearly did, since he could adjust a date, I didn't argue with him. If I had, maybe he'd refuse to do as he said and, two days after arriving in town, our family would've lost everything because of me.

Rather than sitting around the inn on the off chance I'd see Juniper, her brother, or her mother, I went for a drive. I'd just pulled up to a restaurant on the banks of Lake Erie when my cell rang with a call from Pete.

"How'd it go with Hoss?" he asked.

"He told me to show up on Wednesday."

"Gotcha. I've been thinking about something I want to run by you."

"Shoot."

"Does the name Rooker mean anything to do?"

The air left my lungs. "It does."

"How?"

"It's my mother's maiden name."

"Where are you now?" he asked.

I looked up at the sign. "Hoak's."

"Give me twenty minutes, and I'll meet you there."

After walking inside, I sat at a table by the window and ordered a beer. I had a feeling I was going to need it. I'd hold off on the shots, though, since I'd eventually have to drive back to East Aurora.

While I waited, I thought about Juniper, wishing she was with me today. That was hardly fair, though, considering she'd already spent a day with me. I wondered if she'd been to this place and sat where I was, looking out at the frigid lake. Since she'd lived close by all her life, chances were good she had.

"Can I bring you something to eat?" the waitress asked.

"I'll have a salad with grilled chicken, please." I closed the menu and handed it to her.

"You aren't from around here, are you?"

"No, ma'am," I responded.

"We don't get too many cowboys in here. At least not real ones."

I chuckled as she walked away.

"Hey, Pete," I heard her say a few minutes later. "You in for lunch?"

"Meeting someone."

She motioned with her head. "That him?"

"Sure is. Thanks, Lori. Bring me whatever he's having to drink."

When he walked over and sat across from me, I noticed he was wearing street clothes.

"Funny place for you to pick for lunch in the dead of winter," Pete commented.

"Went exploring."

"Right." He looked at the waitress when she delivered his beer, then over at me. "Did you order?"

I nodded.

"Order of wings, please," he said, looking up at her.

"The usual?" she asked.

"Yes, ma'am." He turned from her to me. "You said Rooker was your mother's maiden name."

"It's also my middle name."

"I guess no one's told you it was JD's last name."

My eyes opened wide, and I watched as he retrieved an envelope from his pocket, pulled out some papers, and handed them to me.

"What's this?" I asked.

"Take a look."

The first thing I saw when I unfolded the stack was a family tree like I'd seen on ancestry commercials. On the third row from the top was my mother's name—Patricia Rooker Wheaton. It listed her birth and death date, along with my father's name under spouse.

I went back to the top, where the name James R. Rooker appeared. His spouse was listed as Irene Turner. James and Irene had two children, James D. Rooker and Cena Rooker Covert.

I looked up at Pete. "Mrs. Covert was my mother's aunt?"

He nodded. "So it appears."

I pointed at the name to the left of Cena's. "This is my grandfather."

"That's right. He and his wife had two children, your mother and JD."

"JD was my uncle."

Pete nodded again.

"Holy shit," I said under my breath, finishing the beer in my glass before waving at the waitress for another.

My mind was reeling. I was nine years old when my mother died. I barely remembered her, and I sure as hell didn't recall her or my father mentioning she had relatives in New York.

"It's a clue, at least," said Pete.

"You think that's why I'm here? Just to take over from JD?"

He shrugged. "Seems unlikely that's all it is. I mean, why only for a year?"

I thought about Buck having to spend the same amount of time on the ranch and how he'd gone from never wanting to set foot on it to making it his home. Did my father expect I'd eventually decide to stay here? It didn't make sense. This was my mother's family. Not his. "Truth is, I'm baffled," I said to Pete.

"I would be too if I were you."

"So what is Cena to me? My great aunt?"

"Yeah, and according to this"—he pointed to the family tree—"you might stand to inherit something."

"I don't care about that. In fact, the less I hear about inheritances in general, the better." I put my finger on two more names in my generation, James D. Rooker, III, and John Rooker. "What can you tell me about these two?"

"Jimmy's around. In fact, I believe he might be working with Hoss. Johnny left right after high school. To my knowledge, he's never been back."

"Where'd he go?"

"No clue."

We ate our lunch in silence, and when we finished, I asked Lori for the check. "This one's on me," I said to Pete before walking out.

"Keep in touch," I heard him call out after me.

Two days later, I met with Hoss Schultz. My first impression of him reinforced everything I'd heard. Trouble sat just beneath the surface of this man. It was evident in his hooded eyes and the sneer he hardly tried to hide. Straight off, I decided I wanted nothing to do with the asshole. However, until I knew why I was being forced to spend a year here, I had to make nice.

"I'll give you the rundown before you meet the crew," he began, taking a seat behind the desk of what appeared to be the ranch manager's office. From everything I'd learned from Pete, Schultz wasn't involved in the cattle operation. However, if JD hadn't named a successor before he died, and given what I'd also heard about Mrs. Covert's health, I guessed someone had to have stepped up.

A quick but guarded study of the man told me I wouldn't be answering to him on a daily basis, unless it was inside an office like this one. There wasn't a single callous on his soft hands nor were there scars that every cowboy inevitably had just from mending fences. The numerous scars on the back of mine were a testament to what a bitch barbed wire could be.

"The way the former owners set up the estate is antiquated but functional, at least for now."

The words "former owners" and "functional for now," led me to guess Schultz believed a significant change in who held the property's title was on the horizon.

"In total, there are five thousand acres. Forty-three hundred and fifty are held under a separate deed set aside for the cattle operation."

My best guess was it had been done for tax purposes. It was on the tip of my tongue to ask, but I kept my mouth shut. I'd learn more from the man by what he chose to divulge. More importantly, what he didn't.

If he'd meant it to, the size of the place didn't faze me. It was a tenth of the acreage of Roaring Fork Ranch.

He paused briefly, then continued. "The other six hundred and fifty acres that aren't forested, are utilized for residences, barns, and other outbuildings, including the estate's winery and vineyards."

I nodded once, then waited for him to continue.

His eyes scrunched. "You got any experience with a ranch this size?"

"Not this size, no."

The man sighed and muttered something under his breath.

"What have you got? Three thousand head?"

He looked up at me. "About."

"The last place I was at had closer to thirty-five thousand."

Schultz quickly steeled his reaction, but I saw enough to know he'd heard me.

"What's the size of your crew?" I asked, taking control of the conversation.

"Thirty, give or take."

I didn't react, especially when it became evident the man knew next to nothing about managing a cattle operation. There was no way so few cowboys could manage an operation this big. My guess, if and when I got the chance to look at any ledgers there might be, was their annual head losses were at least ten percent, but probably a *helluva* lot more than that.

"Where are they?" I asked.

He looked up at me.

"The crew."

He didn't respond other than to pick up his phone. He punched the screen several times, then set it down.

"Jed is the foreman. He and the guys will meet you here in thirty."

"We'll meet them at the corral instead."

He raised a brow but, even after I stood, didn't speak. I was almost out the door but turned around. "Is this my office?"

He nodded once.

"How many bunkhouses are there?"

"Jed will answer questions of that nature."

I smirked. The asshole had no idea, in the same way he had no clue how many hands were on the payroll. "What's your role?"

"I don't have anything to do with the cattle."

That much was obvious. "Well, seein' this isn't your office, I'd say you should be the one to leave."

He got up and came around the desk. I had a good foot on the guy and fifty pounds of muscle, which I made sure he noticed as he shuffled past me.

"One more thing. You mentioned the former owners. Who owns the place now?"

He raised a brow. Yeah, I was being heavy-handed with him, but I knew firsthand never to let someone like Hoss Schultz think he'd ever have anything over me.

"I can't answer that yet."

Meaning, he didn't know. *Good.*

As with Hoss, I didn't get a good feeling about Jed. In fact, there wasn't a single man out of the twenty who showed up who impressed me.

Yeah, New York was different than Colorado, but in my experience, cowboys were cowboys regardless of where they hailed from. There was a code we lived by.

I doubted there was one amongst those gathered here who subscribed to it.

"Is this everyone?" I asked Jed.

"Just about."

I leveled a glare at him. "Anyone else not here in fifteen minutes will be removed from the payroll." I stalked into the barn, then returned to the office and started making a list. Near the top was changing the locks on the door and buying a damn space heater. Before that, though, I needed to figure out where I was supposed to live. There wasn't a ranch manager worth two shakes of salt who lived in one of the bunkhouses. It was as much for the cowboys' sake as mine.

I was digging through files I had to admit were meticulously kept when I heard a knock at the door. I was about to tell whoever it was to come in, a practice that would be commonplace at the Roaring Fork. But until I had a better handle on the guys who'd be working for me, it wouldn't be a good idea for them to think they could just walk in.

When I got up and pulled it open, I saw Hoss and Jed head to head a few feet away. "Yeah?"

Schultz got a few more words in before Jed nodded and walked away.

"I came back to give you these," he said, handing me a set of keys. "The cottage a few yards from the barn is where the previous ranch manager lived."

After stuffing them in my pocket, I leaned against the doorjamb. "How long have you two known each other?"

"Jed? Hell, I don't know."

"Guess."

"Few years."

I nodded once, pulled the door closed, and walked away after making sure it was locked. Two things would be updated on my list this afternoon. First, where I'd be living for the next few months. Second, I'd add Jed's name to the list of those who'd be let go.

I wouldn't send him packing right away, though. I needed to get a better lay of the land before I did.

9

Juniper

We'd just finished opening our gifts on Christmas morning when my mother's cell phone rang. Since most of our relatives were here, I couldn't imagine who might be calling.

"Thank you for letting me know, Mrs. Miller," she said a few minutes into the call, looking straight at me.

I knew without her needing to say it that Miss Cena had passed.

I spent the time between Christmas and the week after New Year's looking for more job postings and making a note of the few new ones that had popped up. Rather than look desperate by sending a message when everyone else in the world was still on holiday, I set a reminder to reach out closer to the end of the month.

My mom had called Mrs. Miller a couple of times, asking if there'd be a memorial service for Miss Cena, but she said she wasn't aware of one. If she'd asked whether Cord was still at the Lilacs, she didn't say, and I didn't bring it up either.

Without Miss Cena there, I only had one reason to visit the place again, not that I was ready to. In fact, I might never be.

"Where are you off to?" my mom asked when I came downstairs and grabbed my coat off the rack.

"I'm having dinner with Ross Reynolds."

She raised a brow.

"It's just dinner. I made that perfectly clear."

"I didn't say a word."

"Yeah, you did. I can read your mind."

She shook her head. "My mind is completely blank. Nothing to read."

I chuckled. My mom and I were alike in that our minds were never blank. We both overthought everything down to the most minute detail.

"He's here," I said when I saw his car pull in the driveway. I kissed her cheek and told her I'd see her later.

She waved as I shut the door behind me.

It didn't take long before I realized the mistake I'd made. While I'd said I made it clear we were only having dinner, Ross disregarded it entirely. He was acting as if we were dating again, and when I tried to address it, he responded as if I hadn't said a word.

Finally, when I'd told him I was ready to leave at least three times and he just kept talking, I excused myself, left the table, got my coat from the rack, and walked out. I could've called my mom or brother to come and get me, but it wasn't that long of a trek home and the weather was nice for the beginning of January.

I was about to turn off the main drag onto our street when I saw a black truck drive by. The Colorado plates confirmed it was Cord's. Thankfully, it was dark enough that I doubted he saw me. Halfway down the first block, though, he pulled up beside me and stopped.

"Juniper?"

"Oh, hey, Cord."

"What're you doing out, walking in the cold?"

"It isn't that cold."

"Okay, what are you doing out, walking at this hour?"

I rolled my eyes. "You sound like my nana. It's nine, not midnight."

"Can you get in the truck? I was hoping we could talk."

"It's not a good idea. Besides, my house is right there." I pointed at one a few doors down that was definitely *not* my house. Mine was still two blocks away.

He cut the engine and got out. "I've been trying to get in touch with you."

I knew he had. Who else did I know with a Colorado number? As far as trying to get in touch, he'd only called twice.

I shoved my hands in my coat pockets and sighed. "How are you, Cord?"

"I guess you heard Mrs. Covert passed away."

I nodded. "Mrs. Miller called my mom."

"I never got to meet her," he said, looking down at the ground.

"Too bad. She was a nice lady."

"Look, I don't know what your uncle told you about that day in the tavern…"

"He didn't tell me anything."

Cord's eyes met mine. "Nothing?"

"We didn't talk about it."

"I want to explain. Can we please get in the truck?"

I noticed he wasn't wearing his jacket, so I gave in—stupidly.

He opened the door for me, and I climbed inside.

"It's nice to see you, Juniper," he said once he was behind the wheel and had started the engine.

"Thanks. What did you want to explain?"

He scrubbed his face with his hand, something I'd seen him do more than once the day we spent together. "You know Pete and I were talking about Hoss Schultz."

I nodded.

"When you heard me say I didn't want you to have any part of it, I meant I didn't want you involved with Schultz. As I'm sure you know, he's not a good guy."

"That's not what you said." I'd whispered the words, but as soon as I had, I wished I'd kept them to myself.

"What?" he asked.

"It doesn't matter."

He reached for my hand, but I moved it away. "Juni, talk to me. I've missed you."

I stared at him. "We aren't friends who haven't seen each other for a while, Cord. We spent part of a day together. I showed you around town. That's it." My words came out harsher than I'd intended, but I was still pissed about Ross' behavior at dinner.

"I'm sorry. I never meant—"

"You said, 'If this has anything to do with Juniper, I'm out.' Those were your exact words."

"Taken out of context," he murmured.

"Except it doesn't matter." I put my hand on the door to get out, but he rested his on my arm.

"Wait. Your uncle said he'd explain."

I shook my head and cleared my throat. "Cord, I had a nice time with you that day. I hope you're settling in over at the Lilacs and enjoying the time you have to spend in East Aurora. It's a nice place, and I'm glad I was able to show you around. But that's it, okay?"

He moved his hand down my arm to my wrist. I was wearing gloves, but the area between them and my coat was bare. He drew circles on my skin with his fingertips. "I meant it when I said I missed you."

I cocked my head. "You should get to know more people here. Make some friends."

"I guess. By the way, there's a couple who will be staying in the main house. My understanding is the woman inherited it."

My eyes scrunched. "What did you say?" I held up my hand when he looked like he was going to repeat himself. "Never mind, I heard you. Who is she?"

"I have no idea. I get the impression she doesn't know why Mrs. Covert left it to her."

"What's her name?"

"Samantha. I think her last name is Marquez. Something like that, anyway."

"You said she's with a man? Is he her husband?"

Cord shook his head. "They're definitely a couple, though."

"Hmm." This was an interesting and unexpected development. I groaned and moved my hand away a second time. It was also none of my business. "I'm interviewing for jobs out of state," I blurted.

His eyes were wide. "You're leaving?"

"If someone makes me a good enough offer, I guess I am."

"There's something I need to tell you."

"Okay."

"I regret not kissing you in the movie theater."

"Cord, please, don't be ridiculous. We spent one day—"

"Don't lie, Juni. You wanted me to."

I folded my hands together. "I got caught up in the moment. That's all it was for me. I'm sure that's all it was for you. It's silly that we're even talking about it."

"You can speak for yourself but not for me."

"Right. Good night, Cord." I grabbed the handle at the same time I heard a click. Then it wouldn't move. "You're locking me in here?"

"No, I'm taking you home." He put the truck in gear, pulled away from the curb, and was about to pull in the driveway of the house I'd pointed out earlier.

"I don't live here."

"Huh?"

"I lied. That isn't my house. Mine is a couple of blocks farther down."

"Can I *please* drop you at home, Juniper?"

I sighed. "Sure. Keep going, and when you pass the second stop sign, it's the second house on the left."

He drove slowly and scrubbed his face once more before we got to my driveway. He stopped and put the vehicle in park. "Pete asked me to see what kind of dirt I could get on Schultz. We both agreed we didn't want you or anyone else in your family involved, simply because we believe he's dangerous."

"If this woman you mentioned is inheriting the estate, maybe Schultz won't be a problem anymore."

"Maybe not." His eyes bored into mine. "You're really leaving?"

I took a deep breath. "I'm just looking. I haven't made any decisions yet."

"I hope you don't."

"Is that right? What about you? Aren't you leaving a year from now?"

He sighed. "I am."

"Can you unlock my door, please?" I heard the click and opened it. "Goodbye, Cord."

"Good night, Juni."

"That isn't the same vehicle you left in," my mom said when I came in the front door.

"You're right. Cord dropped me off."

"What happened, sweetheart?" she patted the sofa, and I sat beside her.

"Wait. You can't see the driveway from here."

"I hurried and sat down when I saw you get out and walk up the steps."

I rolled my eyes.

"So, what happened?" she repeated.

"You were also right about Ross. I never should've agreed to have dinner with him. It was like he expected us to just pick up where we left off."

"He's smitten."

"He's obsessed."

"That may be a better word for it." She paused. "So, connect the dots for me. How is it that Cord brought you home?"

I closed my eyes and rested my head on her shoulder. "He saw me walking and gave me a ride."

She leaned away, and her eyes scrunched. "You walked home?"

"It wasn't that far, and it's nice out."

"Nice?"

"For January. Yes."

"Ross made you walk home? I'm going to give that boy a piece of my mind."

"Stop. He's not a boy; he's a man. And I'm sure he would've driven me home had I not stalked out on him at the restaurant."

"That bad?" she asked, resting her head against mine.

"Worse."

"What about Cord?"

"He said Miss Cena left the estate to someone named Samantha Marquez."

She sat up straighter. "What?"

I shrugged. "That's what Cord said anyway."

"My goodness. Jimmy Rooker must be fit to be tied."

I shrugged again. "It's not our business, Mom."

"My darling Juniper, we live in a small town. Everything is our business."

10

Cord

Earlier tonight, I was about to head out to grab some dinner when an SUV pulled up to the barn.

"Hello, can I help you?" I asked when a man and woman got out and walked toward me.

"This is Samantha Marquez, and I'm Beau Barrett."

I tipped my hat to the lady and shook the hand of a man with a British accent.

"Sam has inherited the property," he blurted. Nothing like cutting to the chase.

I thought back to the family tree I'd studied several times since Pete gave it to me, but didn't recall seeing her name on it. "Pardon my manners, ma'am. I'm Cord Wheaton," I said, looking between the two people.

She didn't say anything, but Beau did. "It's our understanding that you were employed by Mrs. Covert to care for her livestock?"

I shifted on my feet. "Not by Mrs. Covert. I never met her. Hoss hired me." That wasn't exactly true, but it was close enough for now.

"Hoss?" he asked.

"Yeah, um, his last name is Schultz. That's all I know besides that he oversees the vineyards and winery. Things have been chaotic since my uncle passed away. Apparently, he and my grandfather worked for the Coverts all their lives, and no one else knew what all they did."

"How long have you worked here?" Samantha asked. Interestingly, she didn't have a similar accent as the man's.

"Since December 20. A few days after my uncle died."

"Who handled the livestock in the time in between?" she asked.

"I'm not sure about that either, other than to say there's a full crew of cowboys on the payroll." That wasn't true, either. There was nothing "full" about the cast of characters I'd been slowly getting to know.

"But you've been hired, yes?"

"Hoss suggested I stick around until the estate was figured out."

"You're from Colorado?" Beau asked.

"Yes, sir," I responded, wishing the guy would stop asking questions. So far, other than to Pete, I hadn't told anyone the circumstances of why I was here. I sure as hell hadn't told Hoss. My opinion of him hadn't changed since the first time we met. In fact, as soon as I learned one of "my" crew had any connection to the man, they went on the sack list.

When the woman audibly shivered, Beau suggested we go inside. I'd never been in the main house and wasn't anxious to tonight.

"We could go into the barn office. It's warm in there," I suggested instead.

They followed me, and I turned the lights and the space heater back on, then motioned toward two of the three chairs in the room.

"Let's see if I can summarize," the Brit began when I took a seat behind the desk. "Your grandfather and uncle worked for Mrs. Covert for many years."

I nodded. "That's right."

"You said you arrived a few days after your uncle died. Had he been ill?"

"I'm not sure, sir." I scrubbed my face with my hand. Might as well cut to the chase in the same way he had. "I guess the question, now, is whether you want me to stay on or if you want to hire someone else."

"We want you to stay on," the woman responded before the man could.

"You will be working for Ms. Marquez, so the decision is hers," he interjected.

"Should I check with Mr. Schultz for the details of your employment?" she asked.

While I answered affirmatively, the truth was, I wasn't sure if Hoss had any inkling as to why I'd turned up at the Lilacs. Once I'd learned JD was my uncle, I figured that was why Schultz thought I'd arrived when I did.

"Understand that this is outside of your job and merely a personal question you do not have to answer."

"Yes, ma'am."

She stood, so I did too. "How old are you, Cord?"

"Twenty-eight, ma'am."

"For the record, I'm twenty-five. Three years younger than you are. You can call me Sam. Him, you still call sir." She pointed to Beau.

"Yes, ma'am, err, Sam."

When I walked them out, they said they'd be in touch.

Since I was on East Coast time, there was a chance Six-pack might still be in his office, so I called to let him know about the new development. I shouldn't have been surprised when the call went to voicemail.

I went into town and ate at the same tavern where I'd initially met with Pete.

I was on my way home from there when I thought I saw Juniper walking down the street. Alone. In the dark. In the middle of winter. There wasn't a chance in hell I'd keep driving without knowing for sure whether it was her.

The minute I was certain, I felt a calmness wash over me. I was so damn happy just to *see* her. And then, I'd blown it, saying the first shit that came to mind without thinking before I spoke.

After dropping her off at her house, I pulled out of the driveway, certain I couldn't have bungled things with her any worse than I had.

Even though I wasn't lying when I said I missed her, should I have said it? More than once? God, it had probably freaked her out.

So often, I found myself wishing I'd handled things differently at the tavern the night when I was with Pete. I should've gone after her and explained. If not then,

I should've called her rather than believe her uncle would take care of it.

The only reason she would've hightailed it out of there, as he'd said, was if her feelings were hurt. I wasn't so insensitive that I hadn't realized that was the case. And yet, I'd let two weeks go by before I finally called. When I didn't hear anything, I gave it one more shot, but she didn't answer or call back.

"You should get to know more people here. Make some friends," she'd said when I told her I missed her a second time. I'd tried that. For a small town, there were a lot of bars in East Aurora, but I'd learned which ones to frequent and which to steer clear of quickly. Anywhere I knew the cowboys who worked at the Lilacs frequented were immediately scratched from my list.

I drove home, but knowing I wouldn't sleep after the way my conversation with Juniper ended, I turned around and went back into town, pulling up to the first open bar I found.

I was about to go inside when I came face-to-face with Beau and Samantha.

"Evenin'," I said, removing my hat.

"Hello, Cord. We were just on our way out, but can we buy you a drink?" Beau asked.

I looked beyond them and noticed a man I'd seen with Schultz a few times. He was looking this way and appeared to be sneering at us. "Nah, but thanks. I don't think I'll stick around."

I turned and walked out.

"What was that about?" Beau asked once we were outside.

"Is there somewhere we can talk? Privately, I mean?" I asked.

"We could return to the Lilacs," he suggested. "Give us twenty minutes?"

"See you there," I said, returning to my truck.

I parked near the cottage, walked up to the main house, and sat on the porch steps. When Beau and Samantha pulled in a few minutes later, I followed them inside.

I removed my hat and sat in the living room after Sam had.

"Cord, are you a wine drinker?" Beau asked when he joined us, carrying a bottle and three glasses.

"I am, thanks."

"Where shall we begin?" he asked after pouring the wine and taking a seat beside Sam.

I set my glass on the table in front of me, leaned forward with my elbows on my knees, then sat up straight and scrubbed my face. "What I'm about to tell you is going to sound crazy."

Sam chuckled. "No crazier than my story."

I smiled. "Guess you're right, ma'am, I mean, Sam. Now, I sound like Dr. Seuss." We all laughed, but what I was about to tell them wasn't the least bit funny. "My father passed away last year."

They both offered their condolences.

"Thanks, but I doubt my siblings are any sorrier than I am that he's gone. The man was a mean *sonuvabitch*."

"Go on," said Beau.

"You'd think death would've put an end to the way the old man manipulated my brothers, sister, and me, but it sure as hell didn't. In fact, it got worse." I looked at Sam. "Sorry for my language."

"No apology necessary. You'll hear plenty of swear words from Beau," she responded, smiling.

"Anyway, our family owns ranchland in Crested Butte, Colorado, called the Roaring Fork." I told them about my dad's trust and how Buck had had to live on the ranch for a period of one year or all of my siblings and I would've lost everything.

"When the year ended, we returned to the lawyer's office, but that's when we learned there was more. As I said, Buck was first. I was next."

"What does that mean?" Sam asked.

"It's why I'm here. Actually, that's what got me here. The why is a mystery."

"Quite conveniently timed, given your uncle had just passed away," Beau commented.

"I think that might have been coincidental." On the other hand, maybe it hadn't been at all. However, until I knew more, I intended to limit how much I speculated. "All the trust said was I was supposed to travel to East Aurora, New York—a place I'd never heard of— and get a job at the Lilacs. And, like my brother, I have to remain here a full year. I hate to disrespect the dead, but I guess it's a good thing my uncle died when he did. I'm not sure I would've been hired on otherwise."

"You don't think your uncle would've given you a job, considering the trust's stipulations?" Beau asked.

I shook my head. "He didn't know me from Adam, sir."

"Was he your father's brother?"

"No. My mother's, and until recently, no one in our family knew she had any siblings."

"An hour ago, I would've said Cena Covert leaving everything to me was the most bizarre thing I'd ever heard, but, Cord, I think you've got me beat," said Sam.

"Not a distinction I desire."

"Believe me, I understand."

"What about the man who hired you? Hoss Schultz?" Beau asked.

"Yes, sir."

"Does he know anything?"

"As I told you earlier, all he said was that he wanted me to stick around until the estate was figured out." I looked between them again. "Have you met him yet?"

"We have not," said Beau.

"I have no reason for thinking this, other than my gut saying I should, but I have a feeling Hoss may have expected someone else would inherit."

"Who did he think would?" Sam asked.

"I have no idea except, that man you saw at the bar? The one who was throwin' daggers at me? It wasn't the first time I've seen him."

"Where else have you run into him?"

"Here. Talkin' to Hoss."

"There's something I need to take care of," Beau said, standing and leaving the room.

"Tell me more about yourself," said Sam.

"There's not much to tell other than my life feels like a movie I'm watching right now."

She chuckled. "You and me both."

When Beau returned, he appeared troubled when he took a seat.

"Everything okay?" Sam asked, probably sensing the same thing I had.

"Yes. We'll chat later."

Sam nodded, and Beau turned to me.

"We'll be meeting with the estate's attorney sometime tomorrow. We'll also make it a point to introduce ourselves to Mr. Schultz."

"Let me know if there's anything I can do to help." I scrubbed my face like I had earlier. As much as I didn't want to broach the subject, I had to. "I know this is a lot to ask, especially since we've just met, but if there's any way I can stay on here, I'd appreciate the opportunity."

"Of course," said Beau, standing. I did the same.

"I guess I don't need to warn you to be mindful what you say to Hoss," I said on my way out after I grabbed my hat.

He shook his head. "You do not."

I was about to take a dinner break the following night when two black SUVs pulled up to the main residence. I walked over when I saw several men get out of each one.

"Can I help you with somethin'?" I asked before noticing the last man to exit the SUV parked farther away. "Decker Ashford?"

"Cord Wheaton? What are you doing here?"

Given he knew my brother Buck and about the situation with the Roaring Fork trust, my answer was a simple one. "My father picked me to be next."

His eyes scrunched. "Seriously?"

"I'm afraid so."

"Shit, Cord. I'm sorry."

"What are you doing here?" I asked.

"Putting a security system in here that's similar to the one we installed out at your place."

I raised a brow. "That extensive?"

Decker nodded. "Beau Barrett and I have mutual friends."

"Speaking of Beau…" I motioned to his and Sam's vehicle as it pulled up and parked.

"Let's catch up later, and you can fill me in on why you're here," he said, walking over to speak with them.

Soon enough, I'd tell him I had no idea why. Maybe he would.

"Do you know him?" Sam asked, approaching me while Decker and Beau chatted.

"Yeah. He and his crew installed a system on our ranch similar to what they're doing for you."

"Small world."

"He also knows my brother Buck."

"The other one who had to stay somewhere for a year?"

"That's right."

"Smaller world."

"I was surprised to see ol' Cord here," I overheard Decker say to Beau. "He's a good guy. Don't know exactly why he's here, but then, I doubt he does, either."

Beau turned to me. "We ran into the man we saw at the bar last night when we arrived at the inn a few minutes ago, which is one of the reasons we returned to the estate."

"Shit," I muttered, looking from him to Sam, who nodded.

"I don't think it's you he hates," she said under her breath.

"Deck, I'd like you to meet Samantha Marquez," said Beau.

"It's a pleasure, miss," Decker responded.

Sam smirked at me, and I laughed.

"He made the mistake of calling me 'ma'am,'" she explained.

After Ashford introduced the three men he'd brought with him, Beau suggested we all go inside.

"Here's where we'll start," said Deck, pointing to a schematic of the main residence. "By the time you go to sleep tonight, the house and one of the barns will be complete, as will the entry gate and most of the perimeter."

Beau had a stunned expression, which Decker caught and chuckled. "We don't mess around, Barrett."

"What can I do to help?" he asked.

"Stay out of our way." Deck looked over at me. "You in?"

"I am, sir," I responded before turning to Beau. "I helped out at the Roaring Fork when Mr. Ashford and his team put a similar system in place."

"What about lodging?" Beau asked Decker.

I cleared my throat. "I, uh, took it upon myself to ask about housekeeping yesterday. Mrs. Miller, who worked for Mrs. Covert for many years, said her staff had cleaned the main residence and the guesthouse per the attorney's request. Not to be morbid or anything, but she mentioned all the bedding was new. I haven't been in this house other than last night, but the guest-house has five bedrooms." I didn't bother mentioning the bunkhouses.

"This one has eight," said Decker, motioning to the schematic and looking over at Sam. "Me and my guys will stay in the guest quarters if that's all right with you."

She responded that they were welcome to stay wherever they'd be comfortable.

Decker said something to the guy he'd introduced as Cru, then asked me and the other two—Snapper and Kick—to join him outside.

"Here's how it's gonna go," he said, handing each of us a set of schematics. "We'll break into teams. Each of you will have three guys helping you. I'll float between you all." After more review, he told the first crew to get started.

"How long did you say you'd be here?" I asked Decker.

He put his hand on my shoulder. "Not as long as you will be, Cord."

11

Juniper

"Hey, I met the woman who's inheriting the Lilacs," said Grayson when he came bounding into the kitchen where my mom and I were making dinner. His cell rang before either of us could respond, and he held up one finger.

"Sure. Of course. Right away, sir," we heard him say.

My mom raised a brow in my direction, and I shrugged.

"Would you mind if my sister rides along? She can help get everything out and ready once we arrive," we overheard him say next.

I put my hands on my hips when his call ended. "What did you just volunteer me for?"

"There's a crew at the Lilacs installing a state-of-the-art security system. That was Beau Barrett. He's the, uh, boyfriend of the new owner. Earlier, when I was helping load their vehicle, I told him our restaurant had great food, and after what he'd tipped me, I said I'd be happy to deliver pizza to them sometime, on me, of course."

"What am *I* helping with, Gray?"

"This." He held out the order he'd jotted on a piece of paper. "Oh, and Beau said he thought Samantha might appreciate having another female to chat with."

"How many people are you serving?" I asked, reading over the list.

"He said fifteen."

"I'll call it in," my mom offered. I handed her the paper, then went upstairs to change. There was no telling whether Cord was one of the fifteen or if I'd even see him. On the off chance I would, I took a quick shower, stuck my hair in a messy bun, then put on a fresh pair of jeans and a sweater.

"Juni, are you ready?" I heard Grayson shout from downstairs just as I finished putting on mascara and some blush.

"Coming," I hollered back.

"You're hoping to see him, aren't you?" he asked once we were on our way to the restaurant to pick up the food.

"I don't want to talk about it."

He nodded. "He seems like a good guy, sis."

Like my mom had to me, I raised a brow in his direction.

"Look, all I'm saying is, when he and I went to get popcorn the day we saw you two at the theater, he said some nice stuff about you."

I shouldn't ask. I did anyway. "What?"

"He said he couldn't explain it, then asked if I'd ever met someone I felt I'd known for years even after only a few hours."

"Couldn't explain what?"

"Why he felt that way about you."

It was the same way I felt about him, not that I'd tell Grayson. Last night, when he'd said he missed me, it was so hard for me not to say I'd missed him too.

"When did they install a gate?" I asked when we pulled up to the estate's entrance after loading the car with enough food to feed three times as many people as he'd said would be eating.

Grayson shrugged. "I can't remember the last time I was here."

"Me either," I said, turning my head away and wiping my tears.

"I'm not sure what to do here," said Gray.

I looked beyond him. "Try pressing the button."

As soon as he had, we heard rustling through a speaker. "Hello, Grayson. Give me a moment to figure out how to open the gate."

"It's opening now," Gray told him, but I no longer heard any background noise.

"He's English? Is she?"

Gray shook his head. "I think they're from California. Oh, and they have a cat named Wanda."

"That's a cool name."

"Right? Better than Buttons."

"We were still in high school when we named her that."

"I didn't name the cat; you did. And if you recall, I protested the choice."

I shrugged, remembering the day my dad had brought the kitten home as a surprise. "Mom was so mad at him," I muttered.

Gray laughed. "She hates cats."

"Hated. Past tense. She loves Buttons."

"Right."

When we pulled up near the house, the first person I saw was Cord. There were two other guys with him.

"Hey, Juni," he said as he walked past me to help unload.

"Hey," I said, following to help.

"Why don't you get the door, and we'll bring all this in?" he offered.

"Uh, sure." I raced up the steps and had my hand on the latch to open it when it hit me that Miss Cena wouldn't be inside. My eyes filled with tears I quickly brushed away.

"That's all of it," Gray said after the four men brought a second load in. "Let me introduce you," he said, leading me over when a man came down the stairs.

"Mr. Barrett, this is my sister, Juniper."

He walked over and shook my hand at the same time a woman who didn't look much older than me came up behind him. "Both of you, please call me Beau. And this is Samantha," he said.

"Sam," she said, shaking my hand too.

"Most everyone calls me Juni."

"What a great name," she commented.

I looked around the kitchen. "I can't remember the last time I was here. It has to have been at least a year. Sorry." I waved my hand in front of my face when I teared up. "Miss Cena was such a lovely woman. I miss her."

"How well did you know her?" Beau asked.

"Not that well. Once her eyesight got bad, I'd visit and read to her a few times a week." Gray's eyes met mine, and I shook my head. The other reason I spent time at the Lilacs wasn't something I wanted to talk about—now or ever.

"Did she say much about her family?"

Gray and I both shuddered. "If you mean her nephews, Miss Cena didn't like to think about them, let alone talk about them. Or one of them, anyway. Johnny was okay."

"Who are the others?" Beau asked.

"Just one. James, but everyone calls him Jimmy." I made a face. "Hard to believe twins could be so different."

"James Rooker?" Sam asked.

I nodded. "That's right." When I glanced over at Cord, our eyes met, but he quickly looked away.

"Did you say his brother's name is Johnny?" Beau asked.

"That's right. He doesn't live around here, though."

"Where does he live?" Sam asked.

"Now that you mention it, I think I remember hearing he went somewhere out west," said Gray, looking over at me. "I can't recall who said it, though. Do you?"

I shook my head. "I don't."

I glanced at Cord again, who was dishing more food on a plate.

"We should let you folks eat," my brother said, nudging me.

"It would be great if you could join us for dinner. As you can see, I'm seriously outnumbered," Sam said to me, motioning to all the men in the room.

Gray shrugged when I turned to him. "Nowhere I need to be."

"Me either, if you're sure you don't mind. I may be biased, since our family owns the place, but I love the Goat's food."

Cord's head shot up. "The Goat?"

"Yeah, have you eaten there?" I asked.

He shook his head. "There's a bar named the same thing in the town where I'm from."

"Interesting. You said somewhere in Colorado, right?" Gray asked.

Cord nodded since he'd just taken a bite of pizza.

Sam and I loaded our plates, and she led me to the other side of the room, where it was quieter.

"I found a box upstairs with a bunch of photos in it. I was wondering if you'd mind taking a look to see if you know anyone in them," she said.

My eyes opened wide. "I'd love to see them."

She looked down at my empty plate. "Did you want to get more?"

I rubbed my stomach. "I'm stuffed. You?"

"Same."

When I took her plate and mine and put them in the trash, I saw Cord talking with Beau. The two were head to head about something that appeared serious.

"Ready?" Sam asked.

"What are the two of you up to?" Beau asked as we passed by.

"I'm going to show Juni the box I found."

"Good idea. I'll be up in a bit."

I couldn't help myself from glancing in Cord's direction. When I did, I couldn't read his expression. If I had to guess, I'd say whatever he and Beau were talking about had upset him.

I gasped when I saw the piles of photographs laid out on the floor, and we sat down to look through them. "These are amazing."

"Some of them aren't labeled," she said, pointing to the pile that had been set aside.

When Sam said something about how sad it was that Miss Cena had lost a daughter so young, I glanced at the photo she held in her hand.

"You look like her," I commented.

"That's what Beau said. I mean, I see it too. There are so many photos of her everywhere."

"My mom used to tell me stories about Miss Cena's life. She didn't speak of it very often. I don't think she ever got over losing her only daughter. I mean, how could she? Then losing her husband the way she did."

"What happened? If you don't mind me asking," said Sam.

"Her brother, Jim, was driving Manley home from somewhere, and I guess he was drunk. There was an accident, and both men died. Her husband was only fifty-four when it happened."

"So sad," Sam murmured. The photo she held in her hand was of Manley and Cena when they were young. "It's confusing, though, right? Jim, JD, Jimmy, then there's Johnny. You said they're twins, right?"

I nodded and watched as she ran her finger over the photo she held in her hand. Then she looked up at me. "Juni, do you know why Cena left everything to me?"

I reached over and put my hand on hers. "I wish I did. All I can say is there was no way she'd let Jimmy get his hands on it."

"He's that bad?"

"Worse. I don't know him, but East Aurora isn't a very big place. There are rumors."

"What rumors?"

"You know, that he drinks too much. Which always leads to him being compared to his grandfather—the one Manley was riding with when he died. Somebody said he gambles. Bets on sports a lot too."

"Do you know much about his dad?"

"From everything I've heard, he was a good guy."

"How did he die?" she asked.

"Cancer." I realized I'd been running at the mouth and most of what I'd said was based on rumors. "I'm sorry for gossiping so much."

"Please don't apologize. If you hadn't come over tonight, there's a lot I wouldn't know. I have one more question if you don't mind."

"I don't mind at all."

"I get that Cena didn't want to leave Jimmy anything, but why didn't she leave it to Johnny?"

"That, I don't know. Like I said, she didn't talk about her family very often."

"What about Jimmy and Johnny's mom?"

"Wait." I looked around for a photo Sam had showed me a few minutes ago of Miss Cena and her son. There was a woman in the background who'd seemed familiar, but I couldn't place her. "That's who this is," I said, picking it up. "JD's wife, err, their mom." I racked my brain, trying to recall what I'd heard about her. "She had an unusual name. From what I remember when Miss Cena said it, it sounded like a cartoon character. A recent one, though. All I can think of is Cruella and Maleficent, and I know it wasn't one of those."

"Juni, was it Ursula?"

"That's it! Wait. Are you okay? You're pale, all of a sudden. Did I say something wrong?"

"How's it going, ladies?" Beau asked, joining us in the bedroom. He went straight over to Sam as soon as he noticed her expression. "What happened?"

"I'm sure it's nothing. Just a coincidence."

"What is?" He looked over at me, then back at her.

"Miss Cena's nephew's wife's name was Ursula," I responded.

"And?" Beau pressed.

"My grandmother had a sister named Ursula," Sam explained.

I held up the photo. "This is her, but it's kind of hard to see what she looked like."

My brother joined us, and we sorted through more piles, but didn't find any others of the woman. When I yawned twice in close succession, Sam noticed and said we should call it a night.

"Sorry. It's been a long day," I said, stifling another yawn.

"I shouldn't have monopolized so much of your time," she said, motioning to all the photos.

"I enjoyed it. I promise. And if you need more help, Beau knows how to reach my brother."

He offered to walk us downstairs, but I told him I knew the way. When Gray and I reached the bottom step, Cord came around the corner.

"Do you have a minute?" he asked.

I looked at Gray.

"Go ahead. I can wait outside," he offered.

"I can give Juni a lift home if you need to leave," said Cord.

My brother yawned. "I am pretty beat."

I raised a brow. Grayson was a night owl, and it was only nine o'clock. There was no way he'd be in bed before midnight. He turned his head so Cord couldn't see and winked.

"If you wouldn't mind," I said, looking up at Cord. Was it my imagination, or did his eyes blaze like they had in the movie theater?

12

Cord

"Okay with you if we head to the cottage so we can give Beau and Sam some solitude?" I asked.

"Actually, I'd love to see the inside of it."

"It isn't much, but it does have a cool stone fireplace."

"Is it where you've been living?" Juni asked.

"Yeah. I guess it's where JD lived the last few years, at least part of the time."

"Cord, I want to apologize—"

"Don't. You have nothing to be sorry for. It's me who mucked everything up."

She took a deep breath in and let it out slowly. "If someone were to ask me about you—about us—I would have no idea what to say. I know you, but I don't."

I nodded. "I feel the same way."

"Grayson told me what you said while you were waiting for popcorn."

We reached the cottage, and I stepped forward to unlock the door, then went ahead of her and turned on the lights. "He did?" I asked once we were both inside and I took her jacket. "Can I get you anything?"

"Are you having something?"

"I've got a bottle of red I opened last night."

"I'll have a glass if there's enough."

I held up the bottle that was still three-quarters full, and she smiled.

"So how are things going here? Are you able to wrangle things?" she asked.

I chuckled. "Truth is most of the horses here are about as elderly as Miss Cena, err, Mrs. Covert was."

"It's okay to call her Miss Cena. Everyone did. In fact, I don't remember anyone calling her Mrs. Covert other than you."

I nodded.

"Sorry, you were talking about the horses when I interrupted you."

"They're all in good health, but they're lacking the kind of energy it takes to *wrangle* a herd as big as this one. I guess I'll need to talk to Sam about that since it would mean investing a significant amount of money. There is one that seems quite a bit younger than the others. Name's Apache. I've taken to riding him." From the corner of my eye, I thought I saw Juni flinch. "Everything okay?" I asked.

"Yeah, fine. Horses can be expensive," she said so quietly I wasn't sure if she meant for me to hear her.

"It isn't just the horses. To be honest, there isn't a single hand I want to keep on the payroll." They were a pretty tight-lipped bunch, so much so I hadn't been able to get a read on whether they were all part of Schultz's crew or if they'd worked for JD. Something told me the former was more likely. While I could've put the hammer on them, I hadn't been here long enough to risk either them ganging up on me or losing the only help I had.

I glanced at Juni, whose eyes had glazed over.

"Sorry, it's not that interesting of a subject." I motioned to the sofa. "Do you have time to sit for a bit?"

"Since you're giving me a ride home, I guess you'd be the one to determine how much time I have."

I wanted to tell her I'd keep her here all night if I could. Longer, in fact. "Okay if I get a fire going?" I asked instead.

"That would be nice."

The wood was already stacked, so all I had to do was light the kindling, which only took a couple of minutes to catch. I got up and turned around, smiling when I saw Juniper sitting in the dead center of the sofa.

"Mind if I join you?" I asked.

"I was hoping you would."

I sat on her left and stretched my arm across the back of the cushions. "Are you warm enough?"

"I'm getting there." She wriggled closer to me.

"Juni—"

"Let me go first, okay?"

I nodded.

"Earlier, I mentioned that Grayson told me what you said at the theater about how sometimes you meet a person and you feel as though you've known them for years even after only a few hours."

"I did say that."

When she turned her head and looked into my eyes, all I could think about was how much I'd wanted to kiss her—that night and now.

"It's how I feel too, and while you said I don't have anything to apologize for, I feel like I do. I was rude to you last night, and I'm sorry."

I reached up and brushed her hair from her face. "You are so beautiful," I murmured.

"Cord, I—"

"No more talking." I leaned forward and kissed her. It was like a whisper, a promise, teasing and taunting, even though I was mad with the desire to ravish her. When she whimpered and grasped the front of my shirt, it was like she'd taken me off a leash, allowing me to break away from all restraints. I pressed my tongue into her mouth and tasted a hint of the wine she'd sipped.

I kissed her slowly, deeply, my tongue winding with hers, and when a second breathy moan escaped her lips, I pulled her onto my lap and eased my hand under her sweater, touching her bare skin.

"Cord, please…"

My desire for her that had been building since the moment we met was like a volcano ready to erupt. But this was too much, too fast. And maybe my name on her lips wasn't pleading with me to take things further. Maybe it was a plea for me to stop. I withdrew my hand, agonizingly pulled my lips from hers, and moved her from my lap.

"Did I do something wrong?" she asked.

I wrapped my arms around her, stroking her hair when she rested her cheek against my chest. "Everything you did was perfect."

"Then, why…"

"Because I asked you here so we could talk. To clear the air between us, not to seduce you."

She turned her head, burying her face in my chest. "What if that's what I want you to do?"

"Then, I will. Soon, but not tonight."

When she pulled away, I sensed surrender. As though, like me, she was giving in to what she knew was right, as difficult as it was.

"I like you, Juniper Chance. Very much, in fact. But there are some things we need to address before we take this any further."

She nodded. "I know."

"You told me you're leaving town."

"I may have exaggerated my departure." Her cheeks flushed, and she lowered her gaze in the way that drove me mad. "I've sent out resumes, but so far, no inter-views. I may have blown my chances."

"What makes you say that?"

"Right after graduation, I had several job offers, but I turned them down. Almost all were on the West Coast, and I wasn't ready to leave the east. A big part of that is how much my parents need my help at the restaurant."

Her mention of it reminded me that I wanted to ask about the name. "You said it's called the Goat?"

"Yeah, kind of weird for a restaurant. I don't know why my dad didn't change it."

"Change it?"

"He bought it from someone else. Why?"

"There's a bar in Crested Butte with the same name."

"That's a coincidence."

Something in my gut told me it might not be, but I didn't have a logical explanation for it. "Do you know who owned it before?"

She shook her head. "No idea, but I'm sure my dad remembers." Juni turned her body to face the fireplace. "You said there were *things* we needed to address. What else?"

"You just said you weren't ready to leave the east. I don't live on the coast, but Colorado is definitely the west. When my year is up, I plan to go home."

"You make it sound like being here is a prison sentence."

I scrubbed my face. Other than to Pete, Beau, and Sam, I hadn't told anyone else here why I was. "My being here wasn't my idea," I confessed.

Her eyes scrunched, and for the third time, I told the story of my father's trust and its stipulations. I explained that if I hadn't come, hadn't gotten the job at the Lilacs, and if I didn't stay a full year—that I couldn't even leave for more than forty-eight hours—my brothers, sister, and I would lose the ranch, along with any other assets contained within the trust.

"What do you mean you can't leave? You can't even go home for a visit?"

"The way it was worded was very specific. It said I have to maintain residency at the Lilacs full-time and cannot leave for more than forty-eight consecutive hours."

"You can't leave the Lilacs?"

I nodded.

"How can that be legal?" she asked.

"When my older brother did his time"—I winked—"he had someone look into it. According to that attorney, it was iron-clad. He said whoever drew it up made sure of it."

Juni stared into the fire. "So you really don't want to be here."

I reached for her hand. "I can tell you that, since I arrived, I found a lot I like about this place."

She took a deep breath and let it out slowly. "I should probably get home."

After dropping her hand, I stood. She did too.

"Juni, I have to ask you something."

"Go ahead."

"I'd like to spend time with you while I'm here. Is that something you'd like too?"

When she didn't respond right away, I knew her answer. I leaned down and brushed her lips with mine, needing one last kiss from her.

"I'll take you home now," I said, standing up straight and squaring my shoulders against the disappointment I knew was inevitable.

"I've never been to Colorado."

My eyes widened. "No?"

She shook her head.

"Do you think you'd like to?" I asked, daring to hope.

"Definitely." She stepped away and grabbed her coat from where I'd set it. "We better go, Cord. If we don't, I might end up in your bed, seduction or not." She winked and I smiled.

Earlier tonight, before I approached Juniper, asking if we could talk, I'd checked with Decker about the installation schedule.

"It's looking like we won't work on your section until tomorrow morning," he said. "However, you know from experience how early we start."

"I'm up before dawn every day, anyway. In fact, I'll have some ranch work to do before I meet up with you," I'd told him.

After dropping Juniper off at home and returning to the Lilacs, I went looking for his crew, anyway.

"Can I help?" I asked when I found him and a few of the guys near the barn.

"Good timing," said Deck. "I could use one more set of hands."

We knocked off after midnight, but like I'd heard him promise Sam and Beau, both the house and the barn were secure. Tomorrow, we'd tackle the perimeter as well as what Deck referred to as hot spots throughout the estate. If someone did manage to get on the property—as unlikely as that was—there would be multiple areas where the system he designed would track movement, particularly from anyone who wasn't identifiable. Even though I'd helped install the one on our ranch, I still had no idea how it all worked, but since we'd caught more than one cattle rustler in the first couple of months after, I was certain it did.

"Get some sleep, and we'll see you in a couple of hours," said Deck, nudging me as we crossed paths on my way back to the cottage.

Rather than get in bed, I stretched out on the sofa where Juniper had been a few short hours ago. I closed my eyes, remembering how our mouths had felt pressed together, her whimpers, and the heat of her skin when I eased my hand under her sweater. Mostly, her parting words had stuck with me.

We better go, Cord. If we don't, I might end up in your bed, seduction or not.

I couldn't remember ever wanting anyone the way I did Juniper. I *yearned* to feel her naked body next to mine. Not just that, but I wanted to know her better. Her words, her smiles, her teasing, her touch—all of it. But then what?

A visit to Colorado was far different than picking up and relocating. Yeah, I was getting way ahead of myself, but I had to. If I didn't, at the end of my year here, I might leave heartbroken.

We made good progress on the perimeter the following day. It was much easier than the installation on the ranch since there was a low stone wall all the way around the property where we extended coverage both inside and out. I was just finishing one section when I received a text from Decker, asking me to come up to the main residence.

"We celebrating something?" I asked when he opened the door and waved me inside and I saw Beau and Sam in an embrace, kissing passionately. I raised a brow. "Did you figure out how Sam's connected to Miss Cena?"

"Nah, I think they're gettin' married," Deck responded.

"Yes, we're getting married, but we also believe we found a link between Cena and my beloved fiancée," said Beau, letting go of Sam. He picked up a picture and handed it to me. "We found this photo taped inside a cupboard. Pilar is Sam's grandmother, and in this photograph, the woman with Manley Junior is identified as having the same unusual name. Also, the date is significant, given Sam's mother was born a year after this was taken."

My eyes opened wide.

"That alone doesn't prove anything in terms of Sam being related to Cena. It'll take DNA to make that determination. That's where you come in. Have you ever had yours tested?" Decker asked.

"I haven't, sir."

"In that case, both you and Sam will get it done at the same time. There's a version of the test law enforcement can push to be expedited. It only takes an hour or two to get the results, depending on how busy the lab is. It'll be definitive enough."

"Sure. Of course," I told him.

"There's a place in town that has the kits. They said they can get it to the lab right away. While you do that, I'll check on my guys' progress."

Decker gave Beau the address of the drugstore.

"Perhaps, while we're out, we could get something for lunch. Cord, do you have time to join us?"

"Sure. I mean, you're engaged, right? And Sam might be my cousin. I'd say we should celebrate."

"I hope we are, Cord," said Sam, looking over the seat at me.

"Me too." I meant that sincerely. I liked Sam straight off and felt an almost brotherly connection to her. To think we could be family made me happy.

As Decker said, the DNA test was simple and only took a couple of minutes for each of us.

"I'll forewarn you that it won't matter where we go. By the time we order and our food is served, Beau will know everyone in the place," Sam informed me as we walked out of the drugstore.

Before I could respond, someone caught my eye. "Fuck," I muttered.

"What?" Sam asked, following my line of sight.

"Jimmy Rooker," Beau muttered.

"There's a place we could eat in the next town over," I suggested. "If he follows us there, we'll know we've got a problem on our hands."

"Cord, did Samantha tell you the bastard's contested Miss Cena's will?" Beau asked.

"On what grounds?"

"I guess it's because he thinks I'm not related to her," said Sam.

"The test we took will tell us one way or another, right?"

She nodded, but I could see worry etched on her face.

Once we were in the vehicle, Beau called Decker and informed him that Jimmy Rooker appeared to be following us.

"He's asked you to text him the name and address of where we're going. He'll have two of his guys there, waiting," he said after ending the brief call.

"Where's the wedding?" I asked in an attempt to change the subject.

They both mentioned spots in California, but when Beau suggested the Lilacs, that would've been my pick, if they'd asked.

"Here's the place," I said, motioning for Beau to turn into the parking lot.

"It says it's been here since 1837," said Sam when we walked in.

"Must be quite good, then," Beau commented.

Historical-looking, black-and-white photos lined the walls throughout the dining area, and when the waitress took our order, Sam asked if it would be okay for us to walk around to look at them.

"That's what they're here for, honey," she said, winking.

The three of us stood, and because the space was tight, I went in one direction and Beau and Sam went in the other. Many of the images appeared to be of customers throughout the years.

I hadn't paid much attention to them the one other time I was here, but they were a fascinating glimpse into the history of the area. One particular image caught my eye. "Hey, look at this," I said as I leaned in to study the photo.

"Is that Cena and Manley?" Beau asked from over my shoulder.

Sam stepped closer. "It says it was taken in 1975, the same year Manley died." The two were holding hands, sitting close enough that their arms touched. "They look so in love," she murmured.

"And they were," said an older gentleman sitting at an adjacent table.

"Did you know them?" Sam asked.

I listened while they chatted about the car accident that killed Mr. Covert and James Rooker, Cena's brother. Pete had told me about it during one of our meetings.

"Hell of a thing, the way Manley died. Worse was how his son went." My ears pricked up.

"What do you mean?" Sam asked.

"Both were killed in car accidents, several years apart, of course. With Junior, though, rumor was his brakes had been tampered with. Couldn't ever prove it. The car veered off the road and went over an embankment straight into Buffalo Creek. The condition of the car made it impossible to prove anything."

Chills spread throughout my body. It wasn't just that I was hearing the story. Something inside me was absolutely certain Junior's death was no accident.

"Some say it was the good-for-nothing nephew did the tampering. Others say Junior had been drinking, but I knew better. After losing his dad that way, he never would've driven while intoxicated."

I motioned to Beau and Sam when the waitress brought our food. I heard them thank the man before joining me at the table.

"Someone should write a book about the Coverts," I said under my breath once we'd taken our seats. "So much needless tragedy."

Sam nodded, and so did Beau.

We'd just finished eating when he received a message on his mobile.

"No sign of Rooker," Beau said after reading it.

On the drive back, the two talked about visiting the Lilac's winery, which I'd never seen.

"Can I come along?" I asked.

"Of course," they both said in unison.

13

Juniper

"Gray came home before you did last night," said my mom while we sat in the kitchen at home before my shift at the Goat.

"I stayed and talked to Cord."

Her eyes bored into mine, and she motioned with her hands for me to go on. "And?"

I shrugged. "He has to work at the Lilacs for a year, but then he plans to return to Colorado."

"Has to?"

I hadn't asked Cord if it was okay for me to talk about what brought him to East Aurora. Until he did, I didn't feel comfortable sharing it. "It's complicated family stuff."

My mother raised a brow.

"Anyway, what I'm getting at is, how much sense does it make to get involved with someone you know is leaving?"

"He could change his mind," she suggested.

"He's adamant, Mom, and where would that leave me? I don't like the idea that in order to be with a man, I'd have to upend my life. Not that he'd necessarily ask me to."

She cocked her head. "Juni…"

"*What?* If you have something to say, say it."

"When you love someone, it isn't about where you live. Home is where they are."

"Why isn't home where I am?" I shook my head. "There's no point in discussing this. His time here is finite. I'll probably keep seeing him, casually, because I think he's a nice guy. That's pretty much the end of the story."

"Maybe there will be a sequel."

I got up to rinse the glass I'd been using, when I saw Uncle Pete pull up in front of the house. He got out of the squad car, then got right back in, turned on the lights and sirens, and sped down the street. By that time, my mom stood beside me.

When my cell rang, I pulled it out of my pocket and saw my brother was calling.

"Hey, Gray. Uncle Pete was just here—"

"Juni, something's going on at the Lilacs. Every available officer is on their way, plus at least one ambulance."

I grabbed my keys off the counter and raced out of the house.

"Juni!" my mom hollered after me, but I didn't stop. If there was an ambulance on its way to the Lilacs, that meant something might have happened to Cord. Or to Sam or Beau. Regardless, there was no way I could sit around, waiting for word.

I took the back way from our house out to the road that led to the estate and waited when I saw another police car with lights flashing heading in my direction. He turned the same way I was going, so I followed.

When we reached the gate, we found it open and we both drove straight in. I pulled up and parked away from all the police cars and off to the side in case one of them, or the ambulance, needed to leave.

Once out of my car, I breathed a sigh of relief when I saw Cord, Beau, and Sam walking up the lawn. Decker Ashford was with them.

"What in the world is going on?" I asked, running over to them, wishing I could rush into Cord's arms and tell him how thankful I was he was okay. Instead, I stopped a few feet from him. "Grayson called and said there were police on the scene here and an ambulance."

Before anyone could answer, Decker's phone went off. He studied the screen, then looked up at Cord, then at Sam.

"Hey, I've got news for you," he said, looking at her, but then turning and pointing at Cord. "And you're lucky to be alive, you idiot. You don't fire a gun when there are nine other guys standing there, ready to shoot somebody."

I was wide-eyed when Cord hung his head and didn't say anything. He'd fired a gun? At who? Is that why an ambulance was here?

"You don't deserve this, Wheaton, but Sam, you're officially related to this putz."

I was stunned. *Sam and Cord were related?* How?

"That means I'm related to Cena, right?" I heard Sam ask.

"Good chance of it," he responded. "You should get confirmation of how closely soon."

"Oh Lord, what is the attorney doing here?" Beau said, but I couldn't take my eyes off Cord. *Something* had happened; that much was obvious.

"I heard on the police scanner that a suspect was apprehended. Was it Jimmy Rooker?" asked the man I now recognized as Paul Creola, a well-known lawyer in town and someone who frequented my parents' restaurant.

"It was," Decker confirmed.

"If you'll excuse us, Samantha and I are going to—"

"Wait!" Mr. Creola shouted. "I have something very important to tell you."

"Can't you tell us tomorrow?" Beau said, leading Sam away.

She stopped walking. "Let's go inside and hear what he has to say."

I realized I was intruding, and as much as I wanted five minutes alone with Cord, I felt uncomfortable being here. "I'll come back another time," I said, taking a step in the direction of my car.

"Wait," said Sam, turning from me to Mr. Creola. "Is there any reason Juni has to leave?" she asked.

"None at all."

Her eyes met mine. "I'd really like you to stay."

"Of course."

They walked in the direction of the house, but I hung back, hoping Cord would approach me. When he did, I took his hand; he was trembling.

"What happened?" I asked.

He wrapped his arms around me and rested his head against mine. "I'll tell you later. I promise. For now, I just want to hold you." We stood that way for a few seconds before Cord said we should go inside.

"As I said, I have important things to tell you," Mr. Creola was saying when we came in the front door. "A few days ago, I informed you that Jimmy Rooker filed a petition to challenge Mrs. Covert's will. The judge denied it today, which means I can give you this." He handed Sam an envelope. "I'm not sure what went on here earlier, but visiting the bank *can* wait until tomorrow. Although I'm going to suggest you go as soon as possible."

"I'd like to go there now," she said to Beau, who nodded. Then she turned to Cord and me. "Will you two go with us?"

When we said we would, Beau handed him a key fob.

We were almost out the door when I heard Decker ask how long Mr. Creola had known Sam was Cena's great-granddaughter?

I gasped, then covered my mouth with my hand. *She was Miss Cena's great-granddaughter?* My mind raced with what it could mean.

"There *is* a letter from Mrs. Covert in the safe-deposit box. It explains everything, not that it's any of your business," Mr. Creola snapped at Decker.

I sat in the front seat with Cord on the way to the bank. Out of everyone in the vehicle, Beau seemed the most agitated. He was holding onto Sam's hand so tightly it had to hurt.

Maybe once they went inside, Cord would be able to tell me what had happened. I still didn't know, other than guessing he'd shot Jimmy Rooker.

"It's exciting that you're related to Sam and also to Miss Cena," I said when we were finally alone.

"It is. I sure wish I'd met her, though. Maybe then I'd have some idea of what I'm doing here."

"Mr. Creola said Miss Cena wrote Sam a letter that explains everything. Maybe it will give you some answers too."

He nodded. "I can't imagine I'm just here to look after horses and cattle for a few months. I suppose it could be so I can find someone to do it after I leave, but I'm sure Sam and Beau could do that on their own."

I reached over and put my hand on his. "You'll figure it out. I'm sure of it."

"Maybe now that Sam is more settled, the security system is in place, and Jimmy Rooker is no longer a threat, I'll be able to work on doing just that."

If Jimmy was dead and Cord had shot him, his attitude toward the man seemed flippant to me. "What happened to him?"

"I shot out his kneecap."

I gasped. "Oh my God."

"It was either that or he would've killed Sam. I couldn't let that happen."

"Is he still alive?"

"Yeah. He'll live."

"That must be painful."

"I'm surprised you couldn't hear him screaming all the way from your house." He looked down at our hands and brushed the back of mine with his thumb. "Jimmy said a lot of shit, and it's all on surveillance footage. I have a feeling he'll be in prison for the rest of his life."

"For attempted murder?" I asked. It didn't seem like that would result in such a long sentence.

Cord shook his head. "Murder. He tampered with Manley's brakes. Miss Cena's son I mean."

My eyes opened wide, and I rested my head against the seat. "Manley died because of him? *Jesus.* Poor Miss Cena. She'd already suffered so much."

"He thought he'd inherit the Lilacs, or at least part of it, once his great-aunt died. I guess he didn't know my siblings or me existed, which would've left just him and his brother to split everything. I can tell you, based on my own experience, when it comes to inheriting something, it doesn't always go the way you'd expect it to."

"Maybe the estate is why you're here."

"According to Decker, who heard it from Beau and the attorney, only Miss Cena's direct descendants can inherit. Jimmy and his brother aren't. Neither am I."

My eyes scrunched. "What would've happened if there weren't any?"

"Everything would be sold and the proceeds given to charity." Cord's eyes met mine. "Same as with my dad's trust."

"Do you think it's a coincidence?"

He shook his head. "Now that I've said it out loud, I don't."

"Me either."

14

Cord

The similarities between Cena's will versus my father's trust were too close for them to be random. But Roscoe Buchtold Wheaton had no relation to Cena Rooker Covert, and given we didn't know a thing about ou r mother's family, it was highly unlikely he would've ever met the woman. In fact, as far as I knew, the man had never left the state of Colorado.

Things definitely weren't adding up, but when had they? I had to think hard to even remember my mom, let alone conversations my parents might have had. Maybe if I mentioned it to Buck or Porter, they might recall something significant.

"I could help you," Juniper said, squeezing my fingers. "I'm sure my mom would too."

"I don't want to impose on anyone." I looked over at her, and she smiled.

"Look at it this way, Cord. If I do, it means we can spend more time together."

"I'd be all for that."

"Me too."

When her cheeks flushed and she lowered her gaze, I wanted to pull her onto my lap and kiss the fuck out of her.

"Here they come," she said, motioning to the bank's front door.

Sam looked as though she'd been crying, but instead of sadness, her expression was almost serene. Beau opened the rear passenger door and helped her in, then went around to the other side and got in too.

"There was a letter," she began. "It explained a lot, and when we return to the Lilacs, I'll let you both read it if you'd like. There were journals too."

"We'll come back another time to fetch those, along with the other contents of the safe-deposit box," Beau added.

"The letter confirmed that Cena Covert was my great-grandmother and her son, Manley, was my grandfather. There wasn't much beyond that, but what she wrote alluded to the journals and that I'd find out more about my family—our family, Cord—by reading them."

I tried my hardest not to get emotional, but looking into Sam's tear-filled eyes, I failed.

I brushed at my own tears, wishing so much I could go back and relive the days when I first arrived in East Aurora. Maybe I wouldn't know any more than I did now, but if I'd pressed, I might have been able to meet Miss Cena.

"Should we return to the Lilacs now?" I asked.

"I know this sounds crazy, but I'm starving," Sam admitted.

"We'd have our pick of restaurants now that we know we won't run into Jimmy Rooker," I said. "I sure could go for one of those burgers they serve at the inn, if the rest of you are game."

"Sounds perfect," said Sam, and when I glanced at Juni, she nodded.

I could tell just by looking at her that she was processing what we'd just learned. No doubt that, like me, she hoped the journals would give some clues about all sorts of things. Selfishly, I hoped they shed light on why my mother had left East Aurora and seemingly never looked back.

When we arrived at the inn, Grayson was just getting off his shift and Beau asked him to join us. First, though, he asked if he could help him with something.

When they took their seats at the table, over twenty minutes later, Beau first apologized for being gone so long, then announced Gray would be working for him, as his assistant. I wasn't sure what that meant or entailed, but Gray seemed happy about it.

"Did you get them?" Sam asked Beau.

"All taken care of, my darling."

Juniper sat between Sam and me, and I overheard them discussing the letter. Then she told Juni she'd arranged for the bank manager to give Beau the journals and asked Juni if she'd be willing to help her sort through them. She enthusiastically agreed to.

That left me feeling out of sorts and without much purpose other than managing the livestock. Something that, based on my experience, wasn't a challenge. Two days from now, the National Western Stock Show that was held in Denver would begin, and I sure wished I was in Colorado instead of here. Even a visit would do me a world of good.

I excused myself like Beau and Grayson had, walked out the front door, and stood on the porch, hoping the cold air would allow me to clear my head and stop me from feeling so damn sorry for myself.

I pulled out my phone, not that now would be the time to call my brothers. Instead, I opened an airline app. There was a nonstop flight from Buffalo to Denver that took four hours each way. That would give me at least thirty at home. Barring flight cancellations, I could probably swing a visit. But would it be worth the risk of me not returning here in time?

I heard the door open behind me but didn't turn around.

"Cord? Are you okay?" Sam asked, coming to stand beside me.

I put my arm around her shoulders. "It's been a *helluva* few weeks."

"That's for sure."

"At least we found out we're related."

She looked up at me and smiled. "That's the *best* news."

"Not inheriting the Lilacs?"

Sam shook her head. "I'm paraphrasing, but in her letter, Cena said all the money in the world isn't as important as being with people you love."

"That's for sure, isn't it?" When I felt her shiver, I led her back inside.

My eyes met Juni's when I approached the table, and I winked. I didn't love her; I didn't know her well enough to. But I knew I could. Even that I eventually would. What would Cena's words mean to me then?

"Cord, have you had the chance to mention the horse issue to Sam or Beau?" Juniper asked.

She knew full well I hadn't, but I appreciated her bringing it up.

"What's wrong?" Sam asked.

I briefly explained about the average age of the stable and that, if the estate could swing it, I wanted to add several younger animals, preferably geldings since they were a little more predictable.

She turned her head from me to Beau, who was seated on her other side.

"It's your decision, darling. I can tell you this much; you could afford to add as many as Cord would like."

"Is that something you can take care of on your own?" she asked me.

"Of course."

"Good."

I reached for Juni's hand under the table, wove my fingers with hers, then leaned over and whispered my thanks.

"Any time," she whispered back.

I ordered the same burger I had my first night in town, and it was good, just not quite as much as I'd remembered. On the other hand, Juni hadn't made this one. Maybe that was the difference.

When we finished eating, Gray offered to give Beau and Sam a lift to the Lilacs so I could take Juniper home. There wasn't a person at the table who didn't pick up on how little sense that made. Why wouldn't she just ride home with him?

"If she doesn't mind, there are a few things I'd like to talk to Juni about," said Sam. "We could do it tomorrow if that would be better."

"Now's good," she responded.

"I can give you a lift later unless you want to swing by and pick up your car," I offered.

"Juni doesn't like driving in the snow at night," Gray said, perhaps a little too quickly.

"Grayson, your matchmaker is showing," Beau teased.

We all laughed, but I wouldn't complain. Like she'd said, the more time we could spend together, the happier we'd both be.

That should've sent me into panic mode, but it didn't. Maybe instead of overthinking being with her, I should let things progress naturally.

When we arrived at the main house, I was about to get out and open Juniper's door for her when I heard Sam say she was sorry, but she was more tired than she thought and hoped Juni wouldn't mind if they got together tomorrow instead.

I shook my head and smiled. "Thanks, Sam."

She reached over the seat and rubbed my shoulder. "What are cousins for, Cord?"

"You're my first, so I have no idea."

"Mine too."

"Maybe, someday, you can meet the rest of us."

She nodded. "I'd really like that."

It reminded me how much I wanted to go home, even if it wasn't for more than a day, but also that it wasn't worth the risk.

"What's on your mind?" Juniper asked after I drove the rest of the way to the cottage. When I took her home later, I'd park the SUV at the house and walk down.

"Nothing much," I said, unlocking the door and turning on the lights.

She stood with her arms folded, not that her expression appeared angry.

"Feelin' sorry for myself."

Juni led me over to the sofa and pushed me so I sat down. Then she moved my arm out of her way and sat on my lap.

"Not feeling sorry for myself now," I said, winking.

"That was the idea."

We kissed for a while, then I moved her from my lap and stood to get the fire started. When I returned, I held out my hand, and she stood too.

"Dance with me?" I asked, pulling her away from the sofa.

Her cheeks flushed. "There's no music."

"That's easily remedied." I walked over to the wireless speaker, switched it on, then queued up a song on my phone. I'd heard it for the first time a couple of days ago, and when I did, all I could think was how much it made me want to dance with the woman now in my arms. The chorus repeated several times while we swayed to the music.

"Excuse me. You look like you love me. You look like you want me," I sang as I nuzzled her hair. "God, you smell good, girl."

She smiled when I tightened my hold around her waist and spun her around the small space.

"One more?" I asked, already knowing I'd set the song to play on repeat. When it started up again, Juni giggled.

"Come here," I said when it ended for the second time, grabbed my phone, and shut down the app before walking over to the sofa.

I stretched out across the cushions and pulled her down beside me.

"Much better," I murmured, grabbing a blanket from the back and spreading it over both of us. "Warm enough?" I asked.

"I am now."

"Thanks again for what you did earlier. About the horses."

She kissed my cheek. "You're welcome."

I was about to fasten my lips to hers when my mobile rang. "Sorry," I muttered, shifting to pull it out of my pocket.

When Juni started to move, I put my free arm around her and kept her close to me. "Buck? What's up?" I asked when I saw his number on the screen.

"Port's been in an accident over in Parlin. Holt and I are headed there now."

"What kind of accident?"

"All we know is that he hit another car and that there are injuries."

I scrubbed my face with my hand. "What can I do?"

"Get in touch with Matt Rice. Let him know he's on his own for the stock show."

"Wait. How bad was Port hurt?"

"Not a scratch, according to the sheriff—"

"I don't get it."

"He was drunk, Cord, and they aren't sure the other driver is going to make it."

"Fuck."

I covered my eyes with my hand, knowing Juni had heard every word. I would've told her anyway, of course, but I hated that she was hearing it the same way I was.

"I'll call Matt. Let me know when you get to Parlin and what you find out."

When I ended the call and set my phone down, Juni shifted again to get up. "Not yet. Please," I whispered.

She relaxed against me, and I held her as close as I could. Yeah, I needed to call Matt Rice, but first, I had to try to wrap my head around everything Buck had said. Porter drove drunk, hit another car, and they weren't sure the driver would make it.

Other than finding out one of my brothers or my sister was dead, this was the worst news I could imagine. I'd say I was shocked, but every one of us knew Porter drank too much. Me especially, since I worked with him day in, day out.

Why hadn't I warned Buck or Holt? Why hadn't I told them how many times I'd taken his keys so he wouldn't get behind the wheel?

I felt Juniper's hand cup my cheek, and God, was it ever what I needed. I looked into her eyes and saw nothing but compassion. As much as I wanted to kiss her, now wasn't the time. I had at least one call to make while I waited to hear from one of my brothers once they reached Parlin.

I eased us both so we were sitting up.

"I'll call Gray to come and get me."

I studied her. Was it because she didn't want to be here or because she wanted to give me privacy?

"I can take you after I make this call. If that's what you want. If you're doing it for me, I'll tell you straight out that I'd rather you stay."

"Then I will."

I brushed her lips with mine before swiping my screen to reach Matt.

"Hey, Cord," he answered. His tone of voice told me he knew why I was calling.

"Have you heard?"

"Yeah. I sure as hell am sorry. My brother's wife is a nurse at the hospital in Gunnison. She called to tell us they brought Porter and Maverick Morris in."

"Mav? Fuck." The kid was a hot-shot, high-school rodeo champ. I doubted he was much over sixteen.

"Shit. Sorry if you didn't know, Cord."

"Buck told me he might not make it."

"He's in surgery now."

"Damn it all to hell," I said under my breath. I knew that, since the kid and his older sister had lost their parents, they'd been struggling to hang onto their ranch. "I can't tell you how sorry I am about this, Matt."

"You weren't behind the wheel, Cord. Porter was. There's nothing for you to apologize for."

"Listen, I'm calling about the National Western."

"Say no more. We'll help. Just let us know what kind of support you need, and we'll give it to you."

I scrubbed my face. "That's the thing. I'm not in Colorado, and there's no way I can get there."

There was silence on the line for several seconds. "What do you mean?" Matt finally asked.

"It's a long damn story, but I'm in New York, and I won't be able to get back in time for the show. I'll let the organizers know the Roaring Fork won't be bringing roughstock. Whatever you were countin' on us to do to assist you, we won't be able to deliver."

"Hold up a minute. Cord, are you in jail or somethin'?"

"Feels like it sometimes, but no, I'm not in any kind of trouble. I just have an obligation here I have to see through, and it means I can't get to the show."

"You do know what kind of money you're talkin' about losing, right?"

"My hands are tied. If there was any way I didn't have to pull out, I wouldn't."

"All right, then. We'll be in touch sometime tomorrow."

I ended the call, noticing Juni looking at something out the window. Before I could ask what, my cell rang again. This time, it was one of the cowboys.

"We've got a situation, Mr. Wheaton. Snow came fast and hard, and it looks like it's gonna be a doozy. We'll have to move quickly to get all the cattle somewhere safe."

I looked up at the ceiling, ready to curse God. "On my way, and…What's your name?"

"Buck."

"Yeah? That's my brother's name. How many of the guys are already out?"

"Not sure, sir."

"Anybody on Apache?"

My eyes scrunched when Juni grimaced and turned her back to me.

"I don't think so."

"Have someone get him ready for me, and tell them not to let anyone else ride him out."

"Yes, sir."

"Sorry, Juni. I gotta get out there."

When she faced me, her brow was furrowed. "It's a bad one, Cord. Snow's coming right off the lake."

I walked over, kissed her quickly, and ran out the door. I hoped to hell she didn't get it into her head to call her brother. There'd be no way he'd be able to get here; that's how much snow had fallen in the last hour.

15

Juniper

I tried pulling a weather app up on my phone, but my signal wasn't strong enough for it to load. There had to be a TV in the cottage, somewhere. When I found one in the bedroom, I turned it on, found the local weather, and sat in a chair near the window.

"Folks, if you aren't somewhere safe and warm, get there as quickly as you can. According to radar reports, what we're experiencing is a bomb cyclone," said the newscaster. He went on to explain the weather phenomenon could generate winds reaching eighty miles per hour and sometimes higher. That kind of wind could uproot fences, utility poles, and trees. Flying debris, blizzard conditions, poor visibility, and structural damage were also possible. I moved the curtain and looked out the window. Snow was already up to the bottom pane.

"Hey, Mom," I said when she picked up.

"Gray said you're at the Lilacs."

"I'm actually at the cottage where Cord lives."

"Do you have power, sweetheart?"

"So far, we do. Before he went out to take care of the cattle, Cord lit the fireplace, so it's warm too and should stay that way if the power does go out."

She gasped. "Did you say Cord is out in this?"

"He had to, Mom. The livestock."

I could hear her talking to someone, but the mic was covered, so I couldn't make out her words.

"I'd send Dad to get you, but he said the roads are already impassable."

"Tell him to stay put. I'm safe. I wouldn't leave anyway until Cord got back. Is Gray home?"

"Yes, he's right here. Do you want to talk to him?"

"No. I just wanted to make sure he was."

"Okay, honey. Keep in touch."

"I will, and please, no heroics from Dad or Gray."

"I'll pass your instructions on."

I ended the call just as the lights flickered and the TV shut off. Seconds later, everything came back on. I checked the time on my phone. Cord had been gone for close to thirty minutes. I knew it could be hours more before he might be back. I tried to keep my eyes open, but after I'd jarred myself awake three or four times, my neck started to ache, so I straightened the blankets and lay on the bed.

"Hey, sleeping beauty."

I opened my eyes and looked up at Cord, who sat beside me on the bed. Snow coated his hair and the scruff of his beard, and when he removed his gloves, his hands looked as blue as his lips did.

"You need to get out of those wet clothes and into warm water. Do you have a tub or just a shower?"

His teeth were chattering. "Both."

"I'll fill the tub. You strip."

"I have to admit; this isn't the way I imagined us getting naked for the first time, Juni."

I smiled. "This isn't us, Cord. It's just you." I pointed to his snow-encrusted jeans. "Get out of those right now." I went into the bathroom across the hall, turned the water on, and checked the temperature. "Okay, it's filling up," I shouted.

I heard his footfalls in the hallway and turned my back before the door opened. "I'll give you some privacy."

"You could stay, although I might not be at my, err, best right now."

I rolled my eyes, not that he could see them. "Get in the water, Cord."

"Damn, you're bossy. I kinda like it."

I heard the water splash, and keeping my back to him, I left the room and shut the door behind me. As I'd anticipated, his clothes were in a heap on the floor. They were heavier than I expected when I picked them up and went in search of a washer and dryer. Before I found either, the lights flickered and we lost power again. This time, it didn't come right back on. I rummaged around in the kitchen, but didn't see any candles.

"Juni?"

"Coming."

"There are candles in the pantry. Is there enough light from the fireplace for you to see in there?" With every word, his voice sounded closer.

"Yeah, looking now."

"In there," he said from right behind me, scaring the daylights out of me. "You can turn around, darlin'. I'm wearing a robe."

I faced him. "I'm not a prude. I just…it's what you said. This isn't how I imagined the first time we were together."

He grabbed the candles from the shelf, set them on the counter, and stepped close enough that our bodies were almost flush. "You imagined it?"

"Of course I did. Didn't you?"

"At least a hundred times."

I shook my head and laughed. "You should get in bed."

"Only if you come with me. I don't want you to get lost in the dark."

"I'll light a candle."

He took a step back, grabbed one from the counter, along with a lighter, lit it, and handed it to me before doing the same with the second. "It'll be warmer if we stay out here, by the fire."

He was right. The bedroom was probably already cold.

He put the candle in a holder I hadn't noticed, took the one from my hand, and placed it in a second, then led me to the sofa.

"Lie down, and I'll go get some blankets."

"I *like* bossy Juni," I heard him mutter as I hurried down the hall.

When I returned, his eyes were closed. I draped the first blanket over him as gently as I could and was about to add another when he grabbed my wrist and pulled me down on top of him.

"Cord!"

"Juni!"

"You need to stay warm in case of frostbite."

"Get under these blankets with me right now, Juniper Chance." His voice was gruff, but he winked. "See, I can be bossy too. By the way, what's your middle name?"

"It's boring."

"Lemme guess. Ann?"

I shook my head, then shifted so I was beside him rather than on him.

"Elizabeth?"

"Nope."

"Hmm. Mary?"

"No, it's—"

He put his hand over my mouth. "No, I want to guess." His eyes bored into mine. "It's Rose, isn't it?"

My eyes scrunched. "How did you know?"

"Juniper Rose Chance. I don't think I've ever heard a more beautiful name."

He snuggled me close, and within seconds, his breathing evened out.

"Cord Wheaton is a beautiful name too," I whispered.

"Cord Rooker Wheaton."

"Really? That's your middle name?"

"Yes, ma'am." His eyes drifted shut again, and this time, he snored.

16

Cord

I leveled my gun and aimed at the *sonuvabitch* who pressed his weapon to Sam's side. His eyes met mine, and in them, I saw pure evil. I was about to pull the trigger when, instead of Sam, Jimmy held the gun against Juni.

"No!" I shouted, racing toward him. *"No!"*

"Cord! Wake up! You're dreaming."

I opened my eyes and looked into Juniper's. "He had you." The words caught in my throat.

She cupped my face with her palm like she had earlier, then stroked my forehead with her fingertips. "It's okay. It was just a dream," she whispered.

"I wanted to kill him."

"But you didn't, and now Sam is safe, and so am I. Go back to sleep. I'll be right here, next to you."

I didn't want to, but the exhaustion I felt was too much for me to fight against. Especially when Juni gently ran her fingers through my hair like my mama used to do. I remembered that now. When I couldn't sleep, she'd sit beside me and do exactly what Juni was.

The next time I woke up, I could hear beeping coming from the kitchen. I moved the blankets, tightened the belt of the robe I still had on, and padded into the kitchen, where Juni was fussing with the microwave.

"Sorry," she said. "I can't get it to shut off."

"It does that after the power comes back on." I hit the button to set the clock, which would make the beeping stop. "What time is it, anyway?"

"A little after seven."

"Shit." I went over to the window and looked outside. Or I would've if it wasn't obscured by a wall of snow. "I need to check with the guys." I glanced around, trying to remember where I'd left my phone.

"It's here," Juni said, picking it up from the dining room table. "It was in your jacket pocket."

I went into the bedroom and got dressed. When I returned to the sofa, I noticed all the clothes I'd had on the night before spread out on the hearth of the fireplace.

"Shit," I repeated when I swiped the screen and saw how many messages had piled up. One said the crew had already checked and the cattle were still secure where we'd herded them the night before.

By the time I'd gotten out to the main barn last night, I realized there was no way in hell we could take the horses out. Instead, we'd piled into trucks and got every one of the herd we could find moved to the closest shelter. I'd driven out the main gate, remembering a back road that would get me to the farthest pasture. Right as it closed behind me, I saw a car drive up and park. When I stopped and asked the kid who had climbed out if I could help him, he told me he was Buck, who I'd spoken to earlier. Rather than sending him to the barns, I told him to climb in, and he rode out with me.

Thankfully, the estate had five large barns in various places on the property where we'd herded as many animals as we could before trying to get the rest to the next closest. I doubted we'd been able to locate them all last night and get them sheltered, but we'd done the best we could.

I read the next message. It was from my brother Buck, saying Maverick Morris had made it through surgery. He was still critical, but they expected him to pull through. His text was delivered at three my time.

Since it was five their time now, I didn't return the call. I would later, though.

Holt had sent a message too. I put my head in my hands when I read that Porter was in jail. "Fucking Port," I said under my breath. I felt Juni sit beside me and reached for her to sit on my lap instead. "Do you know how grateful I am for you right now?" I said, burying my head between her shoulder and jaw.

She didn't say anything, but she held her soft body against mine, and that's what I needed more than anything right now.

"Cord? What happened yesterday? Can you talk about it?"

After the nightmare I'd had, I figured telling Juni might help me work it out of my system. I sighed. "Sam and I had our DNA tested, then got lunch before returning to the Lilacs. Since Decker confirmed no one from Schultz would be at the winery, Beau wanted to see the layout and inspect the equipment. Sam and I went with him. Maybe a half hour later, she said she wanted to go up to the house and make some calls."

"With you so far," she said softly.

"She was gone less than five minutes when alerts from the security system went off on my cell and

Beau's. The surveillance footage loads immediately, so we could see a live version of the breach." I rolled my shoulders when every muscle in my body tightened. "Jimmy Rooker had Sam with a gun held to her side."

She gasped. "Oh my God."

"Beau and I took off running, and by the time we reached where they were, Decker and some of the other guys had them surrounded. I aimed right at the fucker's kneecap, and when I saw his trigger finger move, I shot him. Looking back on it, Decker was right to be pissed at me for doing it. In the split second it took for the bullet to hit him, he could've shot Sam."

"But he didn't."

"No. He didn't. But I gotta tell you, my instincts told me, if he killed her, I'd be next on his list."

"You did what you believed you had to."

"All I could think afterwards was how in the hell did I get here? I'd gone from riding our ranch in Colorado, wrangling cattle and doing other shit like mending fences, to thinking my life might be in danger. Not to mention, fearing for the life of a woman who I might be related to." She squeezed my hand, and I leaned into her. "I'm so glad you're here."

"Me too."

"It was the look in his eyes that really got to me. I saw so much hate. I can't say I've ever encountered anyone I believed was pure evil. Not even my dad, and he was one of the biggest assholes I've ever known." I scrubbed my face. "Sorry, can we change the subject?"

"Of course."

"What do you say we make breakfast?"

"Sounds great." When she smiled, I felt warm all over. How was it that a woman I'd known less than a month could come to mean so much to me? I wouldn't say it out loud, but right now, I never wanted her to leave.

"I'd offer to make it on my own, but I have a feeling you're a better cook than I am."

She smiled. "Before we get started, is your brother okay? Have you heard anything?"

I told her that the driver of the other vehicle had made it through surgery and the prognosis was good. I also said that I was waiting until later this morning to call for an update on Porter, but Holt told me he'd spent the night in jail.

I took eggs and bacon out of the fridge. Thankfully, everything was still cold. I checked the freezer too, and it didn't show signs that anything had thawed. Looking at the snow covering most of the kitchen window, it didn't look like anything was melting outside either.

"I, uh, am not sure when I'll be able to take you home," I said, setting the stuff on the counter.

"I know, but as I told my mom, I'm safe and warm and would rather my dad and brother refrain from trying to come get me." Her forehead furrowed.

"What?" I asked.

"Clothes."

"You're welcome to wear some of mine. You'll swim in them, but if you don't mind, I won't either."

"Maybe just so I can wash what I'm wearing."

Picturing Juni in nothing but one of my flannel shirts made me instantly hard as a rock. "Come here, girl," I said, pulling her into my arms. "I gotta kiss you." I put my arm around her waist and pulled her closer, just not enough that the lower half of our bodies touched. I cupped her cheek with my palm and stared into her eyes. "I'm gonna need you to tell me what's okay and what's not."

She put both hands on my chest. "I was going to say the same thing to you."

I chuckled. "If you leave it to me, I'll have you naked and in my bed—the hell with breakfast."

Her cheeks flushed, and her eyes bored into mine.

"*But* the last thing I want to do is push you into a physical relationship you might not be ready for."

"There are so many uncertainties," she murmured.

"I agree." I kissed her forehead, then released her.

"When you said you had to kiss me, that isn't exactly what I had in mind."

I was about to give her one more like what I'd had in mind when I heard a snowmobile outside. Seconds later, I received an alert on my phone from the security system. I checked the live footage, but couldn't tell who the person getting off the sled was until he removed his helmet and I saw it was Beau. He grabbed something from the back and walked toward us, carrying a shovel. "Beau's here to dig us out," I told Juni.

Based on how high the drifts were by the windows, I figured they were equally as high outside the door, so I knew better than to open it.

"Sam sent a message twenty minutes ago, saying he was on his way to check on us, but it didn't come through until just now," said Juni. "I guess they tried to call, but didn't get an answer."

I had my phone on and the volume up in case I heard from any of my crew or from one of my brothers. I walked over and checked, but didn't see an alert. "Cell coverage must be intermittent."

I could hear Beau shoveling for several minutes, followed by a knock on the door.

"Hey, come on in," I said, looking beyond him. He'd dug out a path from the snowmobile up to where we now stood. All around it, the snow had to be piled up at least four feet. I could see higher drifts too.

He stomped his feet and brushed the flakes off his jacket. "Sam sent me down to make sure you were both all right."

"Hey, sorry about not bringing the SUV back up to the house last night," I said.

He shrugged. "We wouldn't be going anywhere, anyway. The roads are all closed, which also means a plow can't get here to clear the driveway."

"My weather app says more is on the way," said Juni, walking over and handing her phone to me.

"Damn. It's saying maybe another two feet."

"We're in for the duration," said Beau, who then turned to Juni. "Sam was wondering if you wanted me to give you a ride up to the house. She thought maybe you could kill some time, going through Cena's journals."

I had different thoughts about how we could kill time. In fact, if Juni had to stay a week or longer, I had plenty of ideas to keep us busy, none of which involved wearing clothes.

"It's up to you," I said when her eyes met mine.

"I could give her a lift, then come back for you," Beau offered.

"Are there any more of those on the property?" I asked, pointing to the sled.

"At least three or four. My understanding is they're stored in the back of the barn."

"Which barn?"

"The one on the other side of the trees."

Which was the closest to the cottage. I shook my head. Had I known that last night, I would've gone out on one myself and asked a couple of others to as well. We might've found more of the herd by utilizing both snowmobiles and trucks. Once this storm was over, it was time for me to clean house and hire a new group of cowboys.

I realized both Juni and Beau were looking at me as though they expected me to say something.

"I'll check in with the crew, then come up to the house."

"I almost forgot. Sam asked me to inform you the main residence has a generator. Given there's more snow on the way, it might be a good idea for you to plan to spend the night there," said Beau.

Not exactly where I envisioned cuddling Juni's sweet body next to mine later, or even now, but it was for the best.

"Don't stay out in the cold too long," Juni said, walking over to me. "Right now, it's negative ten, and it's supposed to drop even more."

"Bloody hell," Beau muttered.

"What's wrong?" Juni asked.

"I can't very well take you up to the house without something like this." He motioned to the full-body snowsuit he was wearing.

"Maybe there are some in the barn," I suggested.

"Or there's the one I left at the house. I'll be right back." He put on the helmet and walked out the door.

"Are you sure you don't mind?" Juni asked.

"Staying at the main house?"

She nodded.

"The truth?" I asked.

"Please."

I put my arms around her waist. "If I could spend every minute of the next few months alone with you, I would."

She tried to hide it, but I felt her muscles tense. Why had I said months when what I really meant was every day for the rest of my life?

I dropped my arms from around her, took a couple of steps back, and scrubbed my face. *The rest of my life?* Jesus. Where had that come from?

"Juni, listen—"

"I get it, Cord. You're marking the days off on the calendar until you can return to Colorado." She walked over to pick her jacket up from a peg near the door. Put it and her gloves and hat on, then stood near the window.

"It isn't like that," I said, standing next to her.

"No? If someone called and said you could go home right now, or as soon as the snow cleared, I bet you'd be on the first flight out. Wouldn't you?"

"Probably, yeah, but not just because I'd want to leave. There's a lot of shit goin' on at the Roaring Fork right now. My brother's in jail, and God knows what he's gonna be charged with. He may even face a prison sentence. In the meantime, the roughstock business he and I partner in is going to lose the little momentum we've managed to build. We may never be able to regain it, either."

"I get it. You have a full life in Colorado."

"And you have a full life here."

We both heard the snowmobile pull up. When Beau came inside with snow gear, she removed her jacket, and he helped Juni into the suit, not me.

"See you later?" he asked.

"Maybe," I responded when Juni walked out without saying a word.

17

Juniper

It was so cold outside that my nostrils froze, which meant crying would be a terrible idea. If water ran down my cheeks, it would probably freeze there, and I'd end up with frostbite.

Before I put on the helmet Beau had handed me, he also gave me a face mask. "Sorry, should've brought this inside. Snowstorms are somewhat new to me."

"Somewhat?"

"Yes, Miss Chance, this is my first. It's Sam's as well, so be sure to tease her about it equally."

I'd smile if I didn't feel so sad. Why did I have to meet someone like Cord, who I'd be willing to stay snowed in with for the rest of winter, only to know that, a year from now, he'd be halfway across the country with no plans to return to the East Coast?

Life wasn't fair. Actually, as far as I was concerned, right now, it sucked. No one I'd ever dated did it for me the way Cord did. I enjoyed his company and our conversations. Then there was the heat factor, which was off the fucking charts.

When he said I had a full life here, I wanted to tell him I didn't. In fact, outside of my parents and the restaurant, I didn't feel like I had much of a life at all. Except maybe the reason he'd said that was because he was trying to tell me that, even if we spent "every minute of the next few months" together, it didn't mean he'd ask me to go to Colorado with him. To even be thinking about it was ridiculous.

By the time we reached the main house, which only took a few minutes, I'd talked myself out of worrying about Cord. I could stay here, with Sam and Beau, until the roads were clear, then Gray or my dad could come get me. I had no reason to return to the cottage since I hadn't brought anything with me other than my purse and the clothes I was wearing. Thankfully, I hadn't put them in the washer yet.

"Hi," said Sam, walking over when I came inside after shedding my snow clothes in the mudroom—which Beau referred to as the place where dirty winery clothes would go.

"Hey. Crazy storm, huh?" I said.

She smiled. "My first blizzard. Beau's too."

"He mentioned that. I lost count a long time ago," I joked.

"Are you hungry?" she asked.

"Starving, actually, and I'd literally get down on my knees and beg for a cup of coffee."

"I've got a fresh pot that's almost finished brewing." Sam pointed to the coffeemaker. "Miss Cena must've loved the stuff. I don't think I've ever seen one that fancy. Maybe Beau has." She looked around the room. "Wherever he ran off to."

"I think he was heading back to the cottage to, uh, help Cord with something." Just saying his name brought the hurt I'd tamped down back to the surface.

"Am I out of line if I ask what's happening between the two of you?"

"Not at all because it's nothing at all."

She raised a brow.

"As I said to my mom, his time here is finite. He's a nice guy and certainly fun to flirt with, but that's the extent of it."

She nodded, then held up a cup. "How do you take it?"

"A little cream if you have it. No sugar."

"Same as Cord," she said under her breath.

I thought back to the day we'd met at Charlie's Diner for breakfast, and I'd noticed the same thing. It seemed so long ago.

She handed me the cup and motioned to the dining room table, where there was a platter of fruit and slices of coffee cake.

"I can make something more substantial if you'd like," she offered.

"This is perfect." I'd already popped a grape in my mouth and was reaching for a strawberry.

The kitchen didn't look much different than it had when I was here over a year ago, but it felt like it was. Miss Cena's energy had been replaced by Sam's and Beau's. I hadn't realized the depth of her sadness until I contrasted it with their happiness.

"Have you been reading the journals?" I asked.

Her eyes lit up. "I have. I started with the oldest I could find. The first entries are before Cena and Manley married."

"You're kidding! That's fantastic."

"I know. She was so happy. The way she writes about him reminds me of how I feel about Beau."

It was horrible of me to think, let alone say, but I didn't want to read it. Not now, anyway. It would only make me long for the type of relationship I'd probably never have. I turned my head when my eyes filled with tears.

"Juni? What's wrong?" She put her hand on mine.

I could tell her I was emotional over Miss Cena, but I didn't want to lie to Sam. "You know." My voice cracked.

"Cord?"

I nodded. "It's silly, right?"

She shook her head. "Not even a little. He seems like a really good guy. And, actually, Decker Ashford confirmed he was. Plus, he's my cousin." She beamed more than smiled, and it was infectious.

"It's sad that you didn't get to meet Miss Cena, but she'd be so happy you're here and that you and Beau plan to stay. I mean, you do plan to stay, right?"

"I think we fell in love with this place at the same time we fell in love with each other."

I put my hand on my heart. "That's like a greeting card line."

She laughed. "I know. I'm sappy now, I guess."

Her cat, Wanda, jumped up on her lap. "The only downside is that, now, she likes Beau more than me."

"Not true," he said, walking into the kitchen. I was stunned to see Cord right behind him. "She doesn't like me more; I'm just easier to talk into cat treats." He came over, kissed Sam, and scratched the cat's ears.

"Hi, Cord," said Sam.

"Hey, uh, mind if I talk to Juni for a minute?"

Sam winked. "You'll have to ask her."

I'd already pushed my chair back and stood.

He motioned with his head for me to follow him. "Is there somewhere more private we can talk?" he asked once we reached the living room.

"There's a library down the hall." I led him there and closed the door behind us. "What's up?" I asked, switching on the lights. When I turned to face him, he was right behind me.

"I don't want to talk. At least not yet," he said, reaching over to flip the door's lock.

"But—"

Cord stopped my words with his demanding mouth, pressing his tongue against my lips until I opened to him. He angled his head and deepened the kiss at the same time he put one hand on my bottom, holding me still as he rested against me. I wrapped my arms around his neck and added to the intensity of the kiss until I was dizzy with desire.

When he pushed me up against the wall and lifted me until my legs had nowhere to go but around his waist, his hardness pressed against the ache between my legs. I arched but couldn't get close enough to him. Nothing would satisfy me short of Cord being deep inside me.

The clothes that separated our bodies felt paper thin when he thrust against me. I whimpered and tightened my arms, holding him as close to me as I could.

He released my mouth but kissed along my jaw and down my neck.

"Cord."

"Tell me what you want, Juniper."

"Don't stop."

His mouth crushed against mine, his tongue tast ing, exploring, invading. He cupped between my legs, then unfastened my jeans and slid his hand inside my panties.

"God, I can feel how much you want me. You're so wet."

I whimpered again rather than speak when I felt his finger thrust into me and the pad of his thumb press hard against my clit.

"I don't want to spend the night here, Juniper. I want to be alone with you, both of us spread out on a blanket in front of a roaring fire, naked, and doing nothing other than learning the feel of each other's bodies." He added a second finger and pressed harder with his thumb.

A simple okay was as much as my brain could muster.

"I want to know how it feels when my cock is buried deep inside you. To have your heat clench me and, most of all, to experience what it's like when I drive you mad enough with pleasure that you beg me to let you come."

His explicit words drove my passion even higher. "I want that too," I said into his neck, where I'd buried my face.

He curled his fingers, then leaned down and nipped the flesh of my neck. "Beg me, Juni."

"Please, Cord," I cried as my body convulsed in pleasure like none I'd ever known.

He held me close to him, murmuring words I couldn't comprehend until I finally caught my breath. Only then did he lower my legs to the floor, remove his hand from my pants, and refasten my jeans.

"Listen to me, Juniper."

I looked into his eyes.

"I don't want to spend all of our time worrying about what's going to happen months from now. I want us to get to know each other and worry about tomorrow when it gets here. For now, I can't stand the idea of not being with you. You know?"

I nodded.

"Can we do that? Just be together now and let the future figure itself out?" His eyes blazed as he waited for my answer.

"Don't you dare break my heart, Cord Wheaton."

"I won't as long as you promise not to break mine." He kissed me again, then rested his forehead against mine and smiled. "Do you know how much I want to fuck you right now?"

I shuddered and squeezed my legs together, knowing that if he kissed or touched me, I'd be right back on the brink of another orgasm.

"So, um, we kind of just disappeared."

He kissed me once more, then took a step back. "I'm headed out to look for any cattle we missed last night, but I couldn't leave until we talked."

I smiled up at him. "We did a little more than talk."

"You're right. However, it's nowhere near as much as we're gonna do."

"When will you be back?" I asked.

"As soon as I can be."

"I'll be waiting."

He pressed my lips with his one more time before opening the library door and motioning for me to go ahead of him.

After Cord left, I returned to the table where Sam sat reading Miss Cena's journals.

"Everything okay?" she asked.

"Better."

She sighed. "I'm so glad. Listen, I was thinking you might want to start with those." She pointed to a stack that she'd set aside. "Of course, you're welcome to read in whatever order you want to, but since those are dated later, I thought maybe there'd be something in there about Cord's mother leaving the Lilacs."

"Good thinking. I can circle back to the older ones after you're finished."

Periodically, one or both of us would point out a particular passage and mark it with the flags Sam had sitting on the table. Sadly, I'd read through a few of the journals, but hadn't found any mention of Patricia.

"Did everyone call Jimmy and Johnny's father JD?" she asked.

"I never heard him called anything else. Why?"

"Cena talks about Jim. Since her brother was James D. Rooker, his son was a junior, and his grandson was the third, I sometimes have to stop to try to figure out which one she's talking about."

"What does she say about him?"

"That's what's confusing me. It was her brother who was driving the car when he and Manley were killed, right?"

"Yes."

"She clearly didn't care for him, and I suppose, rightly so. But, earlier, when I glanced at the ones you're reading, it sounded more like she was talking about JD. She would've had to have been since those are dated after her brother and Manley died. Anyway, sorry for the interruption. I'm sure you'll see what I mean when you get to those entries."

"I'll keep an eye out."

I'd been so engrossed in reading Miss Cena's words that I lost track of time. Two hours later, I checked my phone but didn't see a message from Cord.

"Does it seem like he's been gone a long time?" I asked Sam.

"Cord? Um, I have no idea how long it takes to look for cattle."

"Me either." I tried to call him, but it went straight to voicemail. I continued calling once every fifteen minutes, but got the same result. When another hour had passed without being able to reach him, I asked Sam if she knew where Beau was.

"Up here," he called out from the second level. "Do you need something?"

"Can you come in here for a minute?" she responded.

"What's up?" he asked, coming to stand behind Sam and rubbing her shoulders.

"We're worried about Cord. He's been gone a long time. Didn't Decker say something about being able to track people within the security system's app? Kind of like a location finder."

"That's correct." Beau was already looking at his phone, presumably at the app Sam had mentioned.

"This is odd. His last location update was thirty minutes ago. I'll see if I can reach him." After a few seconds, he lowered his phone. "No answer."

Pin-and-needle prickles spread throughout my body. "It'll be dark soon."

Beau's eyes met mine. "Understood. I'll round up some of the guys, and we'll go look for him."

When he walked into the other room, I called my mom since my father didn't always answer his phone.

"Hey, sweetheart. How—"

"Is Dad there?"

"Yes, do you want to talk to him?"

"Please."

"Juni? What's wrong?" he asked.

"Cord's been gone over two hours."

"What do you mean gone?"

"He went to see if he could find stray cattle, but he hasn't returned yet."

"Wind is picking up, and we're supposed to get dumped with another round of snow," said my dad.

"Beau is gathering some of the guys who work on the estate to go look for him."

"I'll call Pete. He, Grayson, and I will be there as soon as we can."

I thanked him, ended the call, and looked up at Sam. We reached for each other's hands and held tight.

18

Cord

"Motherfucker," I groaned, opening my eyes and trying to get my bearings. I was on the ground—I knew that much—and my head was pounding like someone had hit me with an anvil. I reached up to where the pain radiated from, and when I brought my hand back down, there was blood on my glove.

I tried to prop myself up on my elbow, but didn't have the strength. Blinking away the spots before my eyes, I patted my jacket, looking for my phone. When I found it, I swiped the screen, but the damned thing was dead. How the hell long had I been out here?

I was conscious, and it was still daylight. Both good signs. I raised my head, looking for some kind of landmark that would tell me where I was. A few feet away was a lean-to. If I could get that far, at least I'd have shelter. As cold as it was, I wouldn't last much longer if I didn't at least try.

I had to drag myself since my every attempt to even get on my knees failed. I made it what I figured was halfway, but the black spots were back, and this time, I couldn't blink them away.

"Fuck!" I cried out with the little strength I had left. What a goddamn way to go. Freezing to death after riding out to find cattle that were probably dead too.

Before everything went black, I saw Juni as if she was standing right in front of me. "Hold on, Cord," she said. "Help is on the way."

I pulled myself up a second time and inched my way into the lean-to. "Hurry, Juniper," I whispered before the darkness overtook me again.

19

"This is the last place where the security app located him," said Beau, pointing to a map of the estate. "As you can see by the outline, then he was almost directly at the perimeter, which means if he ventured farther, he wouldn't have been tracked."

"When was that?" my dad asked.

"Going on an hour."

His gaze met mine. Temperatures were well below freezing. If Cord wasn't found soon, he'd die, if he wasn't dead already.

"We don't have time to waste. Twilight is upon us," said my uncle, who'd divided everyone into teams. There were a total of twenty guys headed out, and they'd found enough snowmobiles in some of the outbuildings for each to have their own. Dad, Grayson, Uncle Pete, and one of the EMTs from the East Aurora fire department rode theirs here.

"There were seven in a storage room in the barn," Beau said. "One of the guys said there are six now."

It made sense. Cord wouldn't have gotten very far if he wasn't on a sled.

I offered to go out with them, but my dad wouldn't have it. Rather than wasting time arguing with him, I let it go. Sitting here, waiting for word, though, felt harder than if I was out in the frigid cold. At least then, I'd be doing something.

The ranch had a comms system, and each person in the search party wore one so they could communicate with each other. Beau left a set with Sam and me so we could hear what was happening in real time. Via the app, we could also follow their locations.

Minutes dragged on like hours as we watched and listened. I tried reading more of Miss Cena's journals, but couldn't concentrate.

"I'm sorry," I said to Sam.

"I don't know what for."

"Not reading."

"Don't worry about it. I can't, either."

I looked up at the clock like I had every few seconds. They'd been gone twenty minutes, and so far, no one had spotted anything other than stray cattle. According to the location tracker, they were getting close to the place where the app had last registered Cord.

"I see something," I heard my brother say a few minutes later.

"Heifer," someone else, whose voice I didn't recognize, responded. "Hold up. There's a lean-to. I'll take a look," he added.

"I see a sled not far from it," said someone else. "It's half buried. Let's start digging."

I had to leave the room. I couldn't listen any longer. I went into the library, closed the door, rested against the wall where Cord had last held me, and cried.

When I returned to the kitchen several minutes later, Sam was ashen.

"They found him."

I wrapped my arms around my midsection. "And?"

She shook her head. "I'm sorry, Juni."

I couldn't make it back to the library before dissolving into tears again. I sat on the sofa in the living room, pulling my knees to my chest. Why hadn't I noticed the time sooner? Why had I waited and called him rather than for help? If I had, maybe Cord would still be alive. I felt like a piece of my heart had broken off and was lodged somewhere in my chest. That's how bad the pain was.

Tears turned into sobs when I thought about every time Cord and I had stopped ourselves from making love, including earlier, in the library. I cried for every time we'd struggled with whether or not it was worth it to get involved with someone whose home was almost two thousand miles away.

From the moment we met, I knew there was something special—different—between Cord and me. And now, he was gone. There were countless things I'd go back and do differently if only I could.

Sam sat beside me on the sofa, both of us crying. He'd been special to her too. He was the first cousin she'd ever known, and while Cord had siblings, no one could take his place, not for her and not for me.

It was close to eight before Sam received a call from Beau. When I sat down at the table next to her after the call ended, she said the snow had let up enough for a medical-transport helicopter to land and that Cord had been taken to a hospital in Buffalo. The men who'd found him, plus the emergency team who arrived on the scene, had taken turns doing two hours of CPR, performing emergency life support, and slowly rewarming his body.

"At the hospital, Cord's body was connected to a machine called an ECMO—extracorporeal membrane oxygenation," she said, looking down at the notes she'd made. "It's used as a last-ditch effort to save patients whose lungs and heart are severely damaged."

"I don't understand. I thought he was…" I couldn't bring myself to say the words.

"Apparently, the doctor who saw Cord when he arrived told Beau there was a fifty-fifty chance he'd survive. A few minutes ago, he returned to tell them Cord's body was warming and his heart was beating on its own."

"He's alive?" I gasped.

She reached over and squeezed my hand. "He is, Juni, but the doctor also said that he's in a coma, and so far, there's no sign of brain activity."

"I don't understand."

Her voice softened. "I think your dad and Grayson are still there. They may know more than Beau."

I returned to the library, closed the door, and called my father.

"Hey, sweetheart. Have you heard the news?" he asked.

"It's very confusing. I was hoping you could explain what's happening."

He reiterated most of what Sam had relayed from Beau but added that Cord's recovery thus far was nothing short of miraculous. "They're optimistic, June-bug," he said. "As long as they are, we will be too."

"What about his family?" I asked.

"His brother is on his way here now with Decker Ashford. Grayson offered to meet them at the airport."

"Dad? Are you still there?" I asked when it sounded as though the call had dropped.

"Sorry, sweetheart. The doctor came out, and I wanted to ask him something."

"I'll let you go for now. How long do you think you'll stay there?"

"Don't you want to know what I asked?"

"Uh, sure."

"I asked if you could see him."

I put my hand over my mouth. "Can I?"

"Yes, sweetheart. In fact, Beau said he'd leave now, pick you and Sam up, and bring you back here."

When I returned to the kitchen to tell her, she was on the phone. "Beau's on his way here," she said, covering the mic.

"My dad told me."

She said something else to him, then ended the call. "Beau said to warn you that Cord looks pretty rough."

"As long as he's alive, I can handle it."

Sam, Cord's brother Buck, and I took turns sitting by Cord's bedside for the next week. The doctors encouraged us to talk to him while we were there. I knew Sam read him Miss Cena's journals. I had no idea what his brother might have said. For me, I struggled. Cord was in a coma, being kept alive by machines and medicines, and even the doctors had said they weren't sure there was much hope for functional survival.

On the eighth day, I stood to excuse myself when the same doctor came in to check on Cord's progress like he did at least once a day.

"You're okay. I'll only be a minute." He held up a light and pulled one of Cord's eyelids open. He did the same thing twice more.

"What is it?" I asked when I saw him smile.

"His eyes are tracking."

"What does that mean?"

"Brain function."

He left, but came back a few minutes later, saying he'd scheduled several tests and that Cord would be out of his room for at least two hours, maybe longer. He also suggested I go home and get some much-needed rest.

"We won't have any concrete results until tomorrow, anyway," he added.

It didn't matter whether I slept or not; I still looked haggard, and I didn't care. Each day, I'd leave the hospital, drive home, and fall asleep, sometimes without changing out of my clothes.

I would've preferred to stay at the cottage, just to feel closer to Cord, but Buck had been staying there since he'd arrived in town.

One thing I didn't do was drive. Either Gray, my parents, Beau, or Decker were always waiting to take me home and bring me back. Tonight was no different.

"Juni, honey?" I rolled over, not realizing I'd drifted off, when my mom stuck her head in my bedroom door. "Sam is trying to reach you."

I felt around on the bed for my phone and saw I'd missed two texts and two calls from her. My heart sank, knowing Cord had to have taken a turn for the worse if she was trying so hard to reach me.

"Hey," I said when she picked up.

"Juni! Have you heard?" She sounded happy.

"I haven't."

"Every test, every scan shows brain activity. He's going to make it, Juni. I know he is. They even removed the breathing tube, and he's doing it on his own."

I'd had so many dreams where Cord came out of the coma and was fine that I had a hard time believing this wasn't one of them.

"Hurry up and get here!"

"On my way," I said, still expecting that, at any time, I'd wake up.

"Good news?" my mom asked when I came downstairs and saw it was daylight.

"Sam said the tests they ran show brain function."

"Are you heading back to the hospital?" she asked after wrapping me in a big hug.

"I have to, Mom."

"I'll drive."

Sam and Beau were still there when I walked into the room. He looked up at me, but she didn't. When I stepped closer, I saw why. Cord's eyes were open, and she was staring into them.

"Juni's here," she told him before standing from the chair where she'd been sitting, and motioning for me to take it.

"Hi," I said, looking into the most beautiful blue eyes I'd ever seen. He blinked twice, and I leaned forward, brushed the hair from his face, and kissed his cheek.

When I was still there a few hours later, Beau asked the hospital staff if they could bring in a chair I could sleep in, not that I did much of it. I woke myself what seemed like every few minutes to check on Cord.

20

Cord

Every time I closed my eyes, I saw someone coming at me. Whoever it was, was covered from head to toe. Between that and the heavy snow and wind, I'd barely seen him, certainly not enough to make out who the fuck it was. I remembered coming to and thinking that it felt like someone had hit me with an anvil. Who knew what it actually was, and it didn't really matter. The guy I'd seen in the middle of a snowstorm intended to kill me. Once he learned he hadn't, I had no doubt he'd return to finish me off.

I'd tried to speak several times, but never managed to get more than a syllable out. "Jun," was the first word I'd tried to say, praying someone heard me, praying that the next time I opened my eyes, I'd see her. When Sam told me she was there, I felt inexplicably relieved. Just her presence soothed me.

Now, staring into her wide eyes, the same feeling swept over me. Sam had been here with me on and off, and so had my brother Buck, but neither of them settled me like Juni did.

She leaned forward and covered my hand with hers. I wanted to pull her closer, but I couldn't get my arm to move. I couldn't get anything to move, but I could feel her touch. That had to be a good sign, didn't it?

My gaze penetrated hers with so many questions, none of which I could articulate. If only she could read my mind.

I blinked a couple of times and tried to speak, but no sound, let alone words, came out.

I knew a guy from high school whose dad had had a stroke so severe that he got what was called locked-in syndrome. He could move his eyes and hear but was otherwise paralyzed and unable to communicate. If that was what was happening to me, I wouldn't fuck-ing want to live.

The door opened, but I couldn't turn my head to see who walked in. "Good morning, Cord," a male voice said. When he came to stand in my line of sight, I figured by the way he was dressed that he was a doctor. "I'm Dr. Oldham. If you can hear and understand me, please blink twice."

I did.

"Excellent. Again, if you remember meeting me previously, blink twice."

Since I didn't, I kept my eyes still.

"Should I step out?" Juni asked.

Not wanting her to leave, I blinked three times.

The doctor smiled. "I think he's trying to tell us you should stay."

I blinked twice.

He covered my hand with his like Juni had. "Can you feel anything?" he asked.

I gave the same response.

Each place he touched on my body, from my forehead to the bottom of my feet, I felt.

"This is excellent progress," he said. "Cord, do you remember being out in the snow?"

I responded that I did.

"Do you recall what happened?"

Again, I gave an affirmative response.

The man pulled a chair closer to the bed, sat down, and leaned forward. "Your recovery is nothing short of a medical miracle. It will take time for your body to recover, but you're already progressing much quicker than I anticipated." He scrubbed his face with his hand, something I always did. "I'm glad you're here, Cord."

I blinked twice, and a tear ran down my cheek. Me too, I wished I could say.

21

Juniper

After Dr. Oldham left, Cord shut his eyes, and his breathing evened out. Hoping he'd remain asleep long enough for me to get my emotions in check, I left the room and made my way to one of the private spaces set aside for families of ICU patients.

"Juni?" The voice sounded so much like Cord's that I jolted.

"Hey, Buck," I said, spinning around to face him.

"I just spoke with the doctor. He said Cord's making good progress. Do you have a minute to talk?"

"Of course." He followed me into the room and shut the door behind him. "I'm not sure what all they've told you," he began.

"Hardly anything," I said, shutting my eyes against the tears that threatened to fall.

He sat beside me and put his hand on my arm. "If you have questions, I'll do my best to answer them."

"I wouldn't know where to start."

"How about if I tell you what I know so far?"

"I'd appreciate it, but…"

"Go on."

"Cord and I…"

He studied me but didn't speak.

"I'm not sure how to put this, but we don't know each other that well. I guess what I'm trying to say is he might not want me to know. You know?"

His smile was sweet when he reached for my hand. "Sam told me the only thing he's said so far is your name. At least as much of it as he could get out. I also saw the way his eyes tracked you when you walked in yesterday. You may say you don't know each other well, but I know my brother. Whatever is between you, you're important to him."

I took a deep breath and let it out slowly, blinking away tears that seemed to fall like clockwork. "Okay."

Buck told me some of the things I already knew about Cord's general condition, then outlined the milestones the doctor had gone over with him. His ability to speak as well as move his extremities would be two major steps in his recovery. From there, they could better assess the amount of brain damage he may have suffered.

"The thing is, there's no precedent for a case like this. Certain tests can be conducted, but they won't tell us anywhere near as much as what Cord will himself as he continues to recover."

My eyes scrunched. "The doctor asked him if he recalled what happened, and he blinked twice, which meant he did. It seemed like an odd question, given he'd just asked Cord if he remembered being out in the snow." I shook my head. "I'm probably making more of it than it was," I mumbled.

Buck leaned against the chair and rubbed the back of his neck. "You're not." He took a deep breath, like I had, and exhaled slowly. "Cord has an injury inconsistent with what we can piece together. There's more to this than him being stuck out in a snowstorm and losing consciousness."

I gasped and covered my mouth with my hand.

"Your uncle can tell you more, but there's an investigation taking place as we speak."

"Do you think someone…?" I couldn't get the rest of the words out, but Buck understood what I was asking.

"Yes, Juni, we do."

My eyes opened wide when I remembered something Cord told me about the stipulations in the trust that had brought him here. "Buck, Cord said he couldn't be away from the Lilacs for more than forty-eight hours. He's been in the hospital longer than that already, and I doubt he'll be released anytime soon."

Buck cocked his head. "He told you about that?"

I nodded.

"I'm surprised," he mumbled, stroking his beard.

"Does this mean your family will lose everything?"

His eyes met mine. "Sorry. Cord sharing that with you stunned me for a minute. Not that there's anything wrong with him doing so. But don't worry. I contacted the attorney we deal with and told him what had happened."

He looked away, and his eyes scrunched.

"What?" I asked.

"I guess there's no point in not telling you since you know the rest, but he already knew."

"Did he say who told him?"

"He didn't." Buck shook his head. "Anyway, what he did say was that he was aware of Cord's condition and the resulting circumstances. He assured me an exception would be made, including allowing him to be moved to a hospital or rehab facility out of state, should it be medically recommended."

"Can you trust him?"

Buck grinned, but the smile quickly left his face. "Hell, no, which is why I asked him to prepare a legal document stating all that and to forward it to my attorney. By the time the plane Decker and I were on landed in Buffalo, he'd received it."

He looked away a second time. "I hate to say it, but it included what would happen should Cord not make it." His eyes filled with tears, and he looked up at the ceiling. "I fucking hate that, instead of being able to focus on the fact that my brother's life hung in the balance, I was worried about our goddamn inheritance."

I put my hand on his. "It wasn't just you. You had to look out for your brothers and sister too."

He studied me. "Here's what I don't get. You said you and Cord didn't know each other that well. Yet, he told you about the messed-up shit my father did and that it affects our siblings. All I can say is Cord isn't one to open up to someone the way he did to you. He trusts you." He shifted our hands and squeezed my fingers. "I'm damn glad he met you. He needs someone like you in his corner to help him get through this."

Could I, though? Yeah, he'd confided in me, but that didn't mean we had enough history for him to allow me to help him. And even if he did, would I know how to go about it? I had no experience with traumatic injury other than my own, and Cord's prognosis was so much worse. What if he refused my involvement? Worse, what if I failed him?

"I should get in there," he said, standing. "Are you headed home?"

I hadn't planned to leave, but since Buck was here, I decided I should give the brothers some time on their own. "I'll just go in and say good night."

When we got to the room, a nurse was coming out the door. "Thank goodness you're back. He's agitated."

I stepped around her and rushed over to the bed. "I'm here, Cord." I took his hand in mine and stared into his wide eyes. "I just left for a few minutes." I glanced over at the monitors, watching as his heart rate and blood pressure slowly came down. Without letting go, I sat in the chair I'd been in earlier.

"Hey, little brother," Buck said, standing behind me. Cord's eyes didn't move. "What do you say we let Juni go home and get some rest?"

He blinked three times, and I looked up at his brother.

"He said no," I told him.

When I turned back to Cord and smiled, I swore he did too.

"I guess that settles it, then," said Buck, chuckling. "How about if I bring you some dinner?"

"Thanks, but I'm not hungry."

Cord's eyes bored into mine.

"It's okay," I said. "I'll get something later."

He blinked three times like he had a few seconds ago, but that wasn't all—Cord squeezed my fingers.

"Do it again," I whispered, and he did.

"Be right back," said Buck, racing from the room. He returned a minute later with the nurse who'd said Cord was agitated.

"I heard you moved your hand," she said to him.

He blinked twice.

"Can you show me?"

This time, the pressure of his fingers was stronger than before.

"Dr. Oldham will want an update," she said, hurrying from the room like Beau had.

"Thank you, Juni," he said, resting his hand on my shoulder.

I wanted to tell him I hadn't done anything; Cord had.

It was after nine by the time Cord fell asleep for more than a few minutes at a time.

"Go get some rest," Buck said when he saw me struggling to keep my eyes open too. "If he wakes up, I'll explain why you aren't here. After the fuss he made about you not eating, my guess is if he could, he'd tell you to go home too."

"I don't want him to get agitated again." I stood and brushed the hair from his forehead.

"I promise I won't leave," said Buck.

I'd sent a message to my brother earlier, telling him I planned to stay longer than I'd originally said. He'd responded he'd let everyone know. Now, I texted again and asked to be picked up. A few minutes later, I received a message from my mom instead, saying she was downstairs, but they wouldn't let her come up.

I responded I'd be right down. Before leaving, I knelt down and kissed Cord's forehead. "I'll be back in the morning," I said more quietly than a whisper.

When I made eye contact with Buck, he nodded once, raised his hand, and waved.

Instead of just meeting my mom when I exited the elevator, I saw my dad and Gray with her. Until they enveloped me in a group hug, I hadn't realized how much I needed it.

"Come on, June-bug. Let's get you home," said my dad, who linked his arm through mine. My mom did the same thing on the opposite side.

"Hey, what about me?" Grayson teased.

"You can read your sister a bedtime story," my dad joked back.

As we walked, I rested my head on my mom's shoulder.

"We'll talk once we're home," she whispered.

I nodded and wiped my tears on her jacket.

"Can I have pancakes?" I asked.

She smiled. "Gray, can you make your sister pancakes?" she said over her opposite shoulder.

"Plain or blueberry?" he asked.

"I think we're out of blueberries," my mom told him.

"I picked some up this morning," said my dad.

The conversation was as mundane as they came, but like the group hug, it was exactly what I needed.

My parents sat at the kitchen table with me, and I told them about Cord's progress while my brother made enough pancakes for all of us.

"I can't help myself from wondering how they knew," said my mom.

"What do you mean?" I asked.

"Cord had no pulse. They could've pronounced him dead. How did they know not to?"

"I actually talked to Pete about that," said my dad. "He told me it's a relatively new protocol that first responders are being trained on all over the country."

"I remember hearing about it," said Gray. "There was another case similar to Cord's, where a drunk college student walked home in a snowstorm. They thought he passed out, and they were able to, uh, bring him back to life, I guess."

"I had no idea," I muttered between forkfuls of pancakes. "So, um, Cord's brother said there's an investigation into what happened."

My eyes met my dad's. "That's right."

"He said Cord had injuries inconsistent with him getting lost in a snowstorm."

"Your uncle thinks someone tried to kill him." My dad reached over and took my hand, and my mom gasped.

"Who would do that?"

"I don't know, sweetheart, but I can tell you this; Cord has some friends in high places. My understanding is there's a private firm assisting in the investigation."

"Decker Ashford."

"That's right. Do you know him?" my dad asked me.

"He helped put in the security system at the Lilacs, but I got the impression that wasn't all he did."

"Your uncle also told me Cord is not without protection."

My eyes opened wide. "What does that mean?"

"Some of the people you see in the ICU aren't doctors, nurses, or family members," my dad responded.

"Why not post a guard outside his door?" I held up my hand before my dad could answer. "Never mind, I get it."

"That's enough talk for tonight," said my mom, standing and taking my hand after I yawned twice in close succession. "Juni needs sleep."

I let her lead me upstairs, and after I took a quick shower, brushed my teeth, and got into pajamas, I found her sitting on the end of my bed.

"How are you holding up?" she asked.

When I shrugged and got under the covers, she stretched out beside me.

"Buck said Cord needed someone like me in his corner to help him get through this."

I felt her nod.

"It almost sent me into a panic, Mom. I mean, I have no experience outside…"

"Of your own?"

"That's right. What if I do the wrong thing? Or what if he doesn't want my help?"

She stretched her arm out, and I rested my head on her shoulder. "As in all things, do the best you can, sweetheart. If you feel overwhelmed, talk to me or someone else. You're Cord's *friend*, Juni. You're not a nurse or a physical therapist."

"He gets upset when I'm not there."

"I would imagine he's terrified right now, and for whatever reason, you're the person who soothes him. The more progress he makes, the better he'll feel on his own."

"What if he doesn't?"

She shifted so she could look into my eyes. "What would Nana say to a question like that?"

"She'd look up at the ceiling, mutter 'God forbid,' then smack me for saying it."

My mom rolled her eyes. "She wouldn't smack you."

"We're talking about Nana, not your mom."

"You're right. She would smack you."

The progress Cord made in the following few days far exceeded the doctors' expectations. He'd gone from being unable to move at all to being able to lift his arms and legs. They didn't believe he was strong enough to try walking yet, but were optimistic he would be within a few days. What seemed to agitate him the most was that he still hadn't recovered the ability to speak beyond a syllable. Even that, he struggled with. Frustration was etched on his face, and being reminded it would take time for him to regain various abilities only increased his irritation that bordered on anger.

Remembering how I'd felt, facing what I considered my journey back to "normal," I knew the last thing he needed was another admonition from me or anyone else, not that it was my place to say anything about it.

A few days ago, Buck had returned to Colorado to be with his wife and baby, and their youngest brother, Holt, came in his place. My understanding was he'd stay for several days, then their sister, Flynn, would arrive.

Sam, Holt, and I took turns being at the hospital during the day. Beau and Gray visited too, and either Holt or I spent most nights there.

"Good morning, Juni," said Holt, standing and stretching when I arrived in the morning after he'd been on the "night shift."

"Good morning," I responded before removing my jacket, then standing by Cord's bedside. He opened his eyes and looked up at me.

"You're…here." He struggled, but that he'd been able to say two words together was progress.

"I am," I exclaimed. "And you're talking."

"He's been a regular chatterbox," muttered Holt.

I looked over at him with wide eyes.

"Sorry. I was kidding. He's only said your name but with increasing frequency."

Cord's eyes scrunched at his brother. "Get…out."

Holt approached on the opposite side of the bed. "Gladly." He leaned over and rested his head against his brother's. "Love you, man," he said before walking out. Two seconds later, he stuck his head back in the door. "Forgot to mention he's gonna try walking today."

"That's great news," I said to Cord, smiling.

His eyes scrunched at me like they had at Holt. "What?"

He shook his head.

"Did I say something wrong?"

When Cord didn't respond and closed his eyes, I pulled out my tablet, sat in the more comfortable chair, and opened the book I was reading. I glanced up at him periodically, standing when I saw a tear run down his cheek.

"What is it?" I asked, stroking his hair.

"So…sorry."

I shook my head. "Stop this. You've nothing to be sorry for."

He lifted his chin. "Tired."

"Then, sleep."

He shook his head again. "You."

He was right. I was exhausted, and while my dad said my being away from the restaurant wasn't adversely affecting the Goat, I still felt bad that other people had to cover my shifts. I simply didn't have the energy to show up after being here all day or night.

Cord lifted his hand, and when I took it, he pulled me closer.

"What?" I asked, but rather than answer, he kept pulling until the upper part of my body was practically on top of him.

"Sleep."

"Cord, I can't get in bed with you. There isn't enough room." I tried to wriggle my hand from his grasp, but he wouldn't let go.

"Sleep," he repeated.

When the orderly came in an hour later to take Cord to rehab, he found me on the bed, stretched out next to him.

"Sorry," I muttered, shifting to get up.

"Stay where you are. This is the best thing I've seen in all the time I've worked here. I'll be back later."

After he left, I looked up at Cord, who was grinning. "Sleep," he repeated, closing his eyes.

22

Cord

"You're an asshole," said my brother Buck.

"Yeah? Fuck off."

"I think I liked you better when you couldn't talk."

"You know where the door is, dickhead. Go home."

I'd been in the hospital for thirty-six days, and while I'd moved from the ICU to a regular room, then to the rehab center, the beds were the same as was the decor. I was sick of being here and sick of my body not being the way it was before some *sonuvabitch* tried to kill me and I almost froze to death.

The doctor said my extreme mood swings were partially due to the medication I still needed to take and might have to for the rest of my life, combined with the length of my hospital stay and the active lifestyle I'd led before my "injury." Not that I'd asked. Buck had.

Just hearing someone use the word injury set me off. I wasn't *injured*. I'd survived an attempted murder, and just barely, at that.

Today, though, I was going home, but not to Colorado. I was headed back to the cottage at the Lilacs.

Buck said he'd done everything he could to get Six-pack to allow me to leave New York State, but in the end, the attorney had said that, unless it was medically necessary for me to be at a hospital or other facility in Colorado, I had to stay where I was. Given Crested Butte didn't have more than urgent care and the medical center in Gunnison was nowhere near as good as this one, Six-pack had refused. Actually, he said the trustee had. Whoever that motherfucker was.

"Why are you here anyway?" I barked at Buck.

"It was my turn," he snapped in response.

"I don't need your help."

His back was to me, but he turned around. "You do. You wanna know why?"

I folded my arms and stared at the wall.

"Because you've run everyone else but Juni and me off, and I can tell you, you keep treating her the way you have been, and she isn't going to show up anymore either."

Nobody—including Juni—got how much I felt like a prisoner in this place. Maybe Porter would, since he'd spent a few nights in jail after the accident, but otherwise, none of my brothers had spent any length of time in the hospital, let alone over a month.

They didn't understand that people I didn't know, and some I did, dictated my schedule from the time I woke up until I went to sleep. Half the time, I feigned it so everyone would leave me the hell alone.

The only person I wanted to be around was Juni, but Buck was right; there were times when I was an asshole even to her. Whenever I snapped in answer to something she said, I felt like shit about it. You'd think it would've made me stop, but it hadn't.

On one of my worst days, when the doctors told me I had to have two of the toes on my left foot amputated because of gangrene, I railed at everyone I came in contact with, but none more than her.

She'd reacted the same way she always did. At first, she didn't respond. Then, after several minutes of silence, she acted like nothing had happened and started up an unrelated conversation. My response that day? I'd lost it.

"Why do you do that? Why don't you leave or at least yell back at me?" I'd shouted.

"Because I understand what you're going through," she'd said in her usual soft tone of voice.

I'd scoffed. "You understand? Right. You have no fucking clue." When she went back to giving me the silent treatment, I told her to leave.

When she didn't come back at all the next day, I was sure I'd managed to drive her away. Every time the door opened, my head shot up, hoping it was her. Which meant I was more of an asshole to everyone who wasn't.

The following morning, when she was finally the one to cross the threshold, I almost wept in relief. I'd apologized several times, but when I asked why she said she understood what I was going through, she clammed up, only saying she was wrong and never should've said it. I knew she was lying, but I let it go.

What she couldn't possibly understand—what no one else could either since I hadn't told anyone outside of Dr. Oldham—was that there was one part of my anatomy that hadn't yet recovered from my ordeal. My cock.

Before the day I almost died, just being around Juni was enough to get a rise out of me, so to speak. Now, even imagining her naked did nothing.

My doc suggested reading material that might help, and I'd tried it. Again, to no avail. Even the porn I'd streamed on my laptop had zero effect.

When Oldham told me to "give it time" as I reported my lack of results, it was all I could do not to tell him to get the hell out, like I had everyone else.

Maybe it would be best if Juni did stop showing up, but the idea I wouldn't see her every day made it hard for me to breathe. Except, what did I have to offer her?

For one, whoever had tried to kill me was still out there, and from what I knew, the police didn't have any leads.

The most obvious theory had been that Hoss Schultz, or someone who worked for him, figured out I'd been spying on him. However, given I hadn't found anything to report to Pete, it made no sense that he'd try to kill me for it.

Plus, Beau confirmed that, after what happened with Jimmy Rooker, Hoss had been more than willing to terminate the contract between the Schultz Brothers and the Lilacs. Him targeting me for that also made no sense. I doubted he was the kind of person who'd give a shit that I'd shot Jimmy. Everything I'd learned about Hoss told me he was a man who was out for no one but himself.

It wasn't until a few days ago, when Pete came to visit me, that I learned the real reason neither Hoss nor anyone associated with him was a suspect.

The day after I shot Jimmy Rooker's kneecap out, the feds had raided Schultz Brothers' main offices, along with every winery, vineyard, brewery, and distillery they held contracts with.

All except the Lilacs, that is. Knowing their assets would be seized, pending an in-depth investigation, Decker Ashford arranged to have Schultz terminate the contract. Since Hoss hadn't known about the raid scheduled to take place the following day, I could only imagine what Deck might've had over him to make him do it.

The last Pete knew was that Hoss and the two brothers he partnered with, along with several of their employees, were under indictment for extortion, racketeering, and conspiracy to commit fraud—among other charges still pending, including attempted murder on the guy who was still lingering in a coma.

None of it changed the fact that someone had tried to kill me, and until they were caught, there was a very real possibility Juni's life might be in danger too.

Secondly, as it related to what I could offer her, I'd be in New York for another ten months, three weeks, and three days. After that, I was going home, and the truth was, I doubted I'd ever set foot in New York again.

Lastly, I was a twenty-eight-year-old guy whose dick didn't work. Who knew if it ever would again?

"I hear you're breaking out of this place," said the orderly who took me down to the rehab center most days and called himself Romeo. I still hadn't figured out if it was his real name.

"You heard right." I was dressed and sitting on the edge of the bed, ready to go like I had been for the last three hours. The only problem was Juni wasn't here. While she hadn't specifically said she would be, I still expected her to come. "So, uh…" I stammered.

"What?" Buck snapped at me.

"Just wondering about Juni. Should we wait?"

My brother's eyes scrunched. "Did you ask her to be here?"

"No, but…"

"It's my day. I'm here. Let's go."

I sure as hell didn't want to stay in this room a minute longer than I had to. It just hurt that she hadn't shown up. I pushed myself off the bed. "I can walk down," I said to Romeo.

"Sorry, man. Hospital policy. Once you're outside the main entrance, you can walk all you want, but until you are, your chariot awaits."

I scowled but sat down. As soon as I had, the chair and Romeo lurched forward.

"What the hell?" I gasped.

"Oh my God. Sorry. Did I hit you?" I heard Juni ask and looked over my shoulder at her and Romeo, who was rubbing his backside. "I didn't think you were leaving until this afternoon, but then I called, and they said you were being discharged this morning." She put her hand on her heart and took several deep breaths. "Thank goodness I made it."

She walked over to the wheelchair, and I reached for her hand. "Thanks. I know it isn't your day." I glared at my brother, who flipped me off.

"Not my day? Are you kidding? I wouldn't have missed this for anything."

I didn't deserve her. Not even a little. But selfishly, I couldn't stand the idea of not seeing her smile, holding her hand, listening to her sweet voice as she read Miss Cena's journals to me, or even the sniffling sounds she made when she got to a sad part. I brought her hand to my lips and kissed the back of it, and she beamed.

"Well? What are we waiting for? Let's go." She motioned with her hand for the rest of us to follow her out the door.

"You don't deserve her," Buck leaned down and whispered, reiterating my thoughts of only moments ago. He was right. I just had no idea how I'd ever let her go.

23

Uncle Pete made me promise not to say a word about what he'd told me earlier this morning. Several times in only the last thirty minutes, I'd had to bite my tongue to stop myself from telling Cord that today—of all the days it could happen—the person who tried to kill him would be arrested.

While it was still the dead of winter, we'd had a week of unusually warm weather, followed by rain that had melted much of the snow, uncovering clues as to what happened that day.

Cord had once said that it felt like someone had hit him in the head with an anvil. He hadn't been far off. The team, which included Decker Ashford and others who worked for him, that went out with my uncle to look for evidence found a pickax buried in the dirt not far from the lean-to where they'd found Cord.

The blood on it was a DNA match to his, and more importantly, they'd been able to lift a partial fingerprint from the handle. There was enough of it for a computer application to find a possible match. Not only that, but one of the ranch hands said he remembered seeing someone on the outside of the estate's perimeter. According to Pete, Decker had access to something called overheads that they used to track the guy and get a positive ID.

Most of what my uncle had said went right over my head, but that didn't take away from the relief I felt, knowing the man who'd tried to kill Cord would soon be in custody.

While he hadn't divulged who would be arrested, I got the impression it was someone local, maybe even someone who might've worked at the Lilacs at one point, but had somehow missed having their profile set up in the estate's new, elaborate security system.

Him stopping by our house to give us the news was the real reason I was late.

"Everything okay?" Cord asked as we waited near the hospital's main entrance for Buck to bring the SUV around.

"Of course," I assured him.

"You seem antsy."

"I'm just excited that you get to go home," I fibbed.

"It isn't my home," he mumbled, but I heard him.

"Sorry. I meant the cottage."

He scrubbed his face, something I hadn't seen him do in so long that I'd forgotten about it. "Look, I'm sorry. I know I've been an asshole—"

"Don't apologize. I understand."

His eyes scrunched, and he studied me.

"What?"

Cord looked up when Buck approached in the SUV. "Nothing," he said, climbing into the front seat and leaving me to sit alone in the back.

My mom had dropped me off at the hospital, so I rode to the Lilacs with them. By the time we got there, I regretted it. It was becoming evident that I was the source of Cord's foul moods. I'd leave, or at least ask someone to come and get me, but I wanted to be there if the news of the arrest was released.

"So, um, is there anything I can do?" I asked when Buck pulled up and parked near the cottage's front door.

Before either Cord or his brother had the chance to answer, my cell phone rang.

"Juni, where are you?" my uncle asked.

"At the Lilacs. We just got here."

"Is Cord there?"

"He is."

"Tell him I'm on my way."

When I turned around, both guys had gone inside. When I followed, I didn't see Buck, but Cord had his hands on his hips.

"That was Pete. He said to tell you he's on his way here."

His gaze bored into mine. "Why?"

My eyes darted back and forth, and I shook my head. "He asked that he be the one to tell you."

"I see." He spun in a slow circle. "Was Mrs. Miller's crew in here?"

"Actually, it was Sam, my mom, and me."

He took a deep breath, then scrubbed his face with his hand.

There wasn't a single time since the night Cord went missing when I'd allowed my anger to rise to the surface. He'd made me mad more times than I could count, but I'd tamped it down, reminding myself how close I came to losing him. Now, though, I'd reached my limit.

"I think what you meant to say was thank you." I turned on my heel and stalked out of the cottage. I no longer cared about being with Cord when Pete told him about the arrest. In fact, I wasn't sure when I'd be ready to be around Cord again, especially when I reached the main residence and he hadn't called out to me or followed.

"Hey, what's going on?" Sam said, coming to the door when I knocked and finding me in tears.

"Can I come in?"

She stepped aside. "Of course."

"First, I should tell you that Cord is home. Actually, he's not *home*—he's here. His words, not mine."

"I saw Buck drive in." She pulled me over to the sofa, and we both sat down. "I'd ask what happened, but I think I already know."

I hung my head. "He's being impossible."

"You're being kind. I would've said he's being an asshole."

"It's like I can't do anything right. He actually seemed angry that we got the cottage ready for his homecoming. I can just imagine how he'll freak out when he sees all the food we made and left in the refrigerator."

Sam's phone vibrated. "Your uncle is here."

I nodded. "Cord is expecting him." I figured within a few minutes, the word would be out, so I said fuck it and told her. "They're making an arrest."

She didn't look surprised. "Decker told Beau and me."

"And here I thought it was a big secret. I didn't even tell Cord when he asked me outright."

Her phone vibrated again. "Beau and your brother are back."

"Good. If you don't mind, I'm going to ask Gray to take me home."

"I understand. I just wish I knew how to knock some sense into him."

"Who? Cord?" Gray asked, coming in through the mudroom with Beau behind him.

I stood. "Can you take me home?"

"Here," he said, tossing me his key fob as he rushed by me, stalking out of the house like I had the cottage.

24

Cord

"Where's Juni?" Pete asked when I opened the door and invited him inside.

"She went up to the house for something."

His eyes scrunched, and he shook his head. "She knew I was on my way."

"She mentioned you wanted to be the one to tell me something, but she didn't say what."

"Yeah, okay. I guess—"

The door flew open, and Grayson came in, slamming it behind him and stalking in my direction.

"What the fuck?" I muttered when he got close enough to jam his index finger into my chest.

"My sister won't say it, so I will. Do you even realize that, if it weren't for her, you wouldn't be alive, asshole?"

Pete stepped forward. "Gray, that's enough."

He shoved his uncle away. "No. I came here with things to say, and I'm not leaving until I do." He took a deep breath. "My sister sat by your fucking bedside for over a month. *A month!* She doesn't even *know* you, but she did it because if she wasn't there, you got *agitated*."

There wasn't a single thing he'd said that I could dispute.

"Do you have any idea how hard it was for her to be back in that hospital? Back on that floor? But she did it. I'm sure it got easier as time went on, but I can guarantee you two things. One, she had a panic attack when she walked in for the first time. Two, she'd never admit it to anyone."

"Grayson," Pete warned again.

He spun around. "Do you think she'd tell him? Of course not." He looked back at me. "But then, I'm sure you haven't asked a single question about Juni or how she was doing. All you cared about was that she was there for you."

I raised both hands. "I understand why you're angry—"

"You're a—"

"Hang on, and let me finish. I get it, okay, and I agree with you. I'm an asshole. But, Gray, the things you're saying make no sense to me. I have no idea what you're talking about, and you're right; I haven't asked."

Pete put his hand on Grayson's shoulder. "Have a seat, son. You've gotten this far. You might as well finish it."

He put his head in his hands. "She's gonna be so mad at me."

Pete ushered him to the sofa. At the same time, Buck came out of the kitchen, carrying a six-pack of beer. I reached for one, cracked it open, and handed it to Juni's brother before taking another for myself.

I sat in the chair facing him. "I'm not going to force you to tell me anything if you're betraying Juni's confidence."

He shook his head. "You need to know. You aren't the only one who almost died on this property."

I leaned forward. "What happened?"

Gray's eyes filled with tears.

"Juniper boarded her horse here, in Miss Cena's stables. She still does, in fact," said Pete when Gray was too emotional to speak.

I looked between both men, waiting for one of them to continue. When Gray didn't, his uncle did. "It happened the summer between her junior and senior year of high school. At the time, she was a contender for a spot on the Olympic equestrian team."

"Her horse got spooked on the approach to a jump and threw her. It isn't uncommon, except the way she landed…" Grayson put his head in his hands again, and his uncle squeezed his shoulder.

"It was a freak accident, and it was bad, Cord," said Pete.

Gray raised his head, and his eyes bored into mine. "She was in the hospital longer than you were."

I didn't need to hear more. The picture Grayson and Pete painted was clear enough. When Juni told me she understood what I was going through, I'd shut her down, and she didn't say another word about it. She came to that hospital every day and spent most nights there, and she never mentioned that she'd once been a patient herself. From the sound of it, she'd been in the ICU, like I was.

I got up and walked toward the door.

"She's gone," said Gray before I opened it.

"What do you mean?"

"She wanted me to take her home, but I gave her my key instead."

"You've got a black SUV, right?"

He nodded. "Yeah, but so does Beau."

"Yours is American. His is German."

"Yeah. So?"

"She's still here." I walked out the door and up to the main house. It took me longer than it should have, which frustrated the fuck out of me, but this was *finally* about Juni, not me. Before I got to the porch steps, I saw her. She was sitting behind the wheel of Gray's vehicle, crying.

As I walked closer, she raised her head, and our eyes met. I hated the hurt and pain I saw reflected in them. I'd done that to the one person who let me off the hook for everything. The one person who'd been patient and understanding and had put her own life on hold to sit with me in a place that held such awful memories for her to cause a panic attack.

I approached the passenger side, heard the lock click, then got in. Thankfully, the SUV was running, so she wasn't sitting out in the freezing cold.

I turned my body to face her, wishing the damned thing had a bench seat rather than buckets, so I could pull her into my arms. Instead, I reached for her hand. She hesitated, then rested it in mine.

"I'm sorry," I began.

Her gaze remained on mine, but her facial expression didn't change.

"As I walked from the cottage here, all I could think was that I hurt the person the most who deserved it the least."

"I'm fine—"

"Don't do that. I *know*. Pete and Grayson told me what happened to you."

She turned her head and pulled her hand from mine. "They had no right."

"I agree that it was your story to tell, but, Juni, you didn't. Why not?"

"It happened a long time ago; it's no longer relevant."

"Is that right? So, five years from now, what happened to me won't be relevant either?" I wished she'd face me again. With every word I said, I felt her pulling farther away.

"What you've gone through is—"

"Not that different from what you did. While I don't know all the details, your brother did tell me you were in the hospital longer than I was."

"My accident was my fault, and someone tried to kill you. I'd say there's a vast difference between the two."

"Look at me, darlin'."

She shook her head.

"Please."

I waited until she finally did to say more. "There is no excuse for the way I've treated you, but I promise that, from this moment on, I'll do everything I can to make it up to you. Juniper, I…"

I couldn't get the words out that I desperately wanted to say. Every day she'd sat by my side, I fell more in love with her, but it wouldn't be fair for me to say it now. First, I had to prove it by my actions. Three words could never make up for the pain I'd caused her.

When I rested my hand on the console between us, she rested her palm on mine.

"I'm sorry I wasn't there when Pete told you about the arrest. I wanted to be."

Her eyes widened when mine did, and I gasped like all the air had left my lungs. "What did you say?"

"Oh my God. He hasn't told you yet. I'm so sorry." She tried to move her hand away, but I wouldn't let her.

"I don't want to hear it from him. You tell me."

"They know who tried to kill you, Cord. By now, he should be in custody. That's what my uncle came here to tell you."

"Who is it?"

"I don't know."

I nodded once, trying to wrap my head around the news and quell the nausea churning in my stomach. Did I even want to know who the person was who'd left me for dead? I remembered the bone-chilling look of evil in Jimmy Rooker's eyes when he'd held the gun against Sam. It was something I never wanted to witness again. How could the person who was arrested not have the same vileness inside him?

"Do you want to go back so Pete can tell you the rest?" she asked in a tone barely above a whisper.

"Not yet. First, I need to know if we can still be friends." As soon as the words left my mouth, I regretted them. Once again, I'd hurt her. "You know, friends plus, uh, more."

"We can still be friends, Cord."

I nodded once. "Understood," I muttered, turning my head to look in the direction of the cottage. I was the one who'd started it. I could hardly fault her for agreeing.

"Pete will probably have to return to the station soon, so if you want to know more about the arrest, you should go talk to him."

"Will you go with me?"

She shook her head. "I'm really tired, Cord. I think I'd rather go home and get some rest."

"Understood," I repeated. "But, Juni—" I stopped talking when she raised her hand.

"Give me some time, okay?"

"Sure. Of course." I opened the door. "See you soon?"

While she nodded, I doubted she meant it. It wasn't any less than I deserved.

"What happened?" Grayson asked, meeting me partway between the SUV and the cottage.

"We talked. I apologized. She's tired and is going home to rest."

He nodded, then ran forward to catch Juni before she left. I watched him get in the SUV, likely asking her what happened like he had me.

Her eyes met mine for a second, then she turned her head and reversed the SUV. I wanted to race after her like Grayson had and beg for her forgiveness again. I didn't, and with every step I took, I regretted not handling things better with her. Why the fuck had I asked her if we could still be friends? I wanted so much more from her.

"You all right?" Buck asked when I came inside.

I shook my head. "I think I've lost her."

He nodded and pulled me into an embrace.

Pete cleared his throat. "Listen, we can do this another time."

I stepped away from Buck. "Now is good unless you need to leave."

"I do, but I wanted you to hear it from me. There's been an arrest, and the case against the suspect is air-tight. What doesn't make any sense is why."

"Unless it's Jimmy Rooker, or someone who went after me for shooting him, I'm at a loss too."

"My thoughts also, but I can assure you James Rooker is locked up tight. Honestly, we can't find a single person who will even admit to knowing the guy. Either way, I'd like to ask you to come to the station and look through a photo array."

"Of course. Let's do it."

"I'd say it doesn't have to happen right away, but the sooner you feel up to it, the better."

"Like I said, let's do it."

Pete nodded and motioned for me to go with him. Buck was right behind me.

"If you follow me in your vehicle, you can leave as soon as you're finished."

Buck said we would and waited until Pete pulled away to do the same. "What happened with Juni?"

"In a nutshell? I apologized, then asked if she thought we could still be friends."

His brow furrowed. "And?"

"We weren't just friends."

"Ah. I see. So she thought you were stating that's all you wanted."

I nodded. "No amount of backpedaling did any good."

"I guess it wouldn't, would it?"

25

Juniper

"Are you sure you don't want me to drive?" Gray asked when I was almost outside the Lilac's gate.

"You're kidding, right?"

"You seem upset."

I shot him a look. "Of course I'm upset. You had no business telling Cord what you did."

"You wouldn't have."

I rolled my eyes. "That's because it isn't this business."

"He said he apologized."

"Gray, you're my brother, I love you, and I appreciate you looking out for me. However, conversations between Cord and me are none of *your* business."

"I know he cares about you."

"Are you fucking kidding me right now?" I glanced over at the expression I expected to see on his face.

"Wow," he muttered.

"I'm not going to apologize. I told you it's none of your concern, and I meant it."

"Wrong. You said it was none of my business. While that's true, there will never be a time in your life when I won't be concerned about you. The same as you will always feel protective of me."

"I don't need your protection with Cord. I just need you to let it be for a bit until I figure out how I feel."

"Understood."

I gripped the steering wheel tighter when he used the same word Cord had.

With the exception of stopping to give my mom a kiss on the cheek when we got home, I went straight upstairs and shut the door. I closed the window blinds, lay on my bed, and hugged my pillow.

The last month had been one of the most emotionally trying times of my life other than when it was me going to rehab every day, learning to walk again. I was damn lucky I wasn't paralyzed after the damage my spinal cord had sustained, not that it made my recovery easy by any means.

Truthfully, I didn't allow myself to spend much time dwelling on it. I was injured, and I recovered. Most people had no idea I'd even had surgery for it unless they saw the scar. Which Cord hadn't and, now, never would. I had thought about how much I'd tell him when that day came, but that no longer mattered.

I opened my eyes when I heard a knock on my bedroom door.

"Hey, Juni. Are you awake?"

"I am now," I said when Gray stuck his head inside. "What do you want?"

"Uncle Pete is here, and he's talking to Mom and Dad about the arrest. I figured you might want to hear it."

"I don't." I rolled over so my back was to him.

"I heard him say something about Cord's mom."

I bolted upright. "Who did?"

"Pete, and the more I stand here talking to you, the less of it I'm hearing."

I followed him down the hallway, and we sat on the stairs where we did as kids when we were supposed to be in bed.

"Decker is digging into it now, but it seems like too much of a coincidence," I heard my uncle say. I looked at Gray, and he shrugged. "I know you're a few years younger, but do either of you remember Brianna Conrad or Joe Wilkins?"

"I remember Joe," said my dad. "Football player, right?"

"Yes, and guess who was voted cutest couple in their senior year?"

Neither of my parents answered.

"I'll give you a hint. Joe was the male half."

"Brianna," guessed my mom.

"Nope. Patricia Rooker."

When I gasped, Gray put his hand over my mouth.

"You might as well come the rest of the way downstairs. We know you're eavesdropping," my dad said in a raised voice.

I was way ahead of my brother.

"How is this relevant?" I asked, pulling out the last empty chair in the kitchen and leaving Gray to lean against the counter.

Uncle Pete shook his head. "I always said you should've been a lawyer."

I rolled my eyes. "Seriously, though."

"The person arrested for attempting to murder Cord was Joseph Wilkins Jr., Joe and Brianna's son."

"Are you saying you think he tried to kill him because Cord is the son of his father's ex-girlfriend?"

The idea of it seemed ridiculous. "How does he even know Cord?"

"According to the man himself, Joe Junior was one of the cowboys at the Lilacs."

"But—"

My uncle held up his hand. "Instead of asking a question after everything I say, why don't you pipe down and listen, brat?"

I stuck my tongue out at him and made a motion with my hand. "Go on."

"To answer the question I didn't let you ask, Cord picked him out of a photo array. He was the only person he recognized out of the twenty cards we had him look at. He said the kid's name—get this—was Buck."

I bit my tongue to stop myself from asking how that, too, was relevant.

"Your next question is how is it that someone who worked on the property missed getting his profile added to the security system. That's still a bit of a mystery, but every cowboy we asked couldn't place him, except Cord, who said he didn't remember ever seeing him *inside* the perimeter."

I sat back in my chair and folded my arms.

"What?" asked my uncle.

"Nothing. Go ahead."

"The kid—who is only seventeen, by the way—has both lawyered up and clammed up. Neither is a surprise. However, I don't believe he acted alone. I think someone pushed him to do it."

"Any idea who?" my dad asked.

"Here's the thing. According to Ashford, Brianna and Patricia were the best of friends. Patricia hightails it out of town, and Brianna marries her ex."

I probably would've scoffed, but in just the limited time I'd been around Decker, it became obvious the man was brilliant. He was the one who'd pieced together that Sam was Miss Cena's great-granddaughter. He'd never make the connection between the guy who'd tried to kill Cord, his mother, plus the kid's parents if he didn't think it was relevant.

"Given you're not supposed to talk about an active investigation, I'm assuming you aren't here just to gossip," I said.

Pete laughed, shook his head, and looked at my dad. "It isn't too late to send her to law school. She'd probably make DA by the time she turned thirty."

My dad smirked. "You could also try to talk her into going to the police academy."

"While this is all very amusing, I'm serious. Why were you talking to my mom and dad about it?"

"To see if we remembered them," my mom answered for him. Of all of us, she was the only one I hadn't seen crack a smile. Not that the subject matter was at all funny, but she usually chimed in when Pete and I were trash-talking each other.

"Do you?" I asked her.

She nodded.

"Well?" I pressed.

"I don't remember Patricia per se, but I do Brianna. She and Joe used to come into the Goat."

My dad raised his head. "That's right, but damn, how long has it been?"

"Years. The last time I saw her, I pulled her aside and suggested she not return."

My mouth gaped. I'd never ever heard my mother say anything like she just had. It was apparent my father was as stunned as I was. "Why?" I asked.

"One night, your Aunt Sue was fit to be tied, and when I asked why, she pointed to Brianna. The other waitresses and the bartender at the time all told stories about how rude she was to them. From what I remember, they said she complained about the service, the food, and even the drinks almost every time she came in, then expected everything to be comped. Whether it was or not, she was one of those people who thought it was funny to leave a penny tip." Her cheeks flushed, and she lowered her gaze. Maybe that's where I'd gotten it from.

My dad put his hand on my mother's shoulder. "You did the right thing, sweetheart."

"I know. I just don't like turning business away."

"We've never hurt for customers," he added.

I glanced up at Gray, whose puzzled expression matched my thinking.

"Okay. So we know Brianna wasn't a nice person. I don't see what that has to do with Cord."

"Me neither," Pete admitted. "However, we're bringing both parents in separately tomorrow to question them."

I looked over at him. "Will Decker be there?"

He grinned. "Damn straight, he will."

After he left, Gray followed me upstairs. "What do you think?" he asked.

"I can't connect the dots, you know?"

"Me neither," he said, repeating what our uncle said.

"Ashford is smart, though."

Gray nodded. "I thought the same thing."

"Do you think Pete told Cord any of this?"

"I know he didn't. That's the part I overheard before I came up to get you. He said he didn't want to mention the possible connection to Cord's mother until they had more to go on."

"I can't help but think Miss Cena would know."

My brother nodded again. "Same."

I tapped my lower lip with my index finger. "Which means there might be something in her journals."

"What are you thinking?" Gray asked.

"I'll call Sam and ask if she'd mind if I came over and looked through them tomorrow."

"I could help," he offered. "Unless Beau has something else he needs me to do."

"Excellent."

Maybe I wasn't ready to address the relationship between Cord and me—or lack of one—but I sure could help Pete figure out the connection between Patricia Rooker and the guy who'd tried to kill him.

When I arrived, at ten the following morning, Cord's truck wasn't parked near the cottage, but there was another black SUV near the main residence. "Is that all guys drive anymore?" I grumbled to Gray, who had the same type of vehicle.

"In the dead of winter, living in the snowbelt? Yes, it is."

"So what do you do for Beau anyway, besides food delivery?"

"You're being awfully surly for a girl who wanted my help."

I looked over at the cottage again, wishing I saw signs of life. Besides having no SUV parked out front, it didn't look like any lights were on, and there was no smoke coming from the chimney.

"Someone would tell us if Cord was back in the hospital, right?" I asked.

"He's with Pete."

"How do you know?"

My brother rolled his eyes. "Because I pay attention. He said it last night before leaving."

"What do you mean?"

"He said that he, Cord, and Decker were meeting this morning."

I didn't remember hearing him say that. "What about Buck?"

"I guess he had to leave last night."

My eyes opened wide. Cord had been alone? Why hadn't someone told me? Wait. Because I'd left after telling Cord to give me time; that's why. Still, I wouldn't have wanted him to be alone on his first night in the cottage. What if something had happened? What if he'd had one of the nightmares that he said only occurred on the nights I wasn't with him?

"Juni?"

I glanced at my brother. "What?"

"I was just making sure you heard me."

Had I? I guess it depended on what the last thing he'd said was. "What are they meeting about?"

Gray reached into his pocket, pulled out his cell, and tapped the screen. "Here. Ask him yourself." He put the phone to my ear.

"Hey, Gray," the voice answered. "How's Juni?"

My mouth gaped, I pulled the phone out of his hand, and looked at the screen. "You called *Cord*?" I mouthed.

Gray smirked.

"Hello? You there?"

"Uh, hey, Cord."

"Juni? Sorry. I thought it was your brother calling."

"It was. He, um, dropped the phone, and I picked it up." I cringed. Why was I lying?

"Where are you?"

"The Lilacs. I'm getting together with Sam this morning to read through more of Miss Cena's journals."

"How long will you be there?"

"We just pulled in, so…I'm not sure."

"Decker, Buck, and I are on our way there now. I was hoping we could talk. You know, about us. Plus, there's stuff Deck wants to talk to all of us about."

I leaned against the seat and shut my eyes. "Yeah, sure," I responded.

"Good. So, uh, see you soon."

"Sure," I repeated, ended the call, and tossed the phone at Gray. "You're a jerk."

"Actually, what I am is the guy who went after Cord on your behalf, had it out with him, and all that's left is for the two of you to kiss and make up."

I shot him a look and got out of the SUV.

"Hey, hold up," he hollered after me as I ran up the porch steps. "Will you wait?" he added when I didn't stop.

I ignored him and knocked. Sam must've been waiting in the foyer because the door opened a second later. I stepped inside and closed it behind me.

"Isn't Gray with you?" she asked at the same time he knocked, then walked in.

"Nice, Juni," he mumbled as he brushed past me.

"Ready to get started?" I asked, not wanting to talk about my brother or Cord or my uncle—pretty much every man was on the list. Even my dad, not that he had any reason to be.

"Sure. I moved the journals from upstairs into the library yesterday. I decided it would be easier to go through them if they were on a shelf in date order."

Why did she have to say the library? If there was any one room in this house I didn't want to set foot in, that was it. I just prayed Cord didn't come looking for us, find us there, and think it was my idea.

On the other hand, I had to agree that making the journals easier to identify by date would be helpful, and looking through them to see what I could find relating to Cord's mother was the reason I was here.

I groaned inwardly. Or thought I had until Sam asked if I was all right.

"I'm fine."

"If you say so," she said, pulling a journal from the shelf and handing it to me. "This is from the year Patricia graduated."

"Have you read it?" I asked.

"I have, but I don't remember any mention of her. It could be that I skimmed over it, thinking it was irrelevant."

Irrelevant. I almost laughed at her word choice. If she'd said it in front of my uncle, he'd probably suggest she become a lawyer too.

Sam had closed the door, and when someone rapped, I almost knocked the water bottle I'd brought with me off the table.

My brother peeked his head in the door. "Decker asked if you could please join us."

Sam stood and motioned for me to follow her. I kept my head mostly down as we walked into the main dining area, where everyone was already seated. There were three open chairs, but Gray's stuff was already on the table near one of them. Another one was next to Beau, and the third was beside Cord. Given it would be weird and awkward if I sat next to Sam's fiancé, I walked over to the chair Cord had stood to pull out for me.

26

Cord

"It's nice to see you," I leaned in and whispered, breathing in Juni's scent. I hadn't slept at all last night once I got into my head that she'd been the one to put fresh sheets on my bed and I'd snuggled into the pillow, pretending it was her.

It should've been. It probably would've been, had I handled things differently.

I'd missed her so much I ached. But, like all the time I spent in the hospital with her by my bedside, that was me thinking selfishly rather than what was best for her. It was probably a relief for her, each time she went home and slept in her own bed.

I scrubbed my face just from thinking about the ever-increasing list of things I wanted to apologize for.

I glanced in her direction, unable to keep myself from looking at her, and her eyes met mine. I wished I'd had a few minutes, at least, to talk to her alone when I arrived.

"Let's get started." Decker stood at the head of the table. "Before we do, I want to remind everyone that everything said here today, and in subsequent meetings, is one hundred percent off the record and is not to leave this room. Metaphorically speaking."

He looked directly at each person seated at the table and waited for them to agree before moving on to the next. It was a conversation he and I had had earlier after we'd left the Goat, where we'd met Pete. When he got to me, I nodded anyway.

"First, I'll run through what we know so far."

Most of what he said was a repeat of what I already knew. The kid who'd tried to kill me, Joseph Wilkins Jr., was the only child of Joseph Sr. and his wife, Brianna Wilkins. Both parents had a connection to my mother. Deck had stumbled upon a website for high school reunions where multiple years' worth of yearbooks from the local high school had been uploaded.

In the one from her senior year, there was a photo of my mother with Joe Sr. They'd been voted cutest couple. It was wild to see my mom at that age. I couldn't recall ever seeing photos of her unless they were taken with us kids. There weren't even any with my dad that I remembered.

I'd taken a screenshot of it when Decker showed it to me, and studied it on my way here. There was something about the guy that looked familiar to me, but I couldn't place him. Joe Junior favored his mother rather than his dad, so that wasn't it. Still, it niggled at me.

In another photo of my mom with Brianna, both were wearing cheerleading outfits and the caption read their names followed by "Best friends and cheer sisters."

Decker was certain that, rather than it being a coincidence, it had had some bearing on the son's actions.

Me? I had a hard time buying it. It made a lot more sense that Jimmy Rooker was somehow involved.

However, the mystery of how Joe Junior had circumvented having his profile entered into the security system was cleared up when I looked for his employment records and couldn't find any.

After Pete said none of the other cowboys recognized the kid, I thought back to the one and only time I'd met him in person. It was the night before my attempted murder, when I was headed out in the snowstorm to get the herd to safety. I'd seen him parked outside the estate gates and asked if I could help him. After he'd said he was Buck, I told him to get in the truck and ride out with me. I couldn't remember seeing him after we met up with the rest of the crew and he went out with a group on snowmobiles. Or at least that's what I thought he'd done.

"Sam and Juni, any luck looking through Miss Cena's journals?" Deck asked.

"Not so far," Sam responded. "We were just about to get started when Gray asked us to join you."

"My gut is telling me the kid's parents are involved in some way. Each of them is being interviewed separately this morning. I expect I'll hear if anything of interest comes of it."

I scrubbed my face again.

"Cord? You got somethin' to say?"

"No, sir." I'd already told him I thought it was a huge stretch to think anyone not connected to Jimmy Rooker would want me dead. Especially my mother's ex-boyfriend and her former best friend.

"Then, let's move on." He looked from Sam to Juni. "What I want the two of you to focus on is anything that mentions either Patricia, Wilkins, or his wife, whose maiden name was Conrad. Also, anything at all about Colorado." He turned to Grayson. "You said you'd heard Johnny Rooker was living out west. Were you able to recall where you'd heard it?"

"No, sir," Gray answered like I had.

"I'm coming up empty there too. Once the guy turned eighteen, it's like he walked off the face of the earth. I even went as far as looking at protective-custody and witness-protection programs, but there wasn't anyone matching his age, name, or social security number. No driver's license in any state, no bank accounts. *Nada*."

Decker stopped talking and studied something on his phone. After several seconds, he raised his head. "Also on that note, no death records either."

While the rest of us waited for him to say something else, he went back to his phone, then cleared his throat.

"The precursors to the present-day internet were developed in the sixties. Functions were specific to military and government applications and, on the rare occasion, academics. If John, or Johnny, Rooker had no involvement with any of the three, the ability to track him, even as recently as thirty years ago, just wasn't there yet." He looked around the room. "Which means prior to twenty years ago, it was a *helluva* lot easier for someone to go off the grid."

He seemed distracted, and I wished he'd just tell us why.

"Do you want us to include Johnny in our search?" Sam asked.

"Affirmative. Given this family named the first-born son the same fucking thing for four generations, keep your eye out for nicknames and initials too. I have a strong feeling that's the key to why this seventeen-year-old kid tried to commit murder."

"Understood," Sam responded.

"Gray will be working with the two of you. He'll have the ability to quickly scan whatever you find and get it over to me. I don't want you or Juni bothering with that. The two of you are most familiar with those journals and will notice things the rest of us might not."

Decker looked over at me. "I want you in with them in case they need any help. If I've got something else for you to follow up on once I hear from Pete, I'll let you know."

"Yes, sir," I responded, but something was bugging me. I'd always known my mom was young when Buck was born, but I hadn't realized the significance of it until right this minute. I swiped the screen of my cell and opened the photo Deck had sent me of Joseph

Wilkins with my mom when they were still in high school. "Holy shit," I said under my breath, looking up at him with wide eyes.

"What is it?" he asked, walking in my direction. I led him out to the front porch.

"Buck was born in December of 1992."

Deck's eyes scrunched. "From what we've been able to piece together, your mom left sometime that year."

"Because she was pregnant?"

He nodded. "I think you're on to something."

"I need a minute."

He squeezed my shoulder. "Take all the time you need."

I walked down the porch steps and to the path that led to the cottage, taking deep breaths as I went.

Based on the yearbook evidence, my mom was at that high school for at least part of her senior year, if not all of it. No doubt Decker would be able to find out if she'd graduated. Hell, even I could by calling the school myself.

There was a chance she'd met my dad that year and he was Buck's father, but it seemed unlikely. To the best of my knowledge, he'd never left Colorado.

Combined with the resemblance between my oldest brother and Joe Wilkins Sr., the logical assumption was that he was Buck's dad.

My mind raced, remembering the physical, mental, and emotional abuse "our" father had inflicted on Buck. We'd all experienced it, but his was by far the worst. Could this be the reason it seemed like Roscoe hated his namesake?

I stomped the snow from my boots, opened the cottage door, and went inside. A minute later, I heard a knock.

"Cord, can I come in?" Juni's sweet voice was like a balm to my soul.

I rushed over and unlocked the door. The first thing she did when she stepped inside was embrace me. We held each other tight but didn't speak. There'd be time for words soon enough. Right now, I hoped she felt my love as much as I did hers.

She was the first to drop her arms and shed her jacket, then took my hand and led me to the sofa, where we huddled close. I wanted to pull her onto my lap, brand the skin under her sweater with the heat of my hand, and kiss her. I did none of those things.

"I think Joe Wilkins is Buck's biological father," I blurted. Her head was on my shoulder, and I felt her nod. "It all adds up in a way his relationship with my dad never did. Not just that. He was born in December of the same year my mom would've graduated."

Juni raised her head, and our eyes met. "Gray said Buck had to leave yesterday."

"Yeah, and now, I can't decide whether that was for the best or if he should've been here to piece it together himself. Or at least raise the question."

"As much as you're reeling right now, I think it's better he isn't here."

I cupped her cheek. "Reeling is a good word for what I'm feeling, but, Juni, there's something more important to me than my immediate family's history. Not something, someone. *You.* I want to make things right between us." I rested my forehead against hers. "I should've been honest about my feelings yesterday. The truth was I was afraid that if I admitted exactly how much you mean to me, it might freak you out."

She smiled.

"Instead, I said words that were also true. I do want to be your friend. But I want so much more with you. Sam said that, in her letter, Miss Cena wrote that all the money in the world isn't as important as being with people you love. I feel that so profoundly right now. *Nothing* is as important."

"Cord—"

"Let me say it, Juniper. Don't stop me."

Her eyes darted back and forth between mine. When she didn't speak, I did.

"I love you. I think I have from the first time I saw you. I remember the next day, when you showed me around and I asked you to tell me your faults. It was because you felt so perfect. Not that you seemed that way. It's how I *felt*. I've never met anyone like you, but more, I've never loved anyone the way I do you."

She reached up and put her finger on my lips. "I need to talk now, Cord."

I nodded, hoping she wasn't about to let me down easy.

"I love you so much that sometimes it feels like my heart will beat out of my chest. The night they found you out in the storm"—she took a deep breath and blinked away tears—"Sam and I thought you were dead." Her voice cracked. "All I could think was how I'd never told you I loved you. Then, when they said you were alive…God, the relief I felt. But I still didn't tell you."

I brushed her lips with mine. "It wasn't the right time, darlin'."

"I know," she whispered.

We sat silently for a few minutes before she spoke again. "Do you think you should check your phone?"

I'd heard it go off at least twice, but I ignored it. When I pulled it out, I saw messages from Decker and Pete. I shoved it in my pocket without reading either of them.

"I have to be the one who tells Buck." Which meant I had to figure out how in the hell I'd get to Colorado and back within forty-eight hours. When I heard my cell go off again, I knew that, as much as I wanted to stay in this cottage with Juni and ignore the rest of the world, I couldn't.

"We should go back to the main house," I said.

Her cell pinged. "My uncle is here."

I stood and held my hand out to her. She took it, and I pulled her into my arms.

"You and I still have a lot to talk about, Juni."

"I'll be ready," she responded, winking.

We walked out of the cottage and saw Pete leaning against the police cruiser with his arms folded.

"How are you doing?" he asked when we got closer.

"To be honest, when it comes to all this shit, I don't have a clue." I squeezed Juni's hand, hoping she knew I wasn't talking about my feelings for her. I loved her, and right now, that felt like the only real thing in my life. When she squeezed back, I hoped it meant she got it.

"I'm sorry to say I've got more to tell you," said Pete.

"Might as well get it all out in the open."

We followed him up the steps and into the house. No one said a word even after we joined them at the table. It appeared they were as shell-shocked as I was. Sam, the first one to get up, walked over and hugged me.

"Thank you," I whispered. I was so grateful to know her. That we were blood relation explained the kinship I'd felt from the moment we met.

She returned to her seat, and Juni and I sat in ours. Gray brought his uncle a chair, and he thanked him, but said he'd rather stand.

Decker got up too. "Pete, why don't you fill us in on the parts you're permitted to from your conversations with Joe Senior and Brianna?"

"There isn't a whole lot that's relevant." He looked at Juni and winked. She smiled at what I figured was an inside joke. "Anyway, right before I concluded the conversation with Joe Senior, I received the message from Decker about Cord's theory, which was as much of a revelation, if you ask me."

"Did you run it by him?" I asked.

"Sure did. When I asked if he was aware Patricia Rooker was pregnant at the time they both graduated, he blanched. Clearly, he was not."

"What about Brianna?" Decker asked.

"Oh, she knew. Not that she'd admit it. Her response was only one of many things I suspect she was untruthful about."

Pete looked from me to Decker, who'd cleared his throat.

"As I said earlier, I strongly believe the link between the father, mother, and Patricia Rooker is the key to why this kid did what he did. However, it doesn't give us a motive for his actions."

"Why Cord, though?" Grayson asked.

"I have a theory, but that's all it is presently," Decker responded.

"What's the next step?" I asked, thinking more about how soon I could travel to Colorado than the investigation into my attempted murder.

"I had to go up the chain of command farther than I expected to, but I was able to get authorization for Decker to interview both parents," said Pete.

My eyes opened wide.

"But not the son. At least not yet," he added.

"When are you talking to Joe Senior and Brianna?" I asked,

"As soon as we return to the station. I was able to convince both parents to stick around. Brianna was less willing than Joe was. However, we only have so much time before their patience runs out—Brianna's especially. I want to keep Joe and Brianna separated until Decker has a chance to speak with both on their own."

"Let's go," Decker said, picking up the bag where he'd already stuffed his laptop. "I'll stay in touch."

"Before you go, I'm assuming you want us to continue looking through the journals?" said Sam.

Decker nodded once. "A slew of questions remain, so yes."

"I'll walk you out." I followed Pete and him to the door.

"My brother needs to hear this from me," I said once we were outside.

Deck's eyes met mine. "Agreed. We'll leave in the morning unless you want to try to travel tonight."

"Wait. *We'll* leave?"

"You heard correctly."

"Why?"

Decker put his hand on my shoulder. "The clock starts ticking the minute you leave the Lilacs property, and you have forty-eight hours to get your ass back here. I'm going to make sure that happens. So we're taking my jet." He leveled his gaze at me. "You have enough on your mind, Wheaton. Let me be the timekeeper."

"I appreciate this."

He squeezed my shoulder. "Buck is a member of my team, but he's also a friend. You are too, Cord. Whatever I can do to ease the burden you and your siblings are carrying, I will."

"I don't know if she'll agree to it, but—"

"Yes. Juni can come with us."

I grinned. "Thanks. For everything. I mean that."

I stayed on the porch a few minutes after Pete and Decker got in the car and left. Was it wrong for me to want Juni to go with me? Was I only thinking of myself again and not of her? I didn't want to be that guy. She had her own life and sure hadn't been able to live it in the last few weeks. Maybe it would be best if I didn't even bring it up.

27

Juniper

I knew how important it was that Sam and I get through as many of Miss Cena's journals as we could, but my concentration was shot. Thankfully, Beau and my brother had offered to help too.

"How's Cord doing?" she asked. "I guess that's a stupid question."

"He's probably in shock," said Gray.

Sam's eyes met mine. "I hate that the Lilacs represents the worst time of his life."

"It also represents the best time," Cord said, walking into the room and straight over to me. He leaned down and kissed my cheek.

"Same for me," said Beau, winking at Sam.

"Oh, jeez," muttered Gray.

"You'll find someone one day who you'll feel the same way I do for your sister," said Cord.

I beamed up at him.

"Can I help?" he asked, leaning in to brush my lips with his.

"The more eyes, the better." I stood and plucked the next journal from the bookshelf.

"What about Mom? She'd probably help too," Gray suggested.

"Yes, please," Sam responded.

"I'll call her," I offered. I stepped out into the hall, then went out to the porch.

She answered the same way she always did. "Hi, sweetheart."

"Hey, Mom. If you're not in the middle of anything, we could use your help reading through Miss Cena's journals."

"Even if I was busy, I'd drop whatever I was doing. I've been hoping I'd get the chance to read them."

"Right now, it'll be more about skimming for specific information."

"On my way."

I looked at the phone to confirm she'd actually hung up, then laughed. I doubted Gray or I had ever really appreciated how amazing our parents were. I know I'd definitely taken them for granted.

"Am I interrupting?" Cord asked, peeking his head out the front door.

"Not at all. I was on my way in."

"Before you do, there's something I want to talk to you about." He rubbed my arms. "Are you warm enough?"

"I wouldn't be opposed to you getting me that way." When he gathered me close, I snuggled against him.

"Decker has offered to fly me out to Colorado so I can talk to my brother in person."

"That's nice of him."

"He's got a jet."

My eyes opened wide. "Wow. I've never known anyone who did. So, when will you leave?"

"Either tonight or tomorrow."

"How long will you be gone?"

"I'm still bound by the trust's stipulation that I'm not away from the property for more than forty-eight hours."

Selfishly, I wanted him to leave tomorrow instead of tonight. On the other hand, he'd be back sooner if they left earlier.

Cord leaned away and looked into my eyes. "Since we met, our relationship has been more one-sided than I want it to be. It seems like you're always doing something for me, taking care of me, looking out for me."

"It isn't one-sided."

"As nice as it is of you to say, it isn't true, and someday soon, I want to start being the one taking care of you, looking out for you. But…" He let go and scrubbed his face. "Not today."

We both laughed.

"I want you to know you can say no and I will completely understand, but would you consider going with me?"

I'd dropped my arms when he did, but threw them around his neck. "Really?"

"Is that a yes?"

"It's an 'of course!'"

"I don't know how this news will affect Buck, but as much of an asshole as our dad was, he might be relieved. There will be the matter of proving it, assuming he'll want to."

"If Joe Wilkins is his father, I wonder why your mom never told him."

"Me too. It's one of so many unanswered questions." He turned me in his arms, and we looked out at the view. "I can't figure out how or when she met my dad. More puzzling is why she'd want to be with him."

"Maybe he was different with her."

Cord rested his head against mine. "Maybe."

I heard a car coming up the drive and was stunned to see my mom. "That was quick," I said when she got out and rushed over to us.

"I was afraid you'd change your mind. Hi, Cord."

"Hey, Patricia. Should we get inside?"

"One sec. Uh, Mom, Cord asked me to go to Colorado with him. It'll be a quick trip, but we might leave as soon as tonight."

She put her hand on her heart. "I envy that trip. I've always wanted to see the Rockies. Maybe someday I will." She winked at Cord.

"Yes, ma'am. I predict you definitely will."

"Do you think Dad will mind if I take more time off?" I asked.

She chuckled. "I'm pretty sure he fired you weeks ago."

I gasped. *"What?"*

"I'm joking. All your dad wants is for you to be happy, sweetheart. I'm sure your job will still be there when and if you want to come back."

When we walked into the library, Sam's gaze met mine. "Did you find something?" I asked.

"Maybe." All eyes turned to her. "Remember I asked if everyone called Jimmy and Johnny's father JD?"

"Yes."

"I also said I got confused because it sounded like she didn't care for him."

"I remember that too."

"Reading it again now, I'm certain she didn't." She handed me the journal, and I read the section she pointed to.

I used to think I was cursed, and maybe I am or maybe it's all Rookers. Bad blood runs deep in our veins. Lives have been lost, others ruined. When will it stop? When will Jim stop? When there are none of us left?

"I was confused because this entry was from after her brother and husband died. Why would she ask when

Jim would stop if that was the case?" Sam said when I finished reading the passage and looked up at her.

"This has to be about JD."

"And look at the date."

It coincided with when Patricia might've discovered she was pregnant.

"We should let Decker know about this," said Gray.

"You're right."

I held out the journal, and he took a photo of the entry, then sent it. When he returned it to me, I kept reading. Most of the entries were reminiscent, but several pages later, there was one with only a few words and dated at the end of June.

It is finished. I pray I've done the right thing.

28

Cord

It was after seven by the time Decker returned, and when he came inside, Pete wasn't with him.

"Everything all right?" I asked when I was the first to greet him.

"Come with me. This is better done at the cottage."

I followed him out the front door and down the trail.

"You got anything stronger than beer in there?" he asked when we were close.

"Bottle of whiskey."

"That'll do."

In the time I'd known him, I never saw Decker beat around the bush, so the longer he remained quiet, the more worried I got about what family secret was about to be uncovered next. I poured two shots and handed him one. He drank it, then asked for another.

"Fuck," I muttered. "Must be pretty bad."

"It is." He shook his head when I offered him a third, then took a seat at the kitchen table.

"Should I have another?" I asked before joining him.

"Nah. You'll be okay."

"Is there someone who won't be?"

"A couple of people." He took a deep breath. "Sorry, interrogations take a fuck of a lot out of me. Just give me a sec, and I'll fill you in."

When he rubbed the back of his neck, rested his elbows on the table, and leaned forward, I got up and pulled two beers from the fridge. He might not want one, but I was getting the impression I would.

"Brianna Wilkins made a full confession, not just to coercing her son to commit murder but to everything stemming back to when your mother left New York," he said when I took a seat and cracked mine open.

I got up again and grabbed the whiskey plus the rest of the six-pack. If whatever he was about to tell me about my mama required two shots of whiskey for him, it was gonna take a whole bottle for me. "Go on."

"What the hell. I'll have another."

I poured for both of us, then rested against the chair.

"First, according to Brianna, Buck is her husband's child. Joe, on the other hand, was blindsided."

I sat and listened to the rest of the story, chugging my beer.

As I'd figured, my mom got pregnant in her senior year of high school. According to Brianna, Joe was the father, but even she hadn't known Patricia was pregnant until the night she saw her for the last time.

"Apparently, your mother asked Brianna to meet her, saying it was urgent and to come to Hamlin Park, where she'd be waiting near the tennis courts. Once there, Patricia said she didn't have much time and that she was leaving town that night. She gave Brianna a letter addressed to Joe, telling him about the baby and how sorry she was. The other thing in the letter was a phone number Brianna didn't recognize."

"She never gave it to Joe, did she?"

"She did not."

"So Joe had no idea my mom was pregnant."

"None whatsoever. And, according to him, he also had no idea she'd left town. It wasn't until a few days later, after being unable to reach her, that he showed up at JD's place, where Patricia had been living. JD told him your mom wanted nothing to do with him and to get the hell off his property. Now, here's the part where I admire the guy. He didn't stop there. By that time, he worried something might have happened to her, maybe even that JD had hurt her. So he paid Miss Cena a call."

"Shit."

Decker nodded. "She told him Patricia was fine but had decided to leave East Aurora and start her life over somewhere else. Joe, of course, was devastated."

"And Brianna was more than happy to console him."

"One thing led to another, and pretty soon, Briana told him *she* was pregnant, and they got engaged. They were married, and a few weeks later, she suffered a miscarriage."

"I see where this is going and have to ask; what does this have to do with me?"

"Brianna's sister works at Hoak's. She was there the day you met with Pete."

"That's when he showed me the family tree."

"You got it."

"She wanted me dead because she thought I'd discover the secret?"

"And Joe would leave her."

I hung my head. "Fuck. That was worth me losing my life over?"

"In my experience, anyone who commits murder, attempted or otherwise, isn't exactly focused on the punishment fitting the crime, if you know what I mean."

"She's insane."

"Yeah, well, let's hope the DA doesn't think so. I'd hate to see her get off for this. Not to mention what she did to her son."

"What will happen to him?"

"He'll be charged the same as she will. Actually, his will be worse since her role was as an accomplice."

"What made her confess all this?"

Decker's eyes bored into mine. "I'm fucking good at what I do. Also, my hands aren't tied in the same way Pete's would've been. For example, I might've led her to believe her son's sentence wouldn't be as lengthy if she gave a statement as to her role in all this. Of course I phrased it in such a way that I had no control over what the DA or judge might do."

"Wow." I shook my head.

Decker cracked another beer open. "I gotta say, the kid is pretty fucked up too, though. I asked if people called him Buck, and he laughed."

I raised a brow. "Do they?"

"No, and that's the sick part. He said it just to fuck with you."

I guess I shouldn't be surprised that a guy who'd take a pickax to a man's head and leave him for dead was just as messed up as his mother.

"The East Aurora PD took over at that point, and I got myself out of there. That statement, along with him meeting up with you outside the estate's perimeter, lends itself to premeditation."

"What about the father?"

"I don't believe he played any part in it. Pete agreed and planned to tell him he was free to go. I was gone before he did."

"Why did my mom go to Colorado? Did the mother say who she left with? It couldn't have been on her own."

"All she said is that after she gave her the letter, Patricia got up, walked across the lawn in the opposite direction from where she'd left her car, and climbed into another one. Brianna said it was too far away and too dark for her to see the make or model. She also said she didn't see who was driving."

I told him about the entry in Miss Cena's journal and how she'd written she hoped she'd done the right thing.

"No doubt she had a hand in this. The other entry Gray sent over was a big help. When I asked Brianna if she had any idea what it meant, she said one of the last things your mom said to her was that her brother—that would be JD—was pushing her to get an abortion."

I poured another shot and downed it.

"Are you supposed to be drinking that much with the medication you're on?" Deck asked.

"You started it."

He chuckled. "I guess I did. I'm also sure that, if I were in your shoes, I'd have finished the bottle by now."

"Brianna had no idea how she ended up in Colorado?"

"She said your mom didn't tell her where she was headed."

"What about the phone number in her letter to Joe?"

"Brianna burned it and says she has no recollection of the area code."

I snarled. "Of course she doesn't."

The personal ramifications of everything I'd just learned came barreling at me. If my mom hadn't gotten pregnant, if her brother had succeeded in pushing her into having an abortion, if she hadn't gone to Colorado and met my dad, Buck, Porter, Holt, Flynn, and me wouldn't exist.

"What do you want to do?" Deck asked.

"If you mean when do I want to leave, that's up to you."

"Is Juni going with us?"

"She wants to."

"First thing tomorrow morning. I don't have it in me to tell this story again tonight, and I doubt you do either." When he stood, I did too, and he put his hand on my shoulder. "You're doin' the right thing by telling Buck all this in person. I admire you for that. Just don't have anything more to drink before you do."

I already felt woozy. "Yes, sir." Before Decker got to the door, I stopped him. "Can you ask Juni to come down?"

"You got it."

I'd never understand why this woman and her son thought killing me would result in her actions all those years ago remaining a secret. Worse, I still had no fucking idea who'd sent me here or why.

If it was just to uncover the secret about Buck's real father, why not send him? Why had the burden of exposing my mother's lies fallen on my shoulders?

In every memory I had of her, and there weren't many, she was loving and kind—the nurturer our father wasn't and could never be. Why did the precious time we'd had with her have to be tainted now? Why couldn't we live the rest of our lives believing we'd had one parent who loved us?

I even dreaded setting foot on the ranch I swore I'd never leave—willingly, anyway. Could my brothers, sister, and I ever purge that earth of what we'd all suffered at the hands of Roscoe Buchtold Wheaton? Especially after I heaped my mother's lies on that pile of horseshit? I couldn't keep the secret, though. Buck deserved to know the truth regardless of the questions it brought, most of which we'd never get answers to.

When I heard a soft knock, followed by the door creaking open, I stood and met Juni halfway. Once she was in my arms, I felt the anger and sadness inside me leave as quickly as it had come.

I closed my eyes and stroked her hair, thanking God she'd given me another chance, that she loved me even with all I'd done to hurt her. I just wished to hell I hadn't had so much to drink in the short time it took Decker to tell me what he'd learned.

"I, uh, might be a little shitfaced," I admitted.

She smiled when I weaved back and forth. "A little?"

"Would you mind if we lie down?"

Juni kept one arm around me and led me into the bedroom.

"Here we go again, you taking care of me instead of the other way around."

"We have the rest of our lives for you to take care of me, Cord," she said, stretching out beside me on the bed after she'd pulled back the covers.

"Did you just ask me to marry you, Juniper Rose?"

"I don't recall asking you anything."

"Damn, I love you."

She unfastened the buttons of my shirt, and I rolled to my side. When she slid it off my shoulders, down my arms, and onto the floor, then unzipped my jeans, I raised my butt, and when she pulled them off, both our eyes opened wide when my erection sprang out and hit my stomach.

I looked up at the ceiling, then at her. "I gotta thank you and God."

She raised a brow, but rather than ask what I meant, she removed her clothes in the same order she had mine. Once naked, she pulled the covers over us and pressed her nude body against mine.

I couldn't say whether it was her bare skin touching mine or my relief that my cock chose this particular moment to work again, but I immediately sobered up.

I reached around her to the drawer of the bedside table and pulled out a condom.

"Let me," she said, taking the packet from my hand.

Every muscle in my body tensed, and I squeezed my eyes closed when I felt her fingers touch me. "Juni, I—"

She leaned forward and swirled her tongue around my nipple as she rolled the latex down my shaft. I grabbed her wrists and shifted both of us so she was on her back. I let go, spread her legs, and eased my body down hers until my mouth was close enough for me to take my first taste. Before I did, I looked up at her.

"I love you, Juni."

She smiled and ran her fingers through my hair. "I love you, Cord."

I scooted farther down, then kissed from the inside of her knee up her thigh, then repeated it on her other leg. Using the fingers of both hands, I spread her open, then licked from her opening to her clit. When I swirled it with my tongue, then clamped my mouth to her and sucked, she came off the bed. I wrapped my arms around her legs to hold her still, then continued to ravish her pussy, fucking her with my tongue in the same way I soon would with my cock, settling her legs over my shoulders so I could reach up and cup her breasts. I caught each nipple between my thumb and forefinger, pulling until she cried out and her essence flooded my tongue.

Unable to wait a moment longer, I raised my body, positioned my hardness where my tongue had been and thrust into her as deep as I could go. Her hands gripped my arms, and her fingernails dug into my flesh.

When she writhed, I stilled her, then raised my head and looked into her eyes.

"The very first time you blushed and lowered your gaze, I thought about this. I wanted to fuck you then, Juni. It was all I could do not to sweep you off your feet, take you back to the inn, and strip you bare. Every minute I spent with you only made me want you more. But as difficult as it was to wait, I'm so glad we did."

Her eyes were wide. "You are?"

I nodded. "Do you want to know why?"

She nodded too.

I began to move, slowly at first. "Because, the way this feels, knowing you love me as much as I love you, transcends everything else I've ever known." I increased my tempo, and Juni clung to me. "I long for the day there is nothing between us. When I can fill you and truly make you mine."

She wrapped her legs around me and pressed deeper, harder, and faster.

"Come, Juniper. Let me feel you."

She cried out my name as her pussy clenched me, and her wetness drenched us both. Her skin glowed with the sheen of our combined sweat, and her eyes, at first glassy and unfocused, bored into mine.

"Let me feel you now, Cord."

When I started to move again, she put her hands on the cheeks of my butt, stilling me.

"Really feel you."

I studied her.

"Make me yours tonight. I don't want to wait. Unless…"

I pulled out of her body, reached between us, removed the condom, then rubbed the head of my penis back and forth, coating myself.

"You're sure this is what you want?"

"If you do."

I couldn't wait a moment more. When I eased myself into her, knowing for the first time in my life how it felt to be flesh to flesh, with nothing between us, I knew I wouldn't last. "Wrap your legs around me," I demanded as much as said. When she did, I thrust hard again and again. "Come with me, Juniper. *Now.*"

I felt her squeeze me, drenching me like she had before, at the same time I buried my face between her shoulder and jaw, nearly weeping as the most powerful climax I'd ever experienced had me shuddering.

Juni held me tight with both her arms and legs. Her fingers stroked my skin, and she leaned up to brush the side of my face with her lips. I turned my head, brought my mouth to hers, and we kissed.

It didn't matter why I was sent here; I knew now why I'd come to East Aurora. Whatever secrets were left to be discovered no longer mattered to me. I was here to meet Juni. The love of my life. Whether I stayed here with her, or she came to Colorado with me, or we went somewhere new to both of us, we'd be together. Nothing in this world was more important than being with the woman I loved. Nothing.

I'd made the decision to go to Colorado to tell my brother what I'd learned, but while Juni and I were there, I had something far more important I needed to do.

29

Cord and I made love throughout the night, which meant at dawn, neither of us wanted to get out of bed.

"I have a meeting scheduled with my crew this morning to let them know I'm leaving town but will be back later this week," Cord said. He scrubbed his face like he so often did. "I have to admit, based on what Buck and Holt told me, they stepped up to help out in my absence. In fact, Jed, who I'd planned to sack, believing he was in cahoots with Hoss Schultz, proved to be a better foreman than I could've predicted."

"That's good news, right?"

"Sure is. There are still a few I believe should be shown the door, but rather than making that decision on my own, I intend to get his read on them."

"I heard there's a horse auction next week."

"I heard that too. I'm hoping we can find a few solid geldings to add to the stable." Cord studied me. "There's something Gray said that I've been meaning to ask you about."

I anticipated the question would eventually come. "Go ahead," I said.

"He said you boarded a horse here."

"I do." I should elaborate so he didn't have to ask, but I couldn't bring myself to.

"Do you still ride, Juni?"

I shut my eyes briefly and shook my head. "I do not."

"Have you since the accident?"

My eyes filled with tears. "No."

"I have one more question."

I nodded.

"Is Apache your horse?"

My voice cracked when I tried to answer, and my tears turned into sobs. I'd tried to ride him several times, but never got beyond bringing him out of the paddock. "I should've sold him long ago, but haven't been able to bring myself to do that either."

Cord brushed away my tears. "I'm glad you haven't."

"It wasn't his fault. It was mine."

"Never said it was, darlin'."

I expected Cord to press me about the animal, maybe even suggest I try riding him again, but he didn't.

"Will you sell the other horses?" I asked after getting my emotions in check.

"That's another thing I want to discuss with you."

"It's been almost two years since I was in the barn. I can't offer any insight."

Cord put his finger on my chin and raised my head. "I have an idea. It's something we planned to do at the Roaring Fork—a therapeutic riding program."

My eyes filled with tears again. "It's a good idea, Cord." When he'd mentioned the average age of the Lilacs' horses, I'd worried about their fate. Knowing there might be a home for them here, after all, was a relief.

"I'd like you to help me with it, Juni."

Every muscle in my body tensed. I was familiar with the kind of program he was talking about and what *helping* might entail. "I don't think I can, Cord."

"Understood."

I felt guilty over his easy acceptance. "I mean, I guess we could talk about it."

He smiled. "That's all I'm asking."

My eyes bored into his. "For now."

He nodded once. "For now."

When he asked me to join him in the barn an hour later, I hesitated. "I don't want to disrupt your meeting."

He put his arm around my shoulders. "You won't."

Cord held my hand as we walked down the path leading from the cottage to the area where the horses were kept. I saw several in the corral, all wearing stable blankets.

As if he'd felt my presence, Apache raised his head, and our eyes met. He walked over to the fence, whinnying. When I reached the place where he stood, I extended the knuckles of one hand towards his muzzle. He closed the distance, and we touched. I slowly turned my hand over and lowered it when Apache leaned closer, breathing into my face. I turned my body slightly, and he rested his head on my shoulder.

"Hello, sweet boy," I whispered through the tears running down my cheeks. "I've missed you so much." We stood like that for a few minutes until he raised his head and neighed. I glanced over my shoulder and saw Cord standing a couple of feet behind us. "You like him too," I said, kissing his nose as I stroked him.

Apache nudged me when I dropped my hand.

"Someone's been spoiling you."

I felt Cord's presence behind me. "Put your hand out," he said. When I did, he placed a carrot in it. I fed it to Apache, then turned to face him.

"Thank you."

"My pleasure." He motioned to the barn. "Shall we?"

I ran my hand down Apache's nose once more, so happy to have seen him and relieved he remembered me.

When we entered through the alley door, all the cowboys who'd been seated, stood. Several of them approached Cord, extending their hands in greeting. With few exceptions, their expressions conveyed admiration and respect for the man they hadn't seen in weeks and might well have never seen again.

The meeting, during which Cord thanked everyone for their hard work in his absence, was brief. While he spoke, I heard his cell phone chime twice. After explaining he would be away from the Lilacs for two more days, he dismissed all but Jed. Then he motioned for me to join them. I listened as he mentioned the horse auction as well as the therapeutic riding program we'd discussed.

He stopped talking when his cell chimed a third time and pulled it from his pocket. "It's Ashford," he said, leaning closer to me. "Do you still want to go along?"

I was stunned. "Have you changed your mind about wanting me—"

"Never."

When my cheeks flushed and I lowered my gaze, Cord turned to Jed. "That's all for now."

"Yes, sir," the other man said, walking away.

As soon as he was out of the barn, Cord wrapped his arm around my waist and pulled our bodies flush together. "I thought I made how much I wanted you more than clear last night."

"You certainly did." My cheeks flushed, but I kept my gaze steady on his. "Except that wasn't what I was asking. If you'd let me finish, I would've asked if you'd changed your mind about wanting me to go with you."

"Never," he repeated.

"Good, because if you had, I might've tried to stow away in your luggage."

Cord shook his head and chuckled. "I love you, June-bug."

Had anyone outside of my family ever called me by the nickname, I would've bristled. But Cord felt like my family—the one he and I would create together. "I can't wait to see Colorado. I'm sure I'll love it."

The playful expression on his face morphed into one more serious. "It won't be a prerequisite for us being together, you know?"

"I do, but Cord, it's your home."

He shook his head. "Home is wherever you and I decide to make it."

I thought back to my mother's words shortly after Cord and I met. "When you love someone, it isn't about where you live. Home is where they are," she'd said. I'd scoffed then, but no more.

"I feel the same way. I don't care where we live as long as we're together."

"You love East Aurora."

"I love you more."

30

Cord

Juni and I slept on the plane ride from the airport in Buffalo until we landed in Gunnison. After deboarding, Decker asked if he could have a moment to speak with me alone.

I wanted to tell him that whatever he had to tell me, he could say in front of Juni. However, he seemed almost as troubled as he'd been yesterday.

"What's up?" I asked after I'd escorted Juni to the SUV waiting for us on the tarmac.

"I made contact with Richard Langley during the flight," he began. "When I asked if we could stop by his office before continuing on to the ranch, he informed me he'd already requested a meeting with the rest of your siblings. It's scheduled to take place at fourteen hundred hours."

I knew from Buck that Porter had been released on bail while awaiting trial, but hadn't heard when that might be.

"I also spoke with Sterling Anderson, who I asked to take a look at the Roaring Fork Trust back when Buck received his orders." The way his brow furrowed concerned me.

"Whatever is on your mind, just say it."

"There may be something we missed."

"*May* be?"

"I'll know more when we meet with the lawyers."

"Decker, is there a chance…" I couldn't bring myself to say the words. If Six-pack had double-crossed us and my siblings and I were about to lose the ranch, I wasn't sure what I'd do. This wasn't about me; it was about the rest of them. If my actions were the cause, I'd never forgive myself.

"Whatever you're thinking, it isn't it."

"We haven't already lost everything?"

Decker scowled. "Of course not. I would never have let that happen."

If those words had been spoken by anyone else, I wondered if I'd believe them. Coming from Deck, I had no doubt he meant it.

"There's still a lot we don't know. Most pertains to your mother coming to Colorado and how she met your father. I also have strong suspicions that Miss Cena played a part in all of it." He looked over at the SUV. "Let's get some lunch. By the time we do, Hammer should be here."

"Hammer?"

"The other attorney."

"Just to clarify, the meeting is in two hours, right?"

Rather than answer, he raised a brow.

"What about my conversation with Buck?" I asked.

"I doubt there will be time for it beforehand. However, the questions Hammer will ask have no bearing on who Buck's biological father is."

I didn't like his answer, but it appeared the wheels had already been set in motion.

The only one of my siblings who hadn't met Juni was Porter, so he was the first I greeted and introduced her to. My brother looked like shit. More than even I'd expected.

Juniper was gracious, like she always was, but I could see by the set of her jaw that her encounter with him left her frazzled.

"Are you okay?" I leaned in and whispered.

"He's in so much pain," she murmured in response.

Now that she'd said it, I agreed. Most of my life, I'd thought my second-oldest brother was more like my father than any of us would've wanted to acknowledge. He was often sullen and argumentative, along with intoxicated.

Buck, on the other hand, who'd suffered more abuse at the hands of my dad than any of us, had never seemed that way. He hadn't bothered trying to conceal his hatred for our old man, but it hadn't soured him on the rest of civilization like it had Porter.

I couldn't help but wonder if something far worse than we knew went on between him and Roscoe, as I'd begun thinking of him.

Buck and Flynn were the last of my siblings to arrive, and with them were his wife, TJ, and their son, Buckaroo.

"I thought maybe we could walk around Gunnison while we wait," I heard TJ say to Juni. When her eyes met mine, I nodded.

"I'd like that," she responded, leaning down to say something to the baby, who was in a stroller.

Just then, another SUV pulled up and a man I didn't recognize got out. Based on Buck's and Decker's reaction, I gathered it was Hammer. The man looked more pissed off than the rest of us combined.

"I'm going to get that fucker disbarred," I heard him mutter to Deck as he swept past him and in the front door of the office.

"Should we go in too?" Buck asked.

Decker shook his head. "Give him a minute." He turned to us. "Each one of you owes me a dollar."

My eyes scrunched. "Not that I care about the amount, but why?"

"Hammer is representing you and the rest of your siblings. I fronted the cash. You can settle up with me later."

"We're going to head to the park," TJ said when she and Juni walked over to the vehicle they'd arrived in.

"I'll let you know when we're finished," Buck said, approaching to kiss her and the baby.

I did the same with Juni. "Have fun," I said.

"You too." She winked.

Last night, we'd talked about how I'd approach the conversation with Buck. I decided he needed to learn about Joe Wilkins Sr. without an audience. I hoped that, once we were done with Six-pack, Buck and I could get some time on our own. How and when he decided to tell our siblings would be up to him.

Hammer came storming out of the front door, looking angrier than he had going in. "The meeting has been postponed by an hour."

Buck, the one who most often spoke up, didn't.

"I'm, um…" I was about to say my time was limited, but there wasn't a person among us who didn't know that.

"Let's go," said Hammer. "Deck, you with me."

"Hold up. What the fuck is going on?" Buck finally asked. If he hadn't, I would've. Porter looked like he was a million miles away while Holt and Flynn appeared shell-shocked.

"I'll explain everything once we're at the hotel. Well, at least as much as I know," he added when Decker raised a brow.

I followed Hammer's vehicle, periodically glancing over at Buck, who sat in the front passenger seat. When I did, I couldn't get the image of Joe Wilkins Sr. out of my head. It was crazy how much he looked like the guy. Not that anyone would've known it until they saw a photo of him when he was younger.

I still had no idea how my brother would react when he learned Roscoe most likely wasn't his father. At least biologically. Not that it would change what he'd gone through as a kid. I wondered if he'd blame our mom. I hated to think he would.

After we climbed out of the vehicle, Hammer led us and Decker into a suite where he told us to take a seat. There were bottles of water already on the table in front of us, so I passed them out to everyone.

"You wanna start, or do you want me to?" Hammer asked Decker.

"I will." The attorney handed him an envelope from which he pulled several documents. "This is the first time any of us, with the exception of Hammer, will see the Roaring Fork Trust in its entirety."

"And I only did about twenty minutes ago," the lawyer clarified.

"What was missing in the previous copies were the introduction as well as the final two pages."

"Does this say who the trustee is?" I asked, immediately turning to the last pages of what was stapled together.

"It does not. However, it gives insight into why we haven't been able to find out," Decker responded.

"The two most important pieces of information contained in what you're looking at is that the trust is not your father's."

I raised my head, as did all of my siblings with the exception of one—Porter. If anything, he looked like he wanted to slide under the table and disappear into a black hole.

"What's the second thing?" Buck asked.

"The trust was filed in New Mexico, one of only three states where what's called a 'ghost trust' is legal. Essentially, what that means is it was written and filed in such a way that the identity of the trustee or trustees is protected," Hammer explained.

"Back to this not being our father's trust," I said. "I don't understand."

"Your father's death was the trigger that set the trust in motion. Otherwise, nothing I can find indicates he was even aware of it," said Hammer.

"But his will…" I began, trying to recall what Sixpack had read to us. The one thing that stuck in my mind was that it had been drafted twelve years ago. I turned to the first page of the document I now held in my hand. It was dated twenty-one years ago, which was two years before our mother died.

"Your father had no assets of his own to distribute to any of you. Everything you might've believed was his was property of the trust."

My eyes met Buck's. He had to be piecing together the same thing I was. The trust was our mother's, and someone was carrying out wishes that appeared to come from beyond her grave.

"Could Cena Covert have been the trustee?" I asked.

"She might've been at one time," answered Deck. "However, according to Langley, the reason he asked everyone but Cord to meet at his office this afternoon is because another codicil was delivered."

That meant Cena may have had something to do with my being summoned to the Lilacs, but depending on what this new document contained, it seemed unlikely she could've orchestrated it as well.

"The LLC is in good standing and in compliance with all the requirements set forth by the State of New Mexico," Hammer reported.

I glanced around the table, stopping when I got to Porter. I'd bet my share of the inheritance that he already knew some of what the rest of us were just now learning. I had nothing to back my belief other than the feeling in my gut.

"You mentioned getting Six-pack disbarred," said Buck. "Is any of how he handled this grounds for it?"

Hammer took a deep breath and let it out slowly. "No."

Buck looked down at the table where his hands rested on the edge. "So all this time, I thought it was the old man trying to stick it to us like he always did. Instead, it was our mother."

Our mother. The trust was created two years before she died. Two years.

I closed my eyes and covered my ears when the blood rushing through my system caused so much pressure in my head that I felt like I might have a stroke.

All I knew was I couldn't allow myself to lose sight of what was happening around me. I lowered my hands. It was *imperative* I pay attention to every nuance, every deep breath or sigh, every furrowed brow, scrunched eyes, or down-turned mouth. It was what I'd always done, paid attention. My nerve endings were on high alert, my eyes—now open—were laser-focused, and my hearing so in tune that when a paperclip hit the table, I jolted.

"Cord? What's wrong?" I heard someone ask from what sounded like far, far away. I couldn't answer, though. My mind was racing too fast.

I raised my head, and my eyes met Buck's. "Take it easy, little brother," I heard him say, his words trailing off as though I was suddenly being transported back in time to when I was a kid no older than seven to Porter's nine and Buck's eleven.

I squeezed my eyes shut against the memory that played in my head like a movie reel. Buck and Porter had walked into the room just as I jumped between my dad and mother, taking the backhand intended for her. I couldn't recall the pain of his strike, only rage.

Hitting me instead of her had stunned him long enough that, when I lunged, screaming and clawing at him, he was too slow to react. Before he could, Buck and Porter had pulled me off him and dragged me out of the room, leaving our mother alone with him.

"We need to get help!" Buck shouted at Porter and me. The two took off running, but I couldn't. I froze, listening to the sound of fists hitting flesh.

The very next thing I heard, a gunshot, sent shock waves through my body. I raced into the house, knowing that if my father had killed my mom, he'd be the next to die.

Instead, I saw my mother standing on the other side of the room, holding a gun. My father was lying on the floor, blood seeping from his arm, and a man I didn't recognize was crouched over him.

"Get the boy out of here!" he shouted.

"You can't let him die," my mother yelled at him.

"I know that. *Now go!*" he bellowed.

In the split second before my mother dropped the gun, lifted me into her arms, and carried me out of the room, my gaze met the man's.

"Who was that?" I asked once we were in her bedroom with the door shut and locked.

"That's not important, sweetheart." She sat on the bed and drew me closer, her shaking hands grasping my upper arms. "Cord, I need you to listen to me."

I nodded.

"What happened tonight…You can never tell anyone. Do you understand me?"

"Is he dead?" I asked.

She shook her head, but her eyes didn't waiver from mine. "Your father is going to be fine. It was all an accident. No one needs to know about it."

My lips trembled, and my eyes filled with tears. "He was going to hit you."

My mother cupped my cheek. "And you, my brave, sweet boy, tried to protect me. Now, I need you to protect me again. Can you do that? Can you keep what happened between us our secret?"

"We need to leave, Mama. He's going to hurt you again."

She shook her head a second time. "He won't. Everything will be taken care of. I promise. I just need you to promise something to me."

"Don't tell."

"That's right, sweet Cordero. And one day, a long, long time from now, I pray when you learn about the decisions I made, you can understand why"—her voice got shaky—"and forgive me."

When I opened my eyes, the first person I saw was Porter. He was seated at the same table I was, with his head hung.

My eyes met Buck's, and his brow furrowed.

"Mom wanted me to forgive her."

"For what?" Buck asked.

"For protecting you."

"For protecting me? When did she ever do that? Do you call what she's doing now protecting us? It's all a fucking game, Cord. Just like it's always been. Face it, our parents—both of them—were fucked up until the day they died." When he got up from the table and walked to the door, I stood too.

"Let him go," said Decker.

I ignored him.

Once outside, I spotted him right away, headed into an outcropping of trees. "Hold up," I hollered. He spun around, and when our eyes met, he stopped walking.

"Anyone else I would tell to fuck off," he said when I got closer to him. "What I don't get is you're the only one, at least so far, who has a right to be as angry as I am." He studied me when I didn't say anything. "Except you're not. You're rambling some bullshit about Mom wanting you to forgive her."

"Not just me. All of us."

Buck weaved his fingers in his hair and bent at the waist, almost as though he was going to be sick. "This is fucking madness." He straightened, and his fists clenched at his sides. "Did you know it was her all along?"

"No. I found out the same way you did."

"I don't fucking get it, Cord."

"There's something I need to tell you that I think will help you understand." I motioned to a picnic table in the shade under a tree. He followed me over and sat when I did.

"As you know, they arrested the kid who tried to kill me."

"Yeah. So?"

"Yesterday, Decker and the East Aurora PD were able to get a confession from his accomplice."

Buck's eyes opened wide.

"It was his mother."

I told him the same story Decker had told me, except this time, without the benefit of alcohol. With the exception of his eyes darting back and forth, Buck remained still.

"Mom was pregnant when she left East Aurora. Her brother was trying to force her to get an abortion." There was no easy way for me to tell him the rest, so I pulled out my phone and swiped the screen. "We believe this man is your father, Buck, and until yesterday, he was completely unaware of your existence."

He studied the image, then stood and walked over to the tree. He leaned against it and lowered his head on his folded arms.

I couldn't predict how he was feeling or what he was thinking. Most likely, he didn't know himself.

When he pushed away from the tree and walked toward the hotel's entrance, I followed.

We returned to the suite, but no one, including Buck or me, said a word when we retook our seats at the table.

"It's time to head back," said Hammer, looking between my brother and me. We all stood and left the suite, and still no one spoke.

The same was true when we arrived at Six-pack's office.

"Cord," he said, approaching me. "It's good to see you here. I hope—"

"Save it," I snapped.

When he nodded and stood behind his chair, I felt like crap for cutting him off, but I was in no mood for small talk.

After a few seconds of silence, he cleared his throat and switched on the recording device that sat in the middle of the table. First, he said the names of each person in attendance and that the purpose of the meeting was for the official reading of an additional codicil to the Roaring Fork Trust.

"The third codicil reads as follows," he began. "The Roaring Fork Trust further stipulates that Porter Hayes Wheaton must report within twenty-four hours to the Morris Ranch, located on Highway 47 in the town of Parlin, Gunnison County, Colorado, and reside on the property for a period of three-hundred and sixty-five consecutive days." The lawyer reached into a large manila envelope and pulled a second smaller one from it, then slid it across the table. "You'll find the remainder of your instructions in what I've just given you. You are forbidden to share its contents with anyone, including your attorney."

Porter, unlike Buck or me, had no reaction beyond grabbing it from the table, pushing his chair back, standing, and leaving the room.

"My year isn't up," I said.

"It makes no difference," Decker answered before Six-pack could. "There's nothing in the trust or the documents themselves that states the codicils have to be assigned or completed consecutively."

"Does the forty-eight-hour rule apply?" Holt asked.

"I can't answer that," Six-pack responded.

"What happens if he's sentenced to prison?" I added.

"I can't answer that either."

"The assets will be liquidated and distributed according to the stipulations set forth in section four-b of the Roaring Fork Trust," Hammer answered, reading from the document he'd snatched from in front of Six-pack.

"What else does it say?" I asked.

Hammer slammed the papers down on the table. "Not a fucking thing."

I felt Buck's eyes on me and looked in his direction. "Cord and I need to leave. *Now*."

I stood and followed him out of the office.

31

Juniper

"I can't shake the feeling that whatever is happening isn't good," said TJ, looking down at her baby suckling her breast beneath a blanket. She glanced at me. "You might not know this, but in my former life, I was a journalist."

"You're right. I didn't know."

"But you know what's happening, don't you?" she prodded.

I looked out at the horizon. "I do not. At least not what's being discussed in the meeting."

"But something else."

I looked at her and nodded.

"It's about Buck," TJ muttered.

"Please don't ask me," I whispered.

She cupped her baby's head with her palm. "Will he be okay?"

"I believe he will be."

The woman nodded. "The person I'm most worried about is Porter."

I thought about her statement for several seconds, then said, "Me too."

"How's Cord?"

For the second time, I thought before I spoke. "He's good."

TJ reached under the blanket, fiddled with something, then moved the baby so his head rested on her shoulder.

The park was close enough to the attorney's office that we'd know when the meeting broke up, in the event we hadn't heard from anyone before that.

I turned my head to check again and saw Cord and Buck walk out of the office and get in one of the SUVs.

"What's going on?" TJ asked.

"I'm not sure."

"Should we—"

"No."

"All right, girlfriend. You need to start talking."

I shook my head. "It isn't my story to tell."

TJ put the baby, who was now sleeping, back in the stroller. "Tell it anyway. I have a sneaking suspicion Buck is going to need you to."

32

Cord

"What happened that night?" Buck asked.

"You and Porter ran off to get help. A few minutes after you left, I heard a gunshot and tore into the house to see what had happened. When I got inside, I saw Roscoe on the floor. Mom had a gun in her hand."

"So it was her who shot him."

"Yeah. At least I think so. They weren't alone in that room, Buck."

His mouth gaped. "Who else was there other than you?"

"A man I didn't recognize. I think he was trying to stop Roscoe's bleeding. He told Mom to get me out of there."

"Do you think he shot him?"

I shook my head. "Mom was holding the gun. Plus, once we were out of the room, she told me I couldn't tell anyone what happened. She made me promise."

"What else?"

"I remember telling her he'd hurt her again. She promised he wouldn't and that everything would be taken care of. Something like that, anyway."

Buck pulled off the main highway and took a gravel road that led to the river flowing between Gunnison and Crested Butte.

"Right after that, she told him she was sick," he said after parking and cutting the engine. "I think she already knew the cancer was too far gone for her to beat it."

"The last thing she said to me that night was she hoped that someday, when I learned about the decisions she'd made, I'd understand why and I forgive her."

Buck stroked his beard. "Here's what I don't get. The ranch belonged to the Wheaton family. How did it end up in our mother's trust?"

"My first question is, how did she end up with Roscoe to begin with?"

"You can call him Dad. It won't bother me."

I shook my head. "I started referring to him as Roscoe a while ago."

My brother studied me. "Why?"

I shrugged. "I hated what he did to us."

Buck picked up a rock and threw it into the river. "Why do you think she never told me?"

"She knew she was dying and was afraid of what he'd do to you if you knew. As long as you didn't, he had to keep up the pretense."

He nodded. "Makes sense."

"My guess is whoever is pulling all our strings now, pulled his while he was still alive." I hung my head.

"You know, if Mom hadn't left East Aurora, if her brother had succeeded in forcing her to have an abortion, none of us would be here."

"You're right."

"There might not even be a Roaring Fork Ranch."

Buck's eyes met mine. "Do you think she ended up with him because of it?"

I shrugged. "No idea. It's all a huge fucking mystery, man. But at the end of the day, here's what I know matters—us. You, me, Porter, Holt, Flynn, TJ, Buckaroo, and the twins."

"And Juni," my brother added.

"Most especially Juni."

"Is she going to be a permanent fixture around here?" he asked.

"In my life? Yes. Around here? I can't answer that."

"I get it."

"Which leads me to the roughstocking business. With both Porter and me gone, I don't see how we can keep it going."

"The same way we have for the last few weeks," said Buck. "Holt has been pitching in when he can, plus we've got about a thousand goddamn cowboys on the payroll. A few of them seem at least somewhat knowledgeable about bulls and broncs."

"Yeah?"

"One guy in particular—Kingston West. Do you remember him? You probably know him as Bridger."

"Of course I do."

"He's taught me a *helluva* lot, I can assure you of that."

Rather than throw it like Buck had, I picked up a flat stone and skipped it across the water. Maybe all was not lost as far as Porter's and my venture. "The important thing is we stay profitable."

Buck nodded. "We're doing better than you think."

"Glad to hear it. I guess that means you won't need me sticking my nose in."

He put his hand on my shoulder. "I'll support whatever decisions you and Juni make, but I will say this;

if the Roaring Fork isn't your home, I'll miss the fuck out of you, Cord."

"Even though I'm an asshole?"

He chuckled. "Especially because you are."

"Speaking of Juni…"

"And TJ…"

"We should get back."

33

Juniper

Whether I was right or wrong in telling TJ that Roscoe Wheaton most likely wasn't Buck's biological father no longer mattered. I'd done it, and there'd be no taking it back.

What I didn't doubt was her love for the man. Without her reassurance, I knew she'd handle it in a way that helped rather than hurt him.

I looked up at the SUV pulling into the parking lot near where we sat, and when I saw TJ stand after Buck got out of the vehicle and the two embraced, I knew I'd done the right thing.

"Babysitting?" Cord asked as he approached where I waited by the stroller.

I rested my head on his shoulder when he sat beside me. "Giving them a moment. How is he?"

"In shock, but otherwise, okay. I think."

I smiled and leaned up to kiss him. "You're a good brother, Cord."

"In the list of things I want you to think I'm good at, that wouldn't be near the top."

"It isn't." I winked.

"So, uh, Porter is leaving. Actually, he already left the attorney's office. Sometime today, he'll leave the ranch."

"Where is he going?"

"To Parlin."

I nodded once. "To help the sister of the man in the accident?"

"He's more of a kid than a man, but yes. That's what we're all assuming."

"Will she accept his help?"

Cord studied me. "You're remarkable."

My cheeks flushed, and I lowered my gaze.

"And sexy as fuck."

"I'm not sure asking a question makes me anything more than nosy."

"It's a million-dollar one, though, isn't it? Will Cici Morris accept help from Porter Wheaton, the man who drove under the influence of alcohol and caused an accident that could have killed her brother? It hasn't been that many years since the two lost their parents, also in a car accident."

"The poor woman. It reminds me of Miss Cena. First, she lost her daughter, then her husband, then her son."

I rested my head on his shoulder.

"What happens now?"

"There's time for me to show you the Roaring Fork, if you're interested. Although I should probably clear it with Decker first."

"I'd love to see it."

He scrubbed his face.

"What?" I asked.

"There are some things I need to tell you. I remembered something today that happened when I was a kid."

I wrapped my arm around his waist.

"How do you do that?"

I raised my head. "What?"

"Know exactly how to soothe me."

I looked over his shoulder at Buck and TJ. "Love."

Decker encouraged Cord to take me to see the ranch, saying we had plenty of time if we wanted to spend the night. I told him I'd be happy to do whatever he felt most comfortable with.

There was room for us to ride with Buck and TJ, even with the baby, Cord's sister, and his brother Holt, who'd arrived with Porter.

"Where do you think Port ran off to?" Cord asked.

"No telling," muttered Buck.

TJ glanced over her shoulder, and our eyes met. It wasn't my place to ask about Porter. We'd been introduced briefly, and all I had to go on as far as his personality was my first impression. TJ probably knew him far better since she and Buck lived on the ranch.

"Whether Port's around or not, I'd like you and me to meet with Kingston West," said Buck.

"I can do that," Cord responded. While he faced me, he wasn't looking at me. Instead, he appeared lost in thought, staring out at the scenery along the ride.

"Almost there," said Cord several minutes later when Buck pulled off the highway. The road we were on wound its way through mountain passes like none I'd ever seen.

When the SUV pulled up to a gate and waited for it to open, I gasped. "It's so beautiful. Even that doesn't do it justice."

"That's the way I felt when I first saw it," said TJ.

My eyes met Cord's, and in them, I saw so many things. Love, definitely. Questions too, though. The thing that surprised me the most was sorrow. Was it because of what he remembered had happened when he was a boy? Was it more or something else? I hoped that, soon, we'd be alone, and when we were, he'd talk to me about the things he was feeling.

"That's our place," Buck said when he drove past a two-story house that sat not far beyond the gates we'd pulled through.

"It sure didn't look like that when we were growing up," Cord commented. "Buck and TJ fixed it up. Saying they brought it back to life is more accurate."

"It's idyllic," I commented as we continued on.

"And that's the main house," Cord said, pointing to a sprawling one-story place that was completely different than the first house but no less breathtaking.

"Is that where you live?" I asked.

"Porter, Holt, and me. Which means the place will be pretty empty for the next few months."

"I'm not living there anymore," Holt said from the seat behind us.

Cord nodded once in acknowledgment but didn't say anything.

"Porter hasn't been, either," his younger brother added.

"Where's he living?" Cord asked.

"He took one of the cabins, and I took another."

No one spoke again, even when Buck parked in front of it.

"I'm gonna show Juni around," Cord said, taking my hand when we got out of the vehicle. Instead of walking toward the house, he went in the direction of the barn. "Let me know when West is available," he shouted behind us.

"Will do," Buck answered.

We walked over to the corral, where several horses stood. Apart from the breathtaking mountains surrounding the ranch, the scene in front of us wasn't much different looking than the Lilacs.

"There's at least one ranch truck we can head out in," he said.

"Cord, um…"

He turned to face me. "What's goin' on, Juni?"

"You already know this, but if there's something you need to talk about, want to talk about, I'm a good listener."

He wrapped his arms around me and pulled me close. "You're more than that, darlin'. I pray to God that someday I can be the one you confide in instead of the other way around."

"You already are."

"I don't know about that, but come on. I'll show you around," he said, dropping his arms, but taking my hand again.

"I love this," I said once we were in the truck that had to be several decades old.

"Wanna know the part I like the best?" He put his arm around my waist, pulled me to the center of the bench seat, then buckled the lap belt. "I like the feel of you right beside me," he said, resting his right hand on my thigh. "It might get a little rough. Hold on tight, darlin'."

I put my hand on his thigh too, squeezing when it was bumpy and also when it wasn't.

"Those are three of the cabins," he said, pointing to the left. "There are five more. I'm not sure which ones my brothers live in."

"They look new."

He shook his head. "Renovated. At one point, Flynn and I wanted to turn this place into a dude ranch. When she got married, we let go of that dream. By then, Port was heavy into roughstock contracting, so I put my energy there."

"So, uh, roughstocking…I mean, I've heard the word before, but what do you do?"

"We supply bulls and broncs for rodeo events. We also breed 'em."

"Just bulls and horses?" I asked.

"Port and I decided early on that we didn't want to get involved in the cattle side of it."

"Why not?"

He shrugged. "Doesn't seem like a fair fight, you know?"

I nodded even though I didn't.

Cord kept driving up a road that got progressively narrower. "You got any issues with heights?"

"Not at all."

He smiled. "Then, I'll show you my favorite spot." He pulled up next to a boulder and cut the engine. The view in front of us stretched on for miles and miles. "That's the ski area," he said, pointing to the right. "The peak is about two thousand feet higher than where we are now, at ten thousand.”

“Do you downhill ski?”

“Used to.”

“Why’d you stop?”

“The older I got, the less time I had for it. What about you?”

“I still do, although the ski areas near East Aurora are pretty tame compared to that,” I said, motioning to the Butte.

He chuckled. “That’s downtown,” he said, pointing to the left. “It looks tiny from here and doesn’t feel much bigger when you’re in it. Wanna walk?”

“Sure.”

He got out of the driver’s side. “Come this way.”

When I scooted closer, he lifted me in his arms and kissed me before carrying me away from the boulder and setting me on my feet. “Ground’s more even over here.”

I turned in a circle, taking it all in. There was what looked like a natural clearing surrounded by aspen and evergreen trees. “It’s gorgeous, Cord,” I said, looking back at the view.

"I think so," he said, staring at me instead of the landscape.

When my cheeks flushed and I lowered my gaze, Cord kissed me again. He pressed his tongue against my lips, and I opened to him.

"When the weather's warmer, I wanna bring you back here, spread a blanket out on the grass, and spend the afternoon making love to you."

"I'd like that."

He cupped my cheek with his palm. "I meant what I said about not living here, Juniper. Sometimes, especially in the last few hours, I wonder if I even could again."

I shook my head. "I cannot imagine anywhere more perfect."

Cord's head cocked. "Not East Aurora?"

"Not even close."

He released me, and I walked closer to the truck, then turned around to look behind me. "Could you build anything up here?"

His eyes scrunched. "Like what?"

"A house or maybe a cabin?"

He studied me but didn't speak.

"That wasn't a rhetorical question, Cord."

"Yeah, I know. I gotta tell you, though. I'm a little speechless. This right here"—he motioned to the clearing—"is where I always dreamed I'd live someday. I just never figured anyone else would want to."

I took his hands and looked into his eyes, remembering how I felt the day he lay in the hospital bed and I saw them for the first time in a way I hadn't before. I knew then I loved him. "I want to."

"Come here." He pulled me over to the boulder next to where he'd parked. "It's getting cold, so I gotta do this quick." He knelt down on one knee, took something from his pocket, then reached for my left hand. My eyes filled with tears when his did.

"I love you more than anything. More than this view or this plot of land, more than wranglin', or anything else I've ever done or anyone I've ever known in my life. Will you marry me, Juniper Rose?"

"Yes, I'll marry you, Cord."

He slid the ring on my finger. "If you want something different—"

I looked down at the simple gold band etched with flowers. "It's perfect."

"That's what Sam said."

I cocked my head.

"She gave it to me while I was still in the hospital. Right before I got out, actually. She said she found it in a box in Miss Cena's closet. There was a note with it that said it belonged to her mother, Irene." He shook his head and smiled. "She told me something else."

"What's that?" I asked, smiling through my tears.

"That if I didn't give this to you when I asked you to marry me, she'd disown me as her cousin."

"She didn't!" I gasped.

Cord nodded. "Those were her exact words."

I studied the ring on my finger. "I couldn't love it, or you, more." I wrapped my arms around him, and we kissed before getting back in the truck when the sun went behind a cloud and the temperature seemed to drop several degrees.

"Looks like there's a storm rolling in."

The sky that had been mostly blue and cloudless when we arrived at the ranch was now gray and getting darker.

Cord put the truck in gear, and by the time we reached the three cabins we'd passed earlier, it was snowing hard.

"Wait for me here," Cord said, pulling up to one. He got out, walked up the porch steps, looked in the window, then reached above the door. He must've found a key because, seconds later, it opened.

I was about to climb out when he raced over to me.

"I can manage, Cord. I'm used to snow," I said, giggling when he picked me up and carried me up the steps and into the cabin.

"Today's the day I start being the one to take care of you," he said, setting me on my feet.

"How about we take care of each other?"

"Sounds perfect to me."

34

Cord

There was a new furnace in the cabin that heated up quickly, but I still lit a fire. Once the kindling sparked, I turned around and looked up at Juni.

"God, you are beautiful," I said, taking in her body that was draped only in a blanket. "How'd you get undressed so quick?"

"I'll show you."

When I stood, she pulled my shirt from my jeans and unfastened it while I lowered them to the floor after toeing off my boots and socks.

"You promised me that, when you got back the night I thought I'd lost you forever, we'd spread out on a blanket in front of a roaring fire and do nothing other than learn the feel of each other's bodies."

"I'm sorry, Juni."

"Don't be. Make it up to me instead."

We had three perfect hours before we decided we couldn't ignore my cell phone any longer. When I checked, there were three messages from Buck and one from Decker. I read his first, then checked the time.

"We have fifteen minutes until Decker shows up here."

Her eyes opened wide.

"At least that was his threat when he reminded me he vowed to get me back to the Lilacs inside of forty-eight hours."

"I thought he said we'd have time to stay the night if we wanted to."

I pointed to the window. "I think the storm is making him nervous."

Juni nodded. "Every storm will make me nervous."

I lay beside her and pulled her into my arms. "I'm going to make you a promise."

"Cord—"

"Let me, Juni."

She nodded.

"I'm not putting myself at risk like that ever again. Even if someone didn't try to bash my head in, going out in that weather wasn't smart. I promise I'll never put you through something like that again. Not intentionally. Now, will you promise me something?"

"Of course."

"No walking home from restaurants by yourself late at night. Especially in the middle of winter."

She rolled her eyes. "Yes, Cord. I promise never to do that again."

"Or have dinner with ex-boyfriends."

She raised a brow.

"What?" I asked.

"Your ex-girlfriends are worse."

I held up both hands. "Hey, I blocked her."

"Maybe you should consider blocking *all* of them."

"How about if I change my phone number?"

She smiled. "That's an even better idea."

We were teasing each other, but what I had to say was something I'd never joke about. "You're the only woman I've ever loved, Juni. The only woman I ever will."

Both of us jumped when my cell phone rang rather than vibrated. "Think you can get dressed in less time than it took you to get naked?"

"I'll race you."

I shook my head.

"What? I told you I was competitive."

"Who do you want to tell first?" I asked on the drive from the cabin to the main house, where Decker said he was waiting.

"Do you want to tell your brothers and sister?"

"Eventually."

Her eyes scrunched. "My parents and Grayson. Uncle Pete too, I guess."

I chuckled. "You guess?"

"He'd be crushed if we didn't. So, there isn't anybody you want to tell right away?"

"There is—Sam."

Juni leaned up and kissed my cheek. "I love that idea, Cord."

Rather than risk not returning to the Lilacs in time, I decided not to meet with Kingston West. There was nothing I could do about the roughstocking business until the end of my year in East Aurora anyway.

The one thing I had wanted to do that I wasn't able to was see Porter. As Buck had said when I asked where he'd disappeared to, there was no telling where he'd gone. Given the Roaring Fork's security system was designed the same way the Lilacs' was, we knew he hadn't returned to the ranch. And when I tried to call him, his phone went straight to voicemail.

Maybe he'd already gone to Parlin, and if that was the case, there wasn't time for me to track him down.

"I'm gonna trust that you can get your ass from the Buffalo Airport to the Lilacs on your own," Decker said when he drove us to the airfield in Gunnison.

"I can ask Pete to pick us up," Juni offered.

"Good idea. Arrange for backup too."

I didn't know whether he was joking or not, but I'd learned a while ago not to ask. I also knew better than to question why we were being transported in his plane and he wasn't going with us.

Once we were in the air, I told Juni the story of what had happened the night my mother shot my father, and how, in the aftermath, she'd said she hoped that one day, when I learned about the decisions she'd made, I'd forgive her.

I also told her we'd learned the trust wasn't our father's, like we'd thought.

"Is it your mother's?" she asked.

"It appears that way. It was drafted two years before she died."

"I think it was. Or is."

Her response intrigued me. "I'm leaning that way too, but why do you believe it is?"

"She wanted Buck to return to the ranch, but not until after your father died. She wanted you to go to the Lilacs, but not until after her brother died. Those are two things she could've decided on before she passed away."

"What about Porter?" I asked.

"That one is harder to figure out."

"I told Buck I thought whoever the trustee is must have had something on Roscoe while he was still alive. Not that it kept him from being an asshole." I scrubbed my face. "The other thing I said was if our mom hadn't left East Aurora, if her brother had succeeded in forcing her to have an abortion, none of us would be here."

"If only Miss Cena was still alive," Juni murmured.

"I wondered if it might be her doin' all this."

She nodded. "Me too. But your point about Porter is a good one. His accident happened after she passed away."

"Only Holt and Flynn are left. I hope there isn't anything they're forced to do. Unfortunately, I think there will be."

"Look at it this way. Buck returning to the ranch had a happy ending. He and TJ seem so in love."

"I wondered if traveling to East Aurora was just so I could meet you. I still think it's part of it."

Juni smiled. "I hope Porter finds happiness."

"Me too." While I nodded and said the words, I wasn't convinced it was possible. It had taken time away from him for me to realize how he seemed to carry a weight on his shoulders that he couldn't bear. So he drank—just like my father had.

"I pray he can exorcise his demons. That may be the best we can hope for." When I reached up to scrub my face, Juni caught my hand and kissed the back of it.

"I love you, Cord."

"And I love you."

By the time we landed, both Juni and I had received a message from Sam saying she and Beau were already at the airport and would give us a ride to the Lilacs.

"So, um, you might want to take your ring off," I said when we deboarded and were walking from the private terminal to the public one.

Juni shook her head. "Nope. I'm *never* taking it off."

"Sam will notice."

"I'm okay if she and Beau know first. We already invited my family to meet us at the Lilacs later."

As I'd anticipated, Sam spotted the ring immediately, and soon, she and Juni were both in tears, hugging.

"Many congratulations," said Beau, shaking my hand. "When's the wedding?"

"We haven't figured that out yet. What about you?"

"Initially, we were talking about Christmas, but I'm a wanker and pushed Sam to move it up."

"When and why?" I asked.

"Mid-May, and don't you want to marry Juniper as soon as she'll agree to it?"

"I guess so. I hadn't really thought about it."

"I have. No way I'm giving Samantha the chance to change her mind."

Epilogue

Cord

December

Juniper and I chose the sixteenth of December as our wedding date, exactly one year from the day we met. We decided on the inn as the site for the same reason. The night before, we stayed in the suite Patricia had given me as an upgrade on my first night in East Aurora, and Juni made us both bacon-cheeseburgers with fries for dinner.

Since I couldn't leave the Lilacs until five days later, my brothers, including Porter, and my sister helped us plan a second "unofficial" ceremony in Crested Butte.

Decker Ashford arranged for his plane to transport us, Juni's parents, her brother, and her nana, plus Beau and Sam there. While he'd be leaving that night, after the party was over, that he'd be there at all meant a lot to me.

No one knew Juni and I were already married long before the "official" ceremony. Not even Sam. Pete had been the hardest one to keep it from since we did it at the East Aurora courthouse, which was in the same building as the police station. It had all worked out, though, since we chose a day he was scheduled to be off. That was ten months ago, less than a week after we'd returned to the Lilacs from Crested Butte with twenty-four hours to spare.

Between then and now, in addition to our secret wedding, Juni and I had gotten the Lilacs Therapeutic Riding Center fully established. More importantly, the day of our grand opening in July, Juni and I arrived at the ribbon cutting side by side, on horseback—her on Apache and me on one of the new geldings I'd named Mojave. It had taken her a few weeks to work up to riding again, but her determination never wavered.

"With you by my side, I can do anything, Cord," she told me repeatedly.

Of course, each time she did, my heart swelled.

I'd offered to bring her horse to Crested Butte, but she'd declined, saying that, given his age, he'd be much happier in the stables at the Lilacs. Since the day after we opened, he'd become a favorite of the kids and adults who visited the center.

"You're deep in thought," she said, resting her head on my shoulder. "It's a long flight. Can you sleep?" she asked.

"I don't want to."

She laughed. "Why not?"

"If I'm sleeping, I can't stare into my beautiful wife's eyes."

Juni beamed in the way that melted my heart. I'd been so pissed off about having to travel to a place I'd never heard of for a reason no one could figure out. Now, I was thankful. There were still so many unanswered questions, but something in my gut told me that, with every new codicil, even the one that had sent Porter to Parlin, we'd discover more.

Juni talked about holding the ceremony on the spot where we planned to build our house, but with the amount of snow that had already fallen, combined with the trek up the hillside, I convinced her we should do it at the same place the after-party was being held.

"At the Goat?" she asked, looking from me to her mom and dad.

"Why not?" said Patricia. "Look, sweetheart, we loved that you had the beautiful ceremony at the inn, which I think was more for us than you, but you and Cord are hardly newlyweds anymore. Why not live it up a little?"

When Juni's mouth gaped and she turned to me, I held up both hands. "I didn't say a word."

"How did you know?" she asked her parents.

"Good Lord, June-bug, do you really think there's anything that happens in East Aurora your mom doesn't find out about?" said her dad, putting his arm around her shoulders. "Come on. Now that the cat's out of the bag, let's get to the party!"

Her mother nudged me. "At least not in the last twenty years. Sorry I can't be more help before that." Her eyes opened wide, and she spun around. "Jay, where's your mother?" she asked Juni's dad.

"Taking a nap," Grayson answered.

"Wake her up."

"Mom, what's going on?" Juni asked.

She leaned closer to both of us. "Why didn't we think to ask the old goat what she remembers?"

"I heard that," said Jay.

"Like that isn't what you call her."

"I'd ask if that's the reason you named your place the Goat, but it's what the previous owner called it, right?" I asked.

Jay chuckled. "We talked about changing it right after we bought it, but never got around to it."

"Do you remember who owned it before you?"

Jay scratched his chin. "I don't remember the man's name. Sorry, Cord. I'm sure I can find it once we're home."

"It's not important. I was just curious."

"I still can't believe someone else named their restaurant the Goat. It's such a weird name," said Patricia a couple of hours later when we were standing at the bar, waiting for a drink.

"My grandfather has a weird sense of humor," said the bartender. "I'm Keltie, by the way."

"Nice to meet you," I said. "I'm Cord Wheaton, this is my wife, Juni, and her parents, Jay and Patricia."

"Oh, good, you guys met," said Holt, walking up to us. "Keltie bought the place from the Rice family."

"Better put, I bought it back from them and at a *much* higher price than they paid for it."

"Hey, Cord," said Juni, who'd wandered to the end of the bar, where she stood studying a photo.

"Yeah, darlin'?"

"Where's Sam?"

"Right here. What's up?"

"Take a look at this," Juni said, pointing.

"Oh my God. That's Ursula!"

"How do you know my Aunt Ursula?" Keltie asked, walking to the far end of the bar, where we stood.

"I, um, don't exactly *know* her," Sam stammered.

"Hey," said Jay, looking over Juni's shoulder. "That looks like the guy I bought our place from."

Keltie's eyes scrunched. "That's my dad."

"What's his name?" Jay asked.

"Victor, but everyone calls him Vic. Our last name is Marquez."

"*Hol-y shit*," I said under my breath when Juni spun around and looked at me with wide eyes.

"So, uh, anyone wanna fill me in on all this?" Keltie asked.

Sam stepped up to the bar. "Pilar Marquez was my grandmother. I'm Samantha."

Keltie looked from Sam to me to Jay. "I think I need a drink." She turned around and grabbed a bottle of bourbon, then lined up several shot glasses. "Raise your hand if you're in."

All five of us did.

"Are you from around here? I've been away for about a year, but I don't remember meeting you before," I said.

"I've only been here a couple of months. When my dad heard the place was for sale, he sent me here to buy it. And run it, not that he mentioned that on the front end." She passed out the shots and raised her glass. "To the Goat."

"To the Goat!" we all responded.

"Did your dad happen to own another restaurant outside of Buffalo, New York?" Jay asked.

"A long time ago. He meant for Aunt Ursula to run it, but she ended up moving."

"Is she still alive?" Sam asked.

Keltie shook her head. "She's been dead twenty years or so. My dad's the only one of the siblings left."

"Where does he live?" I asked.

"New Mexico."

My eyes met Juni's when she grabbed my arm.

"Did she say New Mexico?" she whispered. While the bar was crowded and loud, I knew what she'd asked.

I nodded, looking around for my brothers. Holt, looking as stunned as I felt, still stood with us.

"Get Buck, Port, and Flynn and meet me outside," I told him. "I'll ask Decker to join us."

"On it," he responded.

I wrapped my arm around Juni's waist and rested my forehead against hers.

"Do you think her father could be the trustee?" she asked.

"No idea. However, it is the first solid clue we've found."

I saw Holt wave from across the room. My siblings were following him out the front door. Decker was already with them.

"Here we go," I muttered under my breath as I walked in their direction. Could it be this easy? Would Victor Marquez be able to answer the remaining questions about the Roaring Fork Trust? Somehow, I doubted it.

Keep reading for a sneak peek at
the next book in Heather Slade's
Roaring Fork Ranch series,
Roaring Fork Roughstock

***He carries a secret that could cost him everything.
She must trust the man she swore to hate.
And the truth between them that burns hotter
than the lies keeping them apart.***

PORTER

I came to Morris Ranch to make things right, even though Cici Morris hates me for what she thinks I did to her brother. Keeping my promise to Maverick means living with her contempt, but I can handle that. What I didn't expect was discovering the ranch is being systematically destroyed—or falling for the fiery woman determined to save her family's legacy. Now, someone's threatening not just the ranch but Cici herself, and I'm trapped between the promise I made and protecting the woman I'm falling in love with. If I tell her the truth about that night, I could lose her forever. If I don't, I might lose her anyway.

CICI

I've spent two years rebuilding my life after losing my parents and nearly losing my brother in an accident. The last person I want help from is Porter Wheaton—the man responsible for almost destroying what's left of my family. But with mysterious accidents plaguing the ranch and our finances in shambles, I'm running out of options. Working beside him daily is torture, especially when I start seeing glimpses of a man nothing like the monster I imagined. As we uncover a web of threats surrounding the ranch, I find myself drawn to his quiet strength and unwavering support. But just when I start to trust him, I discover what I believed ended up being wrong—and the truth could change everything I thought I knew about family, loyalty, and love.

1

Porter

I stopped myself from breaking into a run when I left the attorney's office where I'd been given the worst news I could imagine. For the next three hundred and sixty-five days, I'd be living and working on the Morris Ranch, attempting to turn the failing roughstock-contracting business profitable.

If I was unsuccessful, my brothers, sister, and I would lose our own ranch—the Roaring Fork. The reason why we would was troubling in itself, but I couldn't think about that now.

Instead, I had to figure out how in the hell to convince Cecily Morris, who everyone called Cici, to allow me to even set foot on her property. There wasn't a word in the English language strong enough to describe her feelings for me. Hatred, loathing, scorn, among other synonyms, didn't come close.

I knew why; I was just powerless to do anything about it. What she believed—what everyone did—wasn't something I could dispute. Soon, I'd face trial for driving while intoxicated and causing an accident that had almost cost Cici's younger brother, Maverick, his life. It was only by the grace of God he'd lived.

What the police report stated wasn't exactly the way it had all gone down, but as Maverick lay in my arms, breathing what I feared was his last breath, he made me vow to never reveal the truth. When I made the promise, it was as much to God as it was to Mav.

Whether he lived or died, I'd given what I considered a sacred oath to keep the secret he'd pleaded with me to. In exchange, I'd begged the Lord to spare his life.

He'd lived up to his side of the bargain. I'd live up to mine. It didn't matter that I was reviled by everyone in my hometown of Crested Butte, Colorado, along with most everyone who lived in Gunnison County. They could hate me all they wanted. The important thing was for them to never learn the truth. It was the least I could do.

I jumped in the truck I'd parked a block away and drove three miles out of town before finally pulling off the highway and onto a dirt road. Only then, did I reach inside my pocket and withdraw the envelope I'd stuffed in it.

"You'll find the remainder of your instructions in what I've just given you. You are forbidden from sharing its contents with anyone, including your attorney," the lawyer had said when he handed it to me.

Inside, I found a single sheet of paper that had been folded in half. I closed my eyes as I opened it, fearing what it might say.

The words handwritten on the otherwise lily-white paper sent chills down my spine and my stomach churning.

I know what really happened. Soon, everyone will.

Over my dead body, and that was what it might very well come down to.

About the Author

USA Today best-selling author Heather Slade writes shamelessly sexy, edge-of-your seat romantic suspense.

She gave herself the gift of writing a book for her own birthday one year. Sixty-plus books later (and counting), she's having the time of her life.

The women Slade writes are self-confident, strong, with wills of their own, and hearts as big as the Colorado sky. The men are sublimely sexy, seductive alphas who rise to the challenge of capturing the sweet soul of a woman whose heart they'll hold in the palm of their hand forever. Add in a couple of neck-snapping twists and turns, a page-turning mystery, and a swoon-worthy HEA, and you'll be holding one of her books in your hands.

She loves to hear from her readers. You can contact her at heather@heatherslade.com

To keep up with her latest news and releases, please visit her website at www.heatherslade.com to sign up for her newsletter.

MORE FROM AUTHOR HEATHER SLADE

ROMANTIC SUSPENSE

K19 SECURITY SOLUTIONS
TEAM ONE
Razor's Edge
Gunner's Redemption
Mistletoe's Magic
Mantis' Desire
Dutch's Salvation

K19 SECURITY SOLUTIONS
TEAM TWO
Striker's Choice
Monk's Fire
Halo's Oath
Tackle's Honor
Onyx's Awakening

K19 SHADOW OPERATIONS
TEAM ONE
Code Name: Ranger
Code Name: Diesel
Code Name: Wasp
Code Name: Cowboy
Code Name: Mayhem

K19 ALLIED INTELLIGENCE
TEAM ONE
Code Name: Ares
Code Name: Cayman
Code Name: Poseidon
Code Name: Zeppelin
Code Name: Magnet

K19 ALLIED INTELLIGENCE
TEAM TWO
Code Name: Puck
Code Name: Michelangelo
Code Name: Typhon
Code Name: Hornet
Code Name: Reaper

K19 GENESIS CONSORTIUM
TEAM ONE
Blackjack's Ascent
Dagger's Shield
Sundance's Trail
Nomad's Compass
Preacher's Decree

K19 SENTINEL CYBER
TEAM ONE
Code Name: Admiral
Code Name: Dante
Code Name: Grit
Code Name: Tank
Code Name: Atticus

K19 SENTINEL CYBER
TEAM TWO
Code Name: Kodiak
Code Name: Paragon
Code Name: Vex
Code Name: Shredder
Code Name: Jagger

PROTECTORS UNDERCOVER
TEAM ONE
Undercover Agent
Undercover Emissary
Undercover Savior
Undercover Infidel
Undercover Shadow

ROYAL AGENTS OF MI6
Make Me Shiver
Drive Me Wilder
Feel My Pinch
Chase My Shadow
Find My Angel

THE INVINCIBLES
TEAM ONE
Code Name: Deck
Code Name: Edge
Code Name: Grinder
Code Name: Rile
Code Name: Smoke

THE INVINCIBLES
TEAM TWO
Code Name: Buck
Code Name: Irish
Code Name: Saint
Code Name: Hammer
Code Name: Rip

THE UNSTOPPABLES
TEAM ONE
Code Name: Fury
Code Name: Merried

MORE FROM AUTHOR HEATHER SLADE

WINE COUNTRY ROMANCE

BUTLER RANCH
Kade's Worth
Brodie's Promise
Maddox's Truce
Naughton's Secret
Mercer's Vow
Kade's Return
Butler Ranch Christmas

WICKED WINEMAKERS
CENTRAL COAST
FIRST LABEL
Brix's Bid
Ridge's Release
Press' Passion
Zin's Sins
Tryst's Temptation

WICKED WINEMAKERS
CENTRAL COAST
SECOND LABEL
Beau's Beloved
Cru's Crush
Bit's Bliss
Snapper's Seduction
Kick's Kiss

WICKED WINEMAKERS
RUSSIAN RIVER VALLEY
FIRST LABEL
Bas' Blend
Hux's Harvest
Wolf's Want
Oak's Vintage
Cooper's Claim

COWBOY ROMANCE

COWBOYS OF
CRESTED BUTTE
A Cowboy Falls
A Cowboy's Dance
A Cowboy's Kiss
A Cowboy Stays
A Cowboy Wins

ROARING FORK RANCH
Roaring Fork Wrangler
Roaring Fork Roughstock
Roaring Fork Rockstar
Roaring Fork Rooker
Roaring Fork Bridger

SANGRE VISTA RANCH
Thorn's Stand
Stetson's Storm
Maverick's Reckoning
Cinch's Wager
Flints Chance